PRAISE FOR PAUL

THE PRESENCE.

WINNER for science fiction in the 2011 Independent Publisher's Book Awards.

"An exciting read that should prove hard to put down." ~ MidWest Book Review

---

"Science can be a boon to humanity, but it can also be its bane. *The Presence* is a science fiction thriller set in a future where reality is something manufactured by corporations. Sonny Chaco is charged with finding something that resembles law in this world. As he tails one billionaire CEO who may have made those billions with a bit of foul tactics, he finds that the reality-manufacture industry is more tumultuous than he could ever hope, and that throwing in some romance only complicates the complicated. *The Presence* is an EXCITING READ that should prove HARD TO PUT DOWN."

~ *Midwest Book Review*

"*The Presence* is fast-paced thriller, full of smart, interesting characters and suspence. You'll think it's one thing, but it's something else entirely!"

~ *Writer's Digest Magazine*

"It was a FAST READ and I enjoyed the trip that it took me on. It's one of the better hard Sci-Fi books I've read in a long time, and Paul Black is an author I'm looking forward to seeing more from!"

~ *Jordan Mason, themoviepool.com.*

"Author Paul Black brings a fresh look to the near-future fiction-writing genre."

~ *PearlSnapDiscount.com*

"*The Presence* is fast-paced and WELL WRITTEN. Paul Black pulls futuristic tech into a believable and seamless world."

~ *Darcia Helle, author Quiet Furry Books*

PRAISE FOR
PAUL BLACK'S OTHER WORK.

WINNER for genre fiction in the Writer's Digest's International Book Awards.

Gold and Silver medalist for science fiction, ForeWord Magazine's Book of the Year.

"Dallas writer Paul Black makes his first foray into the world of science fiction with *The Tels*. It's a HIGHLY ORIGINAL novel set in the near future and IT MOVES AT LIGHTNING SPEED. Mr. Black has quite an imagination and puts it to good use. The MIND-BENDING PLOT centers on Jonathan Kortel, who is approached by a shadowy group called the Tels, who covet his telekinetic gifts. The ENSUING ACTION IS BIZARRE enough to read like something straight out of The X-Files."

~ *Steve Powers, Dallas Morning News*

"(*The Tels*) is WRITTEN SO SPLENDIDLY, at times I forgot I was reading science fiction – with the emphasis on fiction. The characters are realistic, and the hero is someone you relate to, worry about and wonder if he's going to be able to cope with the reality that is set before him. This is definitely ONE OF THE BEST SCIENCE FICTION NOVELS I've ever read...the BOOK IS REMARKABLE."

~ *Marilyn Meredith, Writer's Digest's 11th Annual Book Awards*

"...Soulware was a BRILLIANTLY EMBROIDERED STORY, mixing science and fiction in a plausible and entertaining way...I absolutely LOVED THIS BOOK!"

~ *Ismael Manzano, G-POP.net*

"A riveting science fiction novel...an imaginatively skilled storyteller."

"This story by Paul Black is as STRONG AND WELL WRITTEN as any of the stories of my heroes: Robert Heinlein, Isaac Asimov, Andre Norton, or Anne McCaffrey. He is one of those writers that we who worship this genre look for every time we pick up the novel of an author who is new to us...The CHARACTERS COME ALIVE for you. You feel right along with them. You can believe the decisions they make. And best of all, nothing is clear-cut and simple. The story brings us to a strong ending while leaving us with the desire for more...I recommend The Tels to every lover of sci-fi. Good work, Paul! Welcome to my bookshelves!"

~ *John Strange, thecityweb.com*

"Paul Black's ENGAGING PROSE promises big things for the future...."

~ *Writer's Notes Magazine*

"...a GREAT READ, full of suspense and action...."

~ *Dallas Entertainment Guide*

"A RIVETING science fiction novel by a gifted author...The Tels would prove a popular addition to any community library Science Fiction collection and documents Paul Black as an IMAGINATIVELY SKILLED STORYTELLER of the first order. Also very highly recommended is the newly published second volume in the Tels series, Soulware, which continues the adventures of Jonathan Kortel in the world of tomorrow."

~ *Midwest Book Review*

"*The Tels* is an addictive read... manages to capture the reader in the first ten pages...*The Tels* has it all."

"Black rises above the Trekkie laser tag spastics found in your typical sci-fi novels resting on the grocery store racks. His sensibilities broaden from machine gun testosterone to discreet fatherhood, from errant sexuality to wry humor. HE DELIVERS A CHARGE OF VENTURE RARELY FOUND IN FIRST-TIME WRITERS. And THE TELS HITS THE MARK as a solid adventure serial, leaving you hanging for the next publication."

~ *Brian Adams, Collegian*

"The Tels is an ADDICTIVE READ from first-time novelist Paul Black, a promising new storyteller on the sci-fi scene. He manages to capture the reader in the first ten pages. He introduces us to a set of intriguing characters in a totally believable possible future. There is a grittiness and sensuality to his writing that pours out of every word in the book. Whether it's his description of the preparation of a good meal, the seduction of a beautiful woman, or a fight to the death, THE TELS HAS IT ALL. Even people who don't read sci-fi will want to read this book. The action is great and would make one hell of a movie. Is Hollywood listening? Paul Black has a winner on his hands. I can hardly wait for the next installment."

~ *Cynthia A., About Towne, ITCN*

"Soulware doesn't miss a beat as it continues Jonathan's story, the story of his quest to find out exactly who he really is and why the Tels are so interested in him. The ending makes it clear that there's more to come, and readers who crave their science-fiction with a hint of weirdness can look forward to the next book in the series."

~ *Steve Powers, Dallas Morning News*

Shelia
Best wishes!

Other books by Paul Black

THE TELS

SOULWARE

NEXUS POINT

THE PRESENCE

A NOVEL

THE SAMSARA EFFECT

PAUL BLACK

NOVEL INSTINCTS
Publishers of Fine Genre Fiction and Non-Fiction

This book is a work of fiction. Names, characters, places, and incidents either are products of the author's imagination or are used fictitiously. Any resemblance to actual events or locations or persons, living or dead, is entirely coincidental.

NOVEL INSTINCTS PUBLISHING
6008 Ross Ave.
Dallas, Texas 75206
www.novelinstincts.com and www.paulblackbooks.com

This book can be ordered on the web at all major retail sites including www.barnesandnoble.com and www.amazon.com.

ISBN: 978-0-9726007-8-1
1. Fiction / Science Fiction / High Tech 2. Fiction / Near-Future

Library of Congress Control Number: 2010934982

Printed in the United States of America.
10 9 8 7 6 5 4 3 2 1

Cover photo: GettyOne.
This book's text is typeset in New Times Roman 11 point/18 point. Its page numbers and chapter heads are in Trade Gothic Bold Condensed and Trade Gothic Bold Eighteen Condensed.

TO WILLIAM GIBSON

~

Who, through his work, taught me how to write.

&

DR. HEIDI SQUIER KRAFT

~

Whose book "Rule Number Two" was the inspiration for the character of Dr. Trenna Anderson. Thank you for your service to our country.

"Let go the past, let go the future, and let go what is in between, transcending the things of time. With your mind free in every direction, you will not return to birth and aging." ~ *Buddha*

Prologue. So help me God.

One sound is certain to wake a mother from the mammalian grip of circadian sleep, and Kimberly Nelson was all too familiar with it. When her brother had worked on the Human Genome Project, he claimed the women in his group had a bet that it wasn't genetically based; they argued it was instinctual, that it went beyond science. All Kimberly knew was that for the last year, the sound of her only son crying had awoken her more times than she could remember. Tonight, however, the voice was different.

She snatched her robe from the bedpost and slipped it on. A cool spring Wisconsin breeze billowed the window curtain.

Her son yelled again.

"I'm coming, Eric," she said. Her husband stirred.

Kimberly followed the reverberating voice of her 8-year-old

through the angular darkness of her family's old farmhouse. Night terrors had become a way of life, but tonight the voice from downstairs barely resembled her child's. Her bare feet slapped against the pine floorboards as she took the stairs two at a time. She grabbed hold of the decorative ball on the banister post, spun off the last stair, and landed at the threshold of the living room.

"Eric, honey?" she asked, straightening. "Are you okay?"

The living room was sliced by moonlight. In a dark corner, standing on top of her grandmother's chaise, was her son. He looked to be holding something, but in the darkness she couldn't tell what.

"Honey, please. Come down from there–"

"Halt! Bewegen Sie nicht oder ich werde Ihre jüdische Weibchenkehle schneiden!"

A deep chill carved through Kimberly. Her son didn't know German. "Eric. What are you saying?"

"Halten Sie auf oder ich werde Sie schießen!"

Something winked out of the darkness, and as if in a terrible dream, Kimberly recognized the barrel of her husband's favorite rifle lowering into a shaft of moonlight. The boy's eyes were partially rolled back, and spittle collected at the corners of his mouth.

"Eric Thomas Nelson! Put your father's gun down!"

"Halt! Erheben Sie Ihre Hände über Ihrem Kopf!" Eric shouted. He motioned upwards with the barrel.

Kimberly reflexively raised her arms, but stopped. "Put that gun down right now, young man–"

"Eric!"

The rifle swung through the shaft of light. Kimberly's eyes followed its path. Standing next to one of the dining room's French doors was the tall, shadowed figure of her husband. He was aiming his handgun directly at their son.

"Boy, if you don't stand down, I'll put you down, so help me God!"

His voice cut through the room with an authority Kimberly had never heard before.

"Scott!" Kimberly screamed. "What are you *doing*?"

In the dim light, Scott Nelson regarded his wife with a detached coolness and cocked the gun's hammer. Kimberly feared his former Special Forces training was gaining the upper hand. He returned his attention to their son.

"Eric," he said gravely, "I'll count to three, and you'll lower that gun. One ..."

Through the shadows, Kimberly could make out her son's head darting from her husband to her.

"Two."

"Ich bin ein Meisterschütze! Prüfen Sie mich nicht!"

"Eric, please!" Tears began to stream down Kimberly's cheeks. "Do what your father says!"

"Three."

1. What the hell?

Deep in the lower levels of the University of Chicago's old Biological Sciences building, surrounded by a drone that only a thousand square feet of industrial computers could make, William Kanter, Ph.D., was seriously considering an offer to join the Genonics Group.

"What do we have?" his assistant asked from somewhere on the other side of the computer stacks.

"Dick," Kanter replied.

The LCD monitor in front of him displayed the latest results from a developmental brain imager he had been slaving over for two years. Unlike an MRI, his design involved a process that worked from the inside out. At the moment, though, all he had was the same damn static he had seen for half a year. He turned down the sound to render it slightly more bearable. Kanter studied the pixels that danced across his screen like a metaphoric middle finger.

"I've got an idea," his assistant said, and he pushed off and rolled his chair across the only open area left in the lab. Kelly was a tall, sinuously muscled streeter who had worked his way out of the South Side of Chicago and earned himself an academic full ride. He was a decent assistant, as grad students went, but Kanter suspected Kelly had come to the lab stoned more times than not. If it weren't for his remarkable ability to write code, Kanter would have canned his ass a semester ago. And now he was into a fad that was all over campus. What was it again, something with leeches?

Kelly slammed into the counter of Kanter's station. "What if we up the sensitivity ratio," he suggested. "You know, way beyond the threshold?"

Kanter, still staring, hardly heard him.

"Doc, are you okay?"

"What did you say?"

Kelly pointed at the console. "Up the ratio."

"It'll trash all the boards. Do you have a spare million?"

Kelly shook his head. His dreadlocks flapped across his forehead. "It won't, trust me."

Right. Trust a stoner. "Define 'up'."

Kelly reached over and dialed the particle ratio halfway into the red.

"Jesus!" Kanter elbowed his assistant away and reset the ratio into the green.

"What?" Kelly asked, gliding towards his station, his legs outstretched. "The system can take it."

Kanter looked back at the screen and caught the flash of an indiscernible image that had blinked, just for a millisecond, out from the bright colors of spectral static. Maybe it had been a head, with the faintest hint of eyes.

"What the *hell*?"

Kelly dropped his legs, his sandals squeaking against the old Formica. "What up?"

Kanter leaned closer to the screen. More static. Maybe he was just tired. "Nothing. Get back to those charts, will you please?"

Kelly pushed off towards his own workstation. "Man, you need to get out more."

Bill Kanter had devoted much of his professional life to finding new ways to image the human body. At 30 he had garnered several honors, including the prestigious Medical Design Excellence Award for developing the first scanning table that used artificial intelligence. Like something out of science fiction, the MedBed could analyze and recommend treatment. Now, however, his quest for a better way to image the brain seemed defeated. The Genonics grant had funded the work to date, but it wasn't a bottomless well. The funding was supposed to cover two years of research, but now he was four months into his third year with little to show, and Genonics had extended an employment offer that was looking better and better. Kanter was beginning to get nervous. Hell, he was, as Kelly liked to say, whacked about it. Or was it thizzy?

"Yo boss?"

"Yeah?"

"There's a party at Hoop's, and a bunch of us are getting together ... just chillin' and shit. You want to go?"

"I don't know if I'm up for being around a lot of people," Kanter said.

Kelly was, by most definitions, brilliant, but Kanter wasn't too sure about the people he chose to hang with. The guy giving the party was named Hoop. He was a big-ass Rastafarian, and Kanter figured there would be lots of marijuana and questionable people, and that was just a little out of his comfort zone.

"I think I'll pass," he said.

"The ladies will be notch."

Beautiful women was something Kelly liked to talk about, but for a guy who was in the lab almost 16 hours a day, Kanter couldn't figure when he had time for dating. "That's tempting."

Kelly peered around the computer stack. "Man, you're younger than me. When's the last time you got *laid*?"

Kanter had to think. "I don't know, maybe–"

Kelly waved him off. "Shit," he said and disappeared behind the stack.

Kanter returned to the static. The metaphor had changed. Now, all he could see was the face of his last girlfriend, Tara. She was smiling and mouthing the words, "Get a life."

*   *   *

"That's it, boss," Kelly said, walking up. "Everything's backed up on the server."

The glow from the desk lamp cast his dreads into a creepy Medusa-like nest of snakes. Through his fatigue, Kanter thought he saw one move. "Thanks. That should do it for tonight."

Kelly started for the lab's exit, but stopped. "You sure you don't want to come?" he said over his shoulder. "You need to chill."

Maybe he *could* use a hit off a blunt. "Nah, thanks," Kanter said. "I've got some things to finish."

Kelly shook his head, and the Medusa resemblance grew even creepier. "Man, you live here." He motioned to the lab. "It'll be waiting."

The apartment Kanter had set up at the back of the lab met his needs, plus he liked being near his work. Literally. "I appreciate the offer. Maybe next time."

Kelly's expression shifted, and he looked older than his years. He walked over and leaned onto the counter. "Man, it's like my daddy used to say just before he died." Kelly's high-pitched voice had grown rich with seriousness. "This life is just too fucking short."

Maybe Kelly's dad was right. It was late; Kanter was beat; and a cold beer sounded good. "Okay," he said. "Go on, and I'll meet you there."

"You better show up." Kelly took a pen off the desk and jotted the party's address on a sticky-pad.

Kanter read it. "I'll be there in thirty minutes."

The lab door clicked shut behind Kelly, and the space filled with the monotonous hum from the stacks. Kanter had come to embrace the sound, even drawing comfort from its white noise. He had told friends it helped him concentrate, although that wasn't completely true. The fact was, ever since he had developed a mild form of tinnitus, sleeping had become difficult, and the lab's white noise partially blocked out the ringing and allowed him to get some rest ... at least for a couple of hours.

The static on his screen jittered. Kanter had always left the latest results (or lack thereof) running as a reminder for his ego. He had been brilliant once, but corporate America only cared about what he would do next. He eyed the static warily, and the pixilated face he had glimpsed before taunted him.

What the hell, Kanter thought. He dialed the ratio into the red.

2. Maybe you'll learn something.

"How did this kid get into his father's gun cabinet? And how did you get this video?"

Trenna Anderson clicked back to the point where the boy pulled the trigger. The angle was high, apparently from a camera mounted in a corner of the ceiling. The living room was dark, and she couldn't make out much until the flash of the gun filled the frame with horrifying details.

"Eric's night terrors have been getting worse," Thomas Prost explained. "My sister's doctor suggested videoing him because he wanted to study what he did during the episodes. They're way out in the sticks, and getting in to their doctor can take weeks."

Anderson watched again as the rifle discharge illuminated the room. The shot went wide of the father. The recoil sent the boy flying backwards over the headboard of the chaise. When the boy landed, the gun fired again and must have hit the video camera, because after the second flash the screen went black. She clicked back and paused on a frame that showed the boy's face. His eyes were partially rolled back, like a character out of a horror film. "You didn't answer my first question."

Tom Prost was a rumpled, thickset man who didn't seem to care about fashion or style. A theoretical geneticist and tenured professor, he had been a good friend ever since Anderson had arrived on the University of Chicago campus. Prost was nice enough, always confiding in her about his latest dating debacle or asking her opinion about this or that. He looked away, then back. "You tell me. You're the kid shrink."

"Tom, I can't help unless you help me." Anderson leaned onto her desk and nudged the picture of her and her dad at the Naval Hospital Camp Pendleton the week before she had shipped out to Iraq. She pushed it back into position next to the photo of her at the surgical unit in Al-Asad. "What about the German Eric was speaking? You said he's never taken a class. Does he watch movies or have any friends who speak it?"

Prost stared at her wall of books like he was grappling to find an answer.

"*Tom?*"

Prost scooted his chair forward and leaned onto her desk. He regarded her through his thick, outdated glasses. "Tren, this is serious."

"You're damn right. Your brother-in-law should have locked his gun cabinet."

"Kim and Scott are good parents. The cabinet was locked. And no, he's never taken German in his life."

His tone suggested Anderson had hit a nerve. "I'm sorry, Tom. Go on."

"Eric has never had an episode like this. Usually he sleepwalks, mumbles to himself, occasionally has a screaming fit, but nothing Kimberly hasn't been able to handle. They consulted with their family doctor because they didn't want Eric to hurt himself. He's already fallen out of bed once and almost knocked himself out." Prost looked away again.

"Tom, what is it?"

"There's something weird about all this." His attention went to her wall of books. "Eric would never point a gun at his parents."

"I could show you a hundred case studies of seemingly perfect kids who turn into monsters overnight. It happens usually around puberty, but I've seen it happen earlier."

"I'm telling you," he said, "Eric wouldn't do this. It's not in his nature. Kim and Scott are fundamentalists ... I'm talking the Right of the far Right. Eric's never been exposed to anything that's bad. Kim censors everything he comes in contact with. And Scott is very responsible. He's taught Eric about gun safety. Hell, he hasn't even taken him hunting yet. Eric knows his butt would be tanned if he so much as looked at Scott's guns."

Prost angrily crossed his legs and accidentally kicked Anderson's desk. Her Academy picture fell flat. "Sorry." He began to right the picture.

Anderson stopped him. "It's okay, don't worry about it. We're talking about your nephew, and you're upset. That's natural."

Prost sighed and rubbed his face. "There're still two things I can't get my head around. One is the German. I had it translated. The first thing he says is: 'Stop, you Jewish bitch, or I'll shoot.'"

"What?"

"Yeah, weird isn't it? All the other stuff is like what a World War II German guard would say to a prisoner ... 'Raise your arms. Shut up. Get in line.' Crap like that."

"Maybe he picked it up off of satellite ... some old war movie."

"No. Kim would never allow him to watch anything like that. There's no way in hell that he could have picked up German. And get this – I had a friend of mine who's a linguistics prof do the translation. Some of the words he's using are colloquial. Tren, what the hell is going on?"

"Can I ask you something?"

"Sure."

"Is there any violence in the home, possibly of a sexual nature?"

Prost shook his head. "No, absolutely not. Kim and Scott are great parents. I can't imagine there's anything like that."

In her years as a pediatric psychologist, Anderson had never seen anything like this. "Tom, without seeing the boy I can't be certain. It could be several things, like delusional disorder, schizophrenia–"

"What about multiple personalities?"

Even though Anderson was progressive in her practice, jumping to dissociative identity disorder was a bit of a stretch, even for her. She took a deep breath. "DID *is* a possibility, but it's usually associated with severe physical or sexual abuse, and we don't have that here."

"But the mind can't just spontaneously have command of a

German dialect. He's eight, for God's sake!"

There was anguish in her friend's voice, and Anderson's heart went out to him.

Prost began pacing. He walked over to her bookshelf and ran his fingers down the spine of an older book. He looked at his fingertips, then wiped them on his pants. "There's something else. The cabinet."

"Right. How did he get the gun?"

"The lock was picked."

"What do you mean picked?"

"It was picked. Granted, it wasn't a modern case. It was our grandfather's. But it has a good lock. Nobody could get into it unless they had a key or was a pro at picking."

"Maybe your brother-in-law left it unlocked ... by accident?"

Prost shot her a look.

"Okay, then explain to me how an 8-year-old could professionally pick his father's gun case, learn colloquial German, and fire a gun that's as big as he is?"

Prost pulled a book from the shelf and turned it over in his hands.

"What?" Anderson asked.

He walked over and handed it to her. She read the cover: Edgar Cayce. Modern Prophet.

Prost grinned for the first time that evening. "This is something you'd find on my shelf, not yours," he said, sitting.

Anderson pensively drew her fingers across its embossed cover. "An old boyfriend gave this to me. You would have liked him. He was into Eastern philosophy."

"Doesn't sound like your kind of guy."

"We all have an experimental phase. So what's this have to do with–" Anderson stopped, remembering the boyfriend and their long talks about life and religion. He was cute: dark wavy hair and a set of green eyes that could melt a woman. Any woman. He had been her bad boy, although her Protestant upbringing wouldn't allow her past his belief in reincarnation. She leafed through the book and stopped at the page where he had written her a note.

"Tom," she said, and closed the book, "Are you suggesting Eric is having a past-life episode?"

"You have a better idea?"

She placed the book on her desk and slid it up to the Iraq picture. Its cover reflected in the frame's glass and created an eerie juxtaposition of Cayce's upside down face between her own and two cot-ridden patients. "I'm not qualified for this. Shouldn't you be talking with ... I don't know, someone who believes in this sort of thing?"

"That's why I think you're the right person for this. You'll be objective. I've read about your work with the inner-city kids. You're good. Real good. I know you said you didn't want to take on any more patients, but my sister's at the end of her rope. Come on, Tren. I need your help."

Anderson's attention went back to her computer and the video. She was already booked to the end of the semester, but this case was just too intriguing. She stared at the paused frame of the Wisconsin boy. His eyes were haunting, and Kimberly Nelson had her arms halfway raised. The rifle looked like a movie prop in the arms of the 8-year-old; its barrel pierced a shaft of moonlight such that Anderson couldn't take her eyes off it. A shiver went through her.

"Okay," she said resignedly. "When can I see him?"

Prost walked around her desk, his arms outstretched. "Thanks,

Tren! This means a lot to me."

Anderson began to stand, but Prost lifted her up and hugged her.

"Well, thank you," she said. She pulled her sweater back onto her shoulder. "This should be interesting."

Prost, gathering his briefcase, looked up. "Who knows," he said, beaming, "maybe you'll even learn something."

3. No way.

The noise from the computer's processing collectively deepened, and the air around Kanter's workstation filled with a burnt electrical smell. It was the same odor he had smelled one Christmas as a little kid, just before the extension cord popped and sent his grandmother into hysterics. He had never seen her move like that before, stomping on the cord and screaming. It was funny now, but back then it scared him so badly he had almost peed his pants.

"There go the IC boards," he said to no one in particular.

Kanter often talked to himself when he worked alone. Most people would call it thinking out loud, but to him it felt like organizing his thoughts. He had concluded that everyone had two parts to their personalities: their rational self and their emotional self. Since he had so much going on in his head at one time, it was better to keep the two parts dialoguing. An old girlfriend had called it "self-lecturing."

Kanter's computer screen had been grey with static for close to a minute. The time was killing him. "Come on!" He slapped the side of the monitor and was about to dial down the ratio when an image surfaced from amid the static. It began oscillating hypnotically. Kanter didn't know how long he had before he would fry the system. He quickly fiddled with the contrast and color levels, but the image wouldn't clean up.

"Damn it!" Kanter eyed the ratio dial. Upping the particle flow would undoubtedly fry the IC and TL boards, but if he didn't try ... well, he had just about exhausted his life savings and was running out of options.

"Screw it," he said and turned the dial to the limit. The acrid odor intensified.

The image remained buried in static; the computer's strain deepened into a range Kanter could feel in his chest; the air seemed to be getting hazy. When he glanced over to the emergency shut-off button on the wall, though, the scene suddenly cleared.

At first, it appeared to be random, grainy video pulls, and Kanter wondered if the University's intranet had migrated into his network. But the point of view was curious, and as he adjusted the color levels, more details emerged.

What the hell is this?

The images were sequencing at a dizzying pace. Kanter slowed the stream to a crawl and studied an old house with a large porch. It looked like it could have been a diorama representing the end of the last century – maybe the 1980s – and the point of view was from the front yard. There was snow on the ground, and the house was a typical two-story farm style found throughout suburban New England. The scene came to life when an older, grey-haired woman with her hair in a ponytail opened the front door and stepped out. She wiped her hands down the front of her flower-patterned apron, walked to the railing, and leaned against one of the columns, all the while looking expectantly to the driveway. Kanter paused the streaming and studied her face, its deep creases a testament to an older and harder way of life. Then the realization of what he was viewing crashed through Kanter's being.

"Mimi," he whispered.

There, quivering in the liquid crystals, was one of his childhood memories. The whole tableau had been captured as if by camcorder, and the point of view was his. He almost didn't recognize his grandmother, which made it hard for him to accept what he was seeing. He started the streaming, and Mimi began waving in surreal slow motion to his parent's car as it pulled into the drive. The point of view shifted to a sled on the snowy ground, then moved back to the car.

My God. Kanter watched in awe as his mother and father presented his baby sister to his grandmother. They beckoned to him, and the point of view rushed toward the porch. He sped up the sequencing, and his boyhood rewound before him.

Jesus, is it all here? Since Kanter had been letting the scan run all evening, he figured it had reached back as far as when he was six. It was unsettling to watch, because he could only remember fragments of his early childhood.

Quickly, the scenes entered his infancy. Kanter paused on one from his bassinette. He must have been a year old, maybe younger, because he had a vague recollection of the wallpaper pattern of dancing ducks and cows. Hadn't that room had been at his parent's first house in Newton? An idea crossed his mind. Would there be any memories of his *birth*?

He started the sequencing again, but the images started breaking up. Fragments flashed by of the kitchen at his parent's first house. A bathtub. His mother's younger face flashed for an instant, pixilated, then dissolved into gray static.

"Come on!" Kanter played with the contrast and brightness controls, but nothing changed. It didn't appear to be a system error, because there were patterns undulating under the static.

Without warning, new images emerged: scenes that looked like they were from the early part of the last century raced across the screen. First, there were images from a hospital room, and then some that might have been from a small European village. He paused the sequencing and studied the scene. It reminded Kanter of a painting he had seen once with a cute med student he had dated. She had dragged him to the Chicago Art Institute to see the Impressionist's wing. There had been a painting of Paris, and it kind of resembled this.

He resumed the sequencing. Now there were carriages and people, and the whole thing was beginning to weird Kanter out. All he had been trying to do was create a better way to map the brain, not project memories onto a screen. And what the hell was he watching now, and why did it look like it was from the 1800s? He checked the readout that calculated the amount of data captured in his scan and saw that he was near the end, but how could that be? If his life's memories comprised the last tenth of the total scan depth, then what kind of data had come before it? He paused the streaming on an image of a middle-aged man trimming his nose hairs. Kanter required a second to realize he was staring at a reflection in a bathroom mirror. The man had wiped an area in the center of the mirror, which created a soft frame of steam around his face. His eyes were keenly trained on the task of grooming, but there was something about them that resonated on an instinctual level.

"No fucking way," Kanter said, pushing back from the workstation.

The scene jittered into patchworks of digitized color. He tried to correct the ratio, but he had already pushed the range to its limit. Suddenly the building's fire alarm pierced the quiet with a staccato of sharp bursts.

"No!" Kanter yelled, and the screen went black.

4. This ho' needs her money.

"Hello, Eric. My name is Trenna Anderson."

Eric Nelson's innocent face stood in stark contrast to the crazed boy from the video. Hands tucked under bouncing legs, he watched Anderson with all the fear of any 8-year-old being asked to talk about something he didn't understand.

"Stop twitching your leg," Kimberly Nelson scolded.

The boy drew his knees tight to his chest and began rocking in the chair.

"Get your feet off Dr. Anderson's–"

"It's okay," Anderson said to Eric. "If you want to rock, I don't mind." She glanced at Kimberly. "It's university property, so what's the harm?"

Eric looked at her from under a wedge of straight cut blond hair, and a faint grin formed at the edge of his mouth. Kimberly didn't acknowledge the remark.

"I think it would be best if the sessions were just me and Eric," Anderson suggested.

Kimberly started to protest, but her brother tapped her knee.

"Dr. Anderson," Prost said, leveraging a diplomatic smile, "is one of the best in the business." His attention went to the wall behind the couch and the photo of Anderson accepting the Mayor's Award for her work with the Chicago Troubled Youth Program. "If she thinks it's best to work with Eric one-on-one, then we should give her a wide berth. Don't you think?"

Kimberly thought for a moment. "All right then," she said, standing.

Kimberly was cuter than Anderson had imagined. Her blond hair was cut in a short utilitarian bob, and she was dressed like she could have been a grad student.

Prost raised an eyebrow at Anderson and stood.

Kimberly brushed a stray lock of hair off her son's forehead. "Now, sweetie, if you need anything, you have mommy's cell phone. Your uncle's number is in the speed dial. You do have it, don't you?"

Eric rolled his eyes and fished the phone from the front pocket of his jeans.

Kimberly smiled approvingly and grabbed her coat off the back of her chair. It was a vintage Army field jacket that reminded Anderson of one her father had. A Ranger chevron was on one arm, a patch that said DEATH FROM ABOVE on the other. Anderson didn't recall Tom saying his sister had been in the military, but maybe that's where she met her husband.

"Kim, why don't I show you around the campus." As Prost helped his sister with her jacket, he made a face at Anderson.

"I think Eric and I are going to get along just fine," Anderson said in reply. She circled her desk and extended her hand.

Kimberly eyed it with trepidation before she shook it half-heartedly.

"How long do you need?" Prost asked.

"A couple of hours," Anderson said. "I'll call you when we're close to being done."

Prost gave a thumbs-up and guided Kimberly toward the door.

Anderson watched them leave, then turned to Eric. "Are you comfortable in that chair, or do you want to be on the couch?"

"Couch, please," Eric said, vigorously nodding.

"Okay then, I'm kicking you out of the chair!" Anderson gripped the top of the wingback, slid it around, and tipped it forward.

Eric giggled heartily as he tumbled off. He ran to the couch and launched himself onto one of the large stuffed animals Anderson kept for therapy sessions. Eric had chosen the tiger and proceeded to hug its head.

"I see you're getting to know Mr. T," she said, sitting in a chair next to the couch. "His real name is Tony, but I call him Mr. T."

Eric punched the tiger's nose, and something shifted inside Anderson. Usually, she detached herself and concentrated on a patient's therapy, but something about Eric was tugging at her sense of professionalism. Maybe it was the harsh contrast from the haunting boy in the video to the playful child now in front of her. Eric smiled, and his dimples deepened. The eyes that had been so full of innocence just a minute before now regarded Anderson with a surprising maturity.

For the next half hour, she went through the standard Q-and-A for a first session. Eric displayed all the attributes of a well-disciplined child and answered the questions with smart, concise statements. Occasionally, the need to do battle with Mr. T snatched his attention away, but it was obvious that Kimberly Nelson had coached her son to respond with the best possible answers.

Anderson had dealt with this kind of scenario before, and for the next 15 minutes, she asked more conceptual and demanding questions. Eric's answers were now filled with lots of "ums" and "I don't knows." Mr. T was absorbing more of a beating.

"Eric, how was the earth formed?"

He brightened. "That's easy," he said. "God made it."

"How did God make the earth?"

"With a wave of his hand!" Eric made a sweeping gesture and fell over sideways on the couch. He giggled and started burrowing under one of the cushions.

"Where you going, silly?"

He kept crawling, and the cushion began to fall off the couch.

Anderson caught it. "Eric," she said with more authority, "I need to ask you a few more questions."

Eric immediately sat up and folded his hands in his lap. He sheepishly bowed his head.

"It's okay," Anderson said, closing her laptop. "You're not in trouble. Now tell me, how've you been sleeping lately?"

The blue eyes regarded her sternly, and he buried his face into the side of Mr. T's head.

Anderson moved closer to the couch. "Honey, is there something wrong?"

The boy shook his head against the tiger.

"Okay. But if everything is all right, why are you hiding your face?"

Eric shrugged.

Anderson broke her protocol and stroked the back of his head. "Is there something you want to tell me?"

Eric lunged, and the eyes that had been cute just a moment before were now partially rolled back. He grabbed her throat and dug in with both thumbs.

"Don't *fuck* with me, sista!" he said. "This bitch has been 'round the block!"

Anderson was so shocked she could hardly comprehend what Eric was saying. He had a surprising amount of strength for such a scrawny kid, and she could barely pry his hands away from her throat. She sat up and held his wrists apart. "That will be quite enough, young man!" He had done some damage; it was hard for Anderson to find her voice. "When I let go," she managed, "I want you to take Mr. T and march back to that chair." She motioned with her head to the wingback.

"The shit you say! That's some attitude coming from a gutter bitch like you!" Eric yanked his arms free and defiantly put his hands on his hips. "This ho' needs her money. Now where is it?"

Anderson was dumbfounded. She stared at Eric, but only the whites of his eyes stared back.

"Well, bitch?"

"W-who am I talking to?"

"Alicia May Tristen," he said, then snapped his fingers in a Z pattern.

* * *

Anderson gingerly accepted the cup of coffee. She took a sip and could feel the bruises where Eric's thumbs had dug in.

"How are you doing?" Prost asked.

"I think the term is 'shock and awe.'"

Prost chuckled. "That was quite an act you put on for Kim. I don't think she has a clue what happened. Why didn't you tell her the truth?"

Anderson leaned back and propped her feet on the coffee table. Mr. T slid against her shoulder.

"*Please*," she said and threw the stuffed animal over the back of the couch. She rubbed her throat and took another sip. "I didn't tell her everything because Kim is a domineering mother and, quite frankly, I think she's in denial." That was only part of the reason, though. The rest was that Anderson's heart had gone out to Eric. Seeing him act out through a different personality had deeply touched her. She wasn't certain what had just happened, and before she could even think about a diagnosis, she needed time to regroup.

Prost walked over to the coffee maker and poured another cup. "Tell me again how Eric snapped out of it."

"I asked Alicia May to leave and Eric to come back. At first, he didn't respond, except to call me a 'white trash bitch' and ask for the money I owed."

Prost shook his head. "That's crazy." He sat in the chair next to the couch and propped his boots onto the coffee table. "What happened then?"

"I just kept asking for Eric. It took about five minutes, but his personality finally surfaced. After that, he went back to being adorable and didn't have any recollection of the episode." Anderson took another swallow and noticed the soreness had subsided.

Prost took his feet off the table and leaned forward onto his knees. He cupped his mug and took a swig. "What do you think is going on here?" His voice was filled with concern.

"It's hard to say so early. We might be dealing with DID. He has many of the classic symptoms."

"But Tren, what about the German?"

"I'm sure that can be explained. After our last conversation, I did a little researching. There was a girl, about Eric's age, in Australia. She had night terrors too, and had spontaneously acquired the ability to speak Japanese. Guess where she learned it?"

Prost shrugged.

"An exchange student at her school. The parents had no idea they were friends. The girl never mentioned it, and since they were never with her during the day, they were clueless. It even made the news. The media was calling her one of those Indigo Children, and the girl played right along until a classmate exposed her."

Prost didn't respond.

"What? You don't believe me?"

"I did a little researching of my own before I came over," Prost said.

"Really, on what?"

"Alicia May."

"How? You were only gone a little over an hour."

"Give three grad students access to the University's bandwidth and the promise of beer, and you can get anything done."

"And?"

"They found an Alicia May Tristen in Orange County, California."

"The name's not *that* unique. I'll bet there's hundreds in the U.S. What's so special about this one?"

"This Alicia May was a crack whore who died eight years ago."

Anderson thought she felt the bruises around her neck start to throb. "Yeah, so?"

Prost stared into his mug and then looked up. "Guess when she died."

It was Anderson's turn to shrug.

"The same day Eric was born."

5. Just learning from the master.

"You are *shitting* me!"

"I'm not, Kelly. You should have seen the imaging. It was un*fucking* believable!" Kanter knocked back the rest of his beer.

Hoop's apartment was a couple of blocks from the Museum of Science and Industry, above a generic Asian restaurant. Kanter hadn't eaten dinner, and the smells of Moo Shu and pork-fried rice were making his stomach growl.

The party was crowded with an eclectic mix of students, peppered with a few out-of-place business types. The fashion tonight seemed all about loud colors and prints, and a few Rastas were holding in their dreads with brightly striped knit hats. One guy's was piled so high it barely cleared the blades of the den's ceiling fan. Someone had wrapped a scarf around the lamp in the kitchen, casting the room in shades of brothel red. The music was a mix of techno and Caribbean pop. Kanter couldn't place the language. He was musing that the whole scene reminded him of a Blaxploitation movie he had watched with a bunch of Kelly's friends, when a girl with a huge Afro and about a dozen strategically placed piercings offered him a joint. What the hell? He was jazzed about his discovery, so why not celebrate?

Kelly's friend Hoop had the body of a linebacker, or at least a linebacker who had been out of the game for a while. He had wedged himself into a heavily duct-taped recliner, from which he eyed Kanter warily. "Careful, mon," Hoop finally said, "that hay will f you up."

Kanter hacked out most of the hit. He had done his share of weed before, but nothing this harsh. "What is this stuff, lawn cuttings from the South Side?" He resumed his coughing fit.

Kelly and Hoop burst out laughing. The two girls who had been sitting with them got up and left.

"So let me get this straight, you two have been trying to develop a new kind of MRI to scan the brain?" Hoop pointed a heavily ringed finger at Kelly. "But in the process, you created a way to see *memories*?"

Kanter shot Kelly a quizzical look.

"Don't let Hoopy here fool you," Kelly said. "Not only does he have the best weed in the city, he also holds a Masters of Computer Sciences from Urbana."

Hoop winked at Kelly from behind a curtain of thick dreadlocks, and Kanter began to sense that Hoop was a father figure to Kelly. Maybe he had raised Kelly, or at least taken him in. Maybe Hoop had inspired Kelly to get into computer science. Their ages seemed about right.

"I think we have," Kanter said. "All thanks to Kelly."

"Nah. I'm just learning from the master." Kelly put a hand on Kanter's shoulder.

"What about the other images you were talking about?" Hoop asked. "The ones earlier in the scan?"

Kanter didn't know how to answer. The implications of the discovery were staggering. "I'm not sure," he said. He lifted the beer bottle to his lips, completely forgetting that it was empty.

Kelly had sunk into a tattered armchair that looked like it came straight from the curb. He pulled two Red Stripes from an ice-filled trashcan and handed one to Kanter. "Doc, it sounds like you've discovered a way to image past lives."

Hoop's bloodshot eyes widened.

Kanter put a hand up. "I don't know if I'd go that far."

"You're playing with Voodoo, mon!" Hoop accepted the other beer from Kelly. He twisted the cap off and flicked it somewhere over Kanter's left shoulder. "You gotta watch yourself."

"Screw Voodoo," Kelly said. "We're talking a full-on Pandora's Box here! Doc, do you know what this means?"

Unfortunately, Kanter did. The legal ramifications alone were staggering, not to mention the moral ones.

"First off, we have to take this slow," Kanter said to Kelly. "We're not sure what we have. For all we know, those other images could be dreams."

"Doc! This is huge. Even if they're dreams, this is going to change everything!"

"Look, we have to run more confirmation tests and make sure the system can handle the extra strain of the increased particle flow."

"We could re-sequence the third and fifth processors," Kelly offered.

Kanter shook his head. "We can't do that. It'll mess with the levels."

"What if we–"

"You need to Rip-tide the data flow," Hoop said from behind the haze of a large joint.

Both Kanter and Kelly lowered their beers.

"That way you take the stress off of the TL boards." Hoop smiled a gummy, gold-enhanced grin and took another hit.

* * *

Kelly leaned back in his chair and stared at the computer screen.

Kanter glanced at his watch. 4:57 a.m. "Well?" he asked.

Kelly started laughing, and his dreads bounced in sync.

"What's so funny?"

"This is too easy. That Hoopy knows his shit."

"It'll work?"

Kelly nodded. "I don't see why not."

Kanter was a software guy and had heard of Rip-tiding. It was an iffy way to get around certain bandwidth issues, used mostly by hackers and those who didn't care about protocols or equipment safety. Since he didn't have any better ideas, he had nothing to lose. On the other hand, maybe that hit back at Hoop's apartment was clouding his judgment.

"I think it's going to double the data stream's capacity." Kelly pointed to the ratio readout. "When you dial into the middle now, it will be like dialing past the previous red. Make sense?"

It did. Kanter wanted to view his past again, but this time without the fear of frying the system.

Kelly passed a hand through his dreads and yawned. "I wonder if it will set off the alarms again?"

"That wasn't us. I think it was the group across the hall. I checked the stacks, and they looked fine. They had heated up, but nothing fried."

"What about the smoke?"

"It's happened before. Those guys do a lot of chemical experiments. I don't ask, so I don't know."

"Probably a damn meth lab."

"Doubtful."

Kelly yawned again and stretched. "I don't know about you, boss, but I'm beat. You going to try again to watch the many lives of Dr. William Kanter?" He snapped his fingers. "Hey, there's another way we can make money ... your own personal soap opera. We could sell it to a network."

Kanter was too tired to laugh. "Let's just see what we have first, okay? Besides, I'm not sure something this important should be packaged. Maybe it should be made available to the world."

"Are you nuts? We're out of money. Even if we do confirm we can image past lives, how we going to perfect it? Hoopy's solution isn't going to keep up. Eventually we have to redesign the boards so they can handle a constant push."

Kelly slipped back to street slang when he was excited, but he was right. Even Kanter knew that the big Rastafarian's solution was a stopgap. In order for them to really confirm what they were looking at, they would have to conduct control testing, probably redesign the applications, and figure a legitimate way around the bandwidth issue. All that took money. Going back to the Genonics' well was a crapshoot. The people he had started with were long gone, and the new suits were slashing budgets that didn't fit their present business model. Even if his discovery were the real thing, most corporations didn't hand out grants on speculation. Either he would have to join the ranks of cubicle America and give up his patent rights, or dip back into his own money, and that wouldn't get them very far ... maybe three months, at best. The idea of starting over at another institution didn't appeal to Kanter at all.

"I don't know, Kelly," he said, rubbing his temples.

Kelly rolled back and folded his arms. "You know, I knew this girl who was a researcher in the pharm department. She funded her work by selling the best–"

"No! I'm not going sell hay or whatever it's called."

Kelly laughed. "I'm just messing with you. Something will come up. It always does." He stood and began collecting his backpack.

"Where are you going?"

Kelly's expression became serious. "Man, it's your soul. It's not my place to watch it."

"Bullshit. You're as much a part of all this as me."

The glow from the computer cast Kelly's face into deep contrasts of brown and black. He hiked his backpack over his shoulder. "It's your discovery, Bill. I'm just learning from the master."

6. Close to the end.

"How's it going?" Prost asked.

"You're breaking up a little," Anderson said.

"There, is that better?"

"Much."

"Great, so how's the hypno session going?"

For the last two weeks, the results from Eric's sessions kept steering Anderson towards a DID diagnosis. Usually severe physical and sexual abuse caused a patient to develop a disturbance of identity, but Anderson couldn't find any trace of an event or series of events. Throughout the sessions Eric had been polite and responsive, but neither the German guard nor Alicia May resurfaced. Anderson figured

Kimberly Nelson had been up to her helicoptering ways and had schooled her son into being the perfect patient, which seemed odd. If Eric were Anderson's son, she would be intent on finding a way to deal with his disorder, not shelter him from it. But mothers like Kimberly were not that uncommon. Anderson had seen her share of parents in denial about their children's conditions. When Anderson had finally told Kimberly about that first session with Eric, she didn't mention the attack. Instead, she had concentrated on walking Kimberly through the ramifications of DID. At first, Kimberly couldn't accept Anderson's thinking, but after some explanation and fueled in part by her bother's insistence, she came to accept that her son might be in need of special therapy.

Anderson peeked around the door and into her office. "Dr. Petrovski is just about to put Eric under."

"God, if Scott knew I was doing this, he'd skin me. I'm just the brother-in-law, you know."

"Who loves his nephew very much. Just keep Kim busy for another couple of hours. What's that noise? Are you in a bathroom?"

A toilet flush muffled Prost's voice. "Of course. Where else can I sneak a call?"

"Are you're sure she's okay with what we're going to do?"

"Yes, I'm sure. Frankly, I'm surprised she's allowing us."

"Given their religious views, I'm surprised she's here at all. Is she going to tell her husband?"

"I don't think so."

"That's not good, but it's her call. So how are you going to keep Kim occupied?"

"I'm going to take her to a movie."

"Make it something long."

"I'll try." A hand dryer came on deep in the background. "Hey Tren?"

"Yes?"

"Thanks."

"My pleasure. I just want to get to the bottom of this and help Eric."

"I know, but you're bending the rules and going way beyond a favor."

"Let me worry about what rules I'm bending. Now go watch the movie. I'll call you when we're finished."

Anderson pocketed her cell and cautiously stepped back to the couch, where Mr. T and Eric were snuggled together. There weren't many treatment options for DID, and because of the Nelson's religious tendencies, she decided to avoid any type of drug therapy. Often psychotherapy with hypnosis was the treatment of choice, but Anderson wasn't skilled in the practice. Petrovski had been recommended to Anderson by the dean of the psychology department. He was very well respected with an impressive list of degrees on his CV. He was sitting on the edge of the coffee table.

"How's it going?" Anderson whispered.

Petrovski glanced up and pressed a finger to his lips.

Sorry, Anderson mouthed.

"Eric," Petrovski said, "when I touch your wrist two times I want you to let everything that bothers you just disappear, all right? Think of a quiet place, away from your school and parents."

Eric, his eyes closed, nodded.

Petrovski touched Eric's wrist twice, and the boy went limp. Mr. T rolled out of his arms and fell to the floor. Anderson picked it up and quietly placed it at the end of the couch.

For the next few minutes, Petrovski led Eric through a series of exercises designed to prepare him for his journey through his past lives. They involved some standard visualization techniques that Petrovski had modified for young children. Depending upon how Eric reacted, Petrovski warned, he might have to shift and conduct a multiple personality session.

"Now, Eric," Petrovski said, "can you introduce me to your German friend?"

Eric shook his head.

"How about Alicia May?"

"I can't," he said, barely above a whisper.

Petrovski frowned and made a notation in his laptop. "Why not?"

Eric's eyelids slowly opened. His eyes were partially rolled back. Petrovski made another notation, clicked on a pocket recorder, and placed it near the corner of the coffee table.

The words that came out of Eric's mouth sounded to Anderson like Native American, but what did she know? They could be Aboriginal or some other tribal language. She was glad Petrovski was recording it.

"Whom am I speaking with?" Petrovski asked.

More tribal speak.

Petrovski made another notation. "Can you tell us where you're from?"

There was a laugh, and the words were more sing-songish. Maybe there was a joke at play, but Anderson and Petrovski would have to wait for the translation.

After about a minute of more tribal language, Eric closed his eyes.

"Am I speaking with Eric now?" Petrovski asked.

Eric nodded.

"All right. When I touch your wrist twice, I want you to wake up feeling rested and alert." He motioned for Anderson to return Mr. T next to Eric.

Afterward, Petrovski tapped Eric's wrist. The boy slowly opened his eyes and began hugging Mr. T.

"Eric, how do you feel?" Petrovski asked.

"Okay. Did I ... change?"

Petrovski glanced at Anderson, his eyebrows raised.

"Yes, dear," Anderson said. "But you were very good and answered all of the doctor's questions."

Eric nodded. "Can I go home now?"

"I think we're finished for today." Petrovski closed his laptop and stood. "You're a very special boy."

"I'll call your mother to come pick you up," Anderson said.

Eric smiled and scrutinized Anderson with those eyes. Something special lurked behind them, and Anderson wanted to find out what.

"Where are your bathrooms?" Petrovski asked.

"They're out the door and down the hall, next to the water fountains. I think the men's is on the other side of the elevators."

"Thank you," Petrovski said and hurried out.

"Eric, do you need to use the bathroom?"

"No, thank you, Dr. Anderson."

She settled into the chair behind her desk and started to shut down her computer. Eric sat on the couch and held Mr. T. She could feel his stare.

"Is there something you want to tell me?" The last time Anderson had asked this question, a crack whore attacked her. She was glad her desk was between them.

The blue eyes studied her for a moment. "When I die," Eric said, "will I become a new person?"

The hairs on the back of Anderson's neck bristled. "I don't know, honey. What do you think?"

The boy pondered the question and smiled. "I think I'm close to the end."

"End of what?"

"Being here."

"I don't understand," Anderson said. "Can you explain what you mean?"

Eric put a finger to his cheek and thought. "I don't think I can fit any more in." He pointed to his heart.

"Any more what?"

The blue eyes blinked. "People," he replied, like it was the obvious answer.

7. Do you feel like God?

"William, this is astounding!"

Kanter had never seen the head of his department so excited. "Pretty incredible, isn't it?"

Phillip Jessel slipped on his horn-rims and leaned closer to the screen. His deep-set eyes squinted under a bushy awning of grey eyebrows. "Are you sure these are *your* memories?"

"I know my own life, Phillip."

"But these could be dreams."

Kanter shook his head. "No. The imaging is too perfect and accurate. And, quite frankly, too boring."

"What about the other, ah ... what should we call them?"

"Past lives?"

Jessel looked at him like a nut. "William, you can't be serious."

"Why not, Phillip? Haven't you ever felt a connection to certain times in history? Something ... I don't know, spiritual?"

"Like Patton?"

"Did he believe in reincarnation?"

The imaging had sequenced into some 18th century Parisian scenes.

"He thought he had been a Roman general, or something like that." Jessel pulled up a chair and sat. "So you think we're looking at one of your past lives?"

"As far as I can tell." Kanter paused the streaming. "See, the scenes are too mundane. I don't dream about brushing my hair or going to the bathroom. And look at the point-of-view. We've calculated it's at the eye level of a woman about five-three. I'm almost six-one."

"You were a woman?"

"What we're looking at has been imprinted through the eyes, so believe me, we can tell."

"I guess you would. So how many lives have you had?"

"So far we've counted nine. Everything from a turn-of-the-century music teacher – which is what you're viewing here – to a medieval innkeeper. Or that's what we think. It's hard to discern since we don't recognize some of the scenes, and there's no sound."

"Nine lives? Were you ever a cat?"

"Funny, Phillip. And no. All human."

"That'll piss the Hindus off." Jessel leaned back and stroked his goatee. "Do you have complete imaging of all your lives?"

"No. It seems that the brain doesn't retain all of the memories."

"The brain doesn't start retaining memories until we're about five.... It's not developed yet. Besides, the brain is developed uniquely from birth. It couldn't have access to memories it never processed."

"Right. That's why we think it's genetic."

"Genetic? How?"

"That part we haven't figured out. Maybe the memories are encoded on a genetic carrier of some sort, the way radio signals are embedded as amplitude or frequency variations on a carrier wave."

"There's a geneticist here at the university I met once at a fundraiser," Jessel said. "He worked on the Human Genome Project. Fascinating stuff. Maybe he could help you. So, tell me, why are the past-life images so fragmented?"

"We're not sure. For us to move forward and process all the data, we have to redesign some of the system. We've only been working on this for a week, and my scan is the only one we've done. We need to run some control tests and scan a broader demographic. The main logic boards have to be upgraded. But … there's an issue."

Jessel regarded Kanter over his horn-rims. He brought out his fatherly look whenever Kanter needed something. Kanter, though he hated to admit it, was the resident celebrity, disliked by most of the tenured professors. He knew Jessel couldn't compete, except when it came to finding money, and he always made sure Kanter was aware of where he stood in the funding pecking order.

"How much do you need, William?" Jessel faced the screen, which had segued to Kanter's life as a tenth-century Italian monk.

"Six million."

"William, that's a lot of money."

"Look at what I've discovered. What the *university's* discovered."

Kanter gestured at the screen. “This could change everything in our society. It will turn religion upside down. The potential is huge!” He leaned back in his chair. “I’m sure there are other universities that would jump at the chance to fund this discovery. Not to mention corporations…”

“Now hold on, William.” The fatherly routine vanished. “You’re not going to Stanford or Duke with this one. And I’ll be damned if you’ll take this back to Genonics.” He chewed one of the ends of his frames. “If this *is* what you think it is, then it needs to stay right here at the University of Chicago. Who knows what this could lead to? This is a damn Pandora’s box, and it needs to be controlled.”

“That’s what Kelly said.”

“Kelly? Your assistant?”

“Yes.”

Jessel pocketed his glasses and folded his arms. “The key to selling this is not to mention the past-life aspect. Hell, the memory imaging alone is revolutionary.... There’re some history professors I know who would kill for this machine! But...”

“What?”

“Money’s tight right now.”

“Phillip!”

“I *know*, William. But I don’t have to tell you what a bunch of asshole conservatives litter the board. This technology hasn’t been independently verified or even thoroughly tested. All you have right now is just a hypothesis of what it can do. If I took this to the board right now, the religious implications alone could kill the project.” Jessel stroked his goatee and stared at the screen.

“Phillip, what are you thinking?”

"There is someone on the board who might be interested in this. Very interested."

"Who's that?"

"Cole Strachan."

"The gaming guy?"

"Strachan Media Group is one of the university's largest benefactors. You've heard of the Strachan Endowment?"

The idealist in Kanter was fighting the realist. He didn't want to sell out to corporate American again. With the MedBed, he had been young and stupid and hadn't listened to his legal counsel. He had taken a lump buyout instead of a percentage and had been screwed out of most of his patents. Kelly once calculated that if Kanter had agreed to just two percent of the total sales for the first two years, he would be worth over $20 million today. Now, Jessel was suggesting he get into bed with a power broker like Strachan. "I don't know. That's not what I was–"

"William, do want this funded or not?"

Kanter had to admit he did, and not because it would make him rich. The world needed to change. He wasn't an overly religious man. He had been raised in middle class Boston by parents who considered themselves Cafeteria Catholics. They were more concerned with being spiritual than religious. Kanter himself had grown to believe there was more to God than what had been written down two thousand years ago.

"Okay. Let me know what I need to do."

Jessel chuckled. "For starters, buy a good suit … or at least borrow one. Strachan is one of these mover-and-shaker types. You're going to have to look the part of someone who knows what they're doing." He eyed Kanter's high-tops and sweatshirt.

"I've got a good suit, don't worry," Kanter said.

"Good, maybe. But current?" He gave him the once-over again. "Doubtful." Jessel turned back to the screen. "Pause this."

Kanter paused the streaming. The image was a distorted reflection of a portly monk. He had picked up a serving tray and was inspecting something in his teeth. The candlelight and warped features of the tray made the scene dreamlike. It was an insignificant moment in an insignificant life.

"What do you feel when you look at this?" Jessel asked.

Kanter had to admit it was weird as hell, especially when he could see what he had looked like. But the odd thing was, he could always feel a connection. Even now, as he studied the image, the sensation washed over him like it had the first time he had seen himself in the past. The intimacy of it was almost overwhelming.

"Have you ever seen one of your past lives do something bad? Like stealing or murder?" Jessel asked.

"I've caught glimpses of some petty thefts, but we can't seem to retrieve a complete life. They get more fragmented the farther back we go. I guess it's possible one of my past lives could have been a murderer or something. I don't know yet."

Jessel leaned back. "This is going to change the judicial system."

"How's that?"

"For instance, say sometime in the future you're charged with murder. All they'll have to do is scan your brain and watch your memories. Case closed."

"Maybe," Kanter said. "But we'll have to determine if these are accurate or not. I'd like to hook this up to a schizophrenic or a psychopath. See if the brain records life as it happens or as it's perceived."

"What do you think?"

"So far it appears to record accurately, but I'm not a good subject.... I'm not crazy enough."

Jessel chuckled.

"The legal issues aren't what concern me," Kanter said. "The courts will figure all that out. It's the religious aspect that's frightening."

"Why?"

"Because," Kanter said, "if you add up all the world's religions that believe in reincarnation, they almost equal Islam or Christianity."

"Why would that be bad?"

"Traditionally, how do the leaders of the world's religions garner their power?"

Jessel thought for a second. "Through control."

"And how do they gain control?"

"Well, if you're a Catholic, through guilt."

Kanter laughed. "You're right about that. But it's really the mystique of religion. Think about it. You're a Hindu, and now you can learn about all your past lives.... Kind of takes the mystery out of it, doesn't it?"

"Okay, but why's that a problem?"

"We're looking at almost a third of the world's population that's going to learn their religions were right, after all."

Jessel's eyebrows went up. "And the religions that don't believe in reincarnation?..."

"Were wrong."

"Which means a lot of very powerful people in this world are going to be out of jobs." Jessel whistled.

"Yeah," Kanter said. "This is going to change everything."

Jessel rolled his eyes. "Great, one more thing for religions to fight about. Wait till the Vatican hears about this."

Both men went back to staring at the monk. An uneasy quiet settled around them.

"Tell me, William, do you feel like God?"

Kanter thought for a moment. "No. More like Robert Oppenheimer."

8. Good luck.

Ulrich Boxler picked a piece of lint off the sleeve of his uniform and flicked it. His gaze followed as it fell delicately to the terrazzo floor. Ever since he had been a boy growing up in Berne, Switzerland, he had thought that Michelangelo had designed the uniforms. But barely a week into his training, he learned that Commandant Jules Repond had designed them in 1914. He liked the berets but hated the helmets. The strap dug into his neck, and after a hot afternoon of parades, the helmet became unbearable. Today, though, there were no ceremonies scheduled, and the black beret was in order.

Boxler had been a Vatican Guard for five years. He was proud of this fact, since many of the guards left after two years for more lucrative jobs in private law enforcement. He had considered following suit, but his devotion to the Holy Father was unwavering.

When the commandant entered the cramped office, Boxler stood to attention.

"Please, sit," the commandant said while he took his seat.

Boxler sat, yet didn't lean back against the chair.

The commandant slipped on a pair of reading glasses, which somewhat diminished his imposing demeanor. He regarded Boxler over the half-rims.

"What are you staring at?" he asked.

"Nothing, sir," Boxler said.

"You are one of my best men." The commandant's scrutiny went to a stack of papers.

"Thank you, sir."

"Have you ever been to the city of Chicago?"

The question caught Boxler off guard. "Sir?"

The commandant's pale grey eyes lifted. He removed the glasses and tossed them on the stack. "I have an unusual assignment for you." His voice was low and measured. "It is of the utmost importance to the Church."

Boxler's pulse quickened. He sat up straighter.

"Everything you need to know is in this file. Read it, then destroy all the contents." The commandant opened a drawer and removed a large manila envelope. He handed it to Boxler. "I would tell you more, but I don't trust these walls."

Boxler spun the heavy folder around and passed his fingers over the Papal seal. The arms of the Holy See were perfectly formed in the blood red wax.

"Ulrich?"

Boxler looked up and found his commandant staring. His hands were folded on the desk, his fingers fidgeting nervously across his knuckles.

"This assignment comes directly from His Eminence," he said. "I have chosen you because of your knowledge of American culture and your skills with its language. This will be the most important assignment we have ever undertaken. You will not be able to contact us until it is finished, so all the decisions you make will be your own. Do you have any questions?"

Boxler looked at the seal. He was in shock. "No, sir," he croaked.

"Excellent." The commandant stood and extended his hand. Rarely had he shown this kind of personal interaction.

Boxler jumped to his feet and took it.

"God be with you, my son. The Holy Father is counting on you."

9. The soul man.

"I can't believe you're dragging me all the way across campus without an appointment." Anderson flipped up the collar of her leather coat and leaned into the cold Chicago night. She had found it on the sale rack a couple of weeks ago at the downtown Macys and hadn't figured she'd have the chance to wear it until next winter.

"The guy will be there," Prost said. "Jessel told me he never leaves. He practically has an apartment in the back of his lab."

They rounded the corner of the Regenstein Library. A blast of wind punched Anderson in the face. "God, it's freezing. Isn't this April?" She pulled the collar tight to her neck and held it there as she walked.

"So much for global warming," Prost said.

"Tell me again why I'm joining you?"

"Jessel called this morning and told me about this researcher–"

"What's his name again?"

"William Kanter. He's the guy who invented the MedBed."

"That was all over the news a while back. Didn't he win some award?"

"I think it was the Gates. And he just invented something that can image memories."

They rounded another building that blocked the wind. Anderson released her collar and plunged her hands into her coat pockets. She could barely feel her fingertips. "You're kidding me. Real memories?"

"Are there any other kind?"

"That's incredible." They walked through the smoky haze surrounding a group of college kids gathered around a cigarette butt container. Anderson held her breath and exhaled when they cleared. "So, why are you seeing him?"

"Jessel thinks that my background in genetics can help Kanter."

"What's genetics have to do with memories?"

"Well, for starters, his machine also seems to image past lives–"

Anderson abruptly stopped.

"–and he thinks it might be related to a gene," Prost continued, walking ahead. "But I don't think–" He did a double take over his shoulder and saw Anderson several paces behind.

"You're joking, right?" she said.

"I'm not," Prost replied. "Jessel saw it. The man was so excited, he could barely get the words out."

Anderson caught up. "Is this why you're having me tag along?"

"Come on, Tren. What do you have to lose? The hypno-whatever hasn't gone anywhere. You've been working with Eric for almost a month and aren't any closer to a diagnosis. At the very least, you'll have gotten some exercise."

Prost's humor didn't sit well with Anderson. "Really, Tom, *past* lives? Next thing you'll be saying is that Kanter is communicating with spirits."

Prost stepped closer. "You need to start opening your mind to all this." His tone was serious and from the heart. "We're running out of options for Eric."

"What do you mean?"

"He fell again the other night ... sleepwalking."

"Is he all right?"

"Yes, thank God. But next time, he might really do some damage."

Anderson had been trained as a clinical psychologist with an emphasis on school psychology, and she taught intro and specialty courses at the university. She had an open mind toward certain fringe practices like neurolinguistic programming and had decided to use Petrovski only because she was getting close to the limit of her expertise. She didn't want to give up on Eric because that would mean bringing in specialists, and from what she knew about the Nelson's financial situation, that was out of the question.

"Okay," she said. "Let's go see the soul man."

* * *

The first floor of the old Biological Sciences building was littered with crates and trash. After the new BS building opened, the departments had scavenged several of the floors and set up makeshift labs. Anderson and Prost had to descend two flights of stairs because the elevator was held up.

"What's that odor?" Anderson asked when she opened the door to the basement level.

"Stale pizza?" Prost guessed. "Pepperoni with olives, I'd say."

They came to the elevator and found it propped open with a large FedEx tube. A gangly undergrad was stacking various boxes onto a four-wheeler. His arms were heavily sleeved with dark, gothic tattoos.

"Excuse me," Prost said. "Can you tell us where Dr. Kanter's–"

The kid looked up through a greasy forelock and pointed a black-nailed finger towards the main hall before he resumed stacking.

They made their way through more crates and trash, in some places turning sideways just to slide by.

"You never told me what that language was that Eric spoke during the first hypno session," Prost said, struggling by a tall crate. Packing labels from several shipping firms covered the upper half of its wooden frame.

"Inuit," Anderson replied.

"Really?"

"That's what Petrovski said."

"What's his take on Eric's condition?"

"He's cautious about formulating an opinion without more sessions, but I think he's leaning toward multiple personality disorder."

"And how much is he charging?"

"I know, right? He did offer one bizarre theory. Something about Eric's soul leaving and a new one taking its place."

"Walk-ins," Prost said.

"Yeah, that's it. He said it was related to ancient Hindu spiritualism.

I found it a little too 'out there' for my taste."

"Today it's connected with the New Age movement, or what's left of it." Prost turned to negotiate another tall crate. "Some people believe that groups of souls can occupy one person."

"Well, that's one way to explain MPD." Anderson's sweater caught on the crate. "Hold on, I'm snagged."

Prost sidestepped back to her. "Here, let me help. I can get to it." He reached and unhooked Anderson's sweater, but in the process grazed her breasts. He quickly withdrew his hand. "Jeez, Tren, I'm sorry."

"Don't worry, that was the most fun I've had all year. Was it good for you?"

Prost laughed.

The hall past the crate was remarkably clean. There was only one door, and it had Kanter's name written in Sharpie on the glass.

Prost knocked and tried the handle. The door was unlocked. "Dr. Kanter?" he asked, opening.

"Over here," a voice said from deep in the space.

They maneuvered through tall stacks of processing computers, and Anderson caught two mini-supercomputers out of the corner of her eye. The place was dark with the exception of isolated islands of light at three workstations.

They walked into a small open area and found a grad student hunched over an exposed processor panel. The guy had pulled the unit out from the middle of a rack and had it filleted on top of a red tool cart.

"Excuse me," Prost asked. "I'm looking for Dr. Kanter."

The student turned and flipped up his magnifying goggles. He had about a day's growth and a cleft chin that could have come straight out of central casting. His dark green eyes considered Anderson.

"I'm Kanter."

"Hello, Dr. Kanter," Prost said and extended a hand. "I'm Tom Prost."

"You're the guy Phillip mentioned. He said you might be stopping by."

"I hope you don't mind us dropping in so late."

"No problem," Kanter said. "I'm always up."

Anderson noticed that his left eye was a distinctly different shade of green than his right. He smiled, and soft dimples appeared at the corners of his mouth.

"I'm sorry," Prost said. "This is Dr. Trenna Anderson."

"Are you in genetics also?" Kanter asked, shaking Anderson's hand.

"Trenna," Prost cut in, "is one of the city's premier pediatric psychologists."

Kanter made a face. "No offense, but didn't Phillip mention we were trying to keep this quiet ... at least until we can confirm what we have?"

Prost hesitated.

"Dr. Kanter, I have a patient that might be able to benefit from your discovery," Anderson offered. "He's a little boy who's having some extreme psychiatric episodes."

Kanter's expression grew serious. "Really? That's terrible."

"I hope you don't mind me tagging along with Tom."

"It's okay. Come on. I'll show you what we've created." He headed into the dark. "It's really pretty fucking cool." Kanter stopped and questioned his statement. "I'm sorry ... my language. I've been working alone way too long. Please." He gestured to a narrow passage between the computer stacks.

They came to another open area where a lone workstation sat tucked against a large cement column. Its lamp was the only light, and it bathed the desk in a spot of cool halogen. As Anderson approached, she glimpsed a bed and a small workout machine in a shadowy, distant corner.

"Welcome to my office," Kanter said.

In the light, Anderson noticed how Kanter was dressed. He wore a pair of classic Converse high-tops, faded jeans, and a University of Chicago sweatshirt. It was hooded, and the two drawstrings had miniature screwdrivers tied to them. He peeled off the magnifying glasses and passed a hand through his wavy brown hair.

"Phillip said you had created a machine that can image memories?" Prost asked.

Kanter nodded. "That's right. We've only been able to view my own scan, but the results are unbelievable. Check it out."

Kanter sat at the station. Anderson and Prost pulled up two chairs and crowded around the monitor.

For the next hour, Anderson was transfixed on the images that passed across the large LCD. Prost seemed equally amazed. She didn't quite believe what she was watching, but the images were compelling. It crossed her mind that Kanter might be faking it for some notoriety fix, but he didn't seem the type. Besides, he had already garnered a modest celebrity with his MedBed invention.

"You know, I never get tired of watching them," Kanter said just above a whisper.

"How many lives have you had?" Anderson couldn't believe the words had just come out of her mouth.

"Nine," Kanter replied. "And please don't do the joke about 'Have you been a cat.'"

"How many hours can be recorded?" Prost asked.

"I guess that depends on how many past lives you've had," Kanter said. "So far my data stream is more than two-and-a-half million hours long."

"But that's more than nine lives."

"Right. So we know we haven't recovered them all."

"How do you think it works? I mean, where's all this coming from?" Anderson asked.

"We think it's genetic," Kanter said.

"Interesting," Prost remarked. "Why do you think that?"

Kanter spun and faced them for the first time since he had sat. "The brain can't retain information the senses haven't processed, right? The next best guess is that there's a gene that harbors the information. And it's passed on somehow."

"But that implies that the memories of past lives are carried forward from parent to child," Prost said. "Is that what your data is showing?"

Kanter's demeanor sank. He started playing with one of the screwdrivers. "I was afraid you were going to say that. No, there's nothing in the data that shows that. The past lives are all over the place."

"Don't get me wrong," Prost said. "Even though I'm a geneticist, I have my metaphysical side. There is some basis for after-life in quantum theory."

"I wondered about that," Kanter said. "I've read some of Chopra's work."

"You two want to fill me in?" Anderson asked.

"Simply put," Prost said. "Consciousness can't be explained physically, with genetics and chemistry. But because quantum physics suggests that everything *is* energy, there's a school of thought that believes, someday, that consciousness will be explained. It's a little hard to grasp without a solid knowledge of quantum theory."

Anderson's head was beginning to spin, and Prost picked up on it.

"Here's another way to look at it," he continued. "Science believes that the brain creates consciousness through the processing of our experiences. But what if the brain were more like a satellite dish that received our consciousness from another source? That would suggest a greater consciousness existing on another plane. Even Einstein, towards the end of his life, began to believe in an intelligent design principle for the universe."

"Excuse me," Anderson said. "Since we're basically talking about a person's soul, isn't there another element to take into consideration?"

"What's that?" Kanter asked.

"I don't know. Faith? Mystery?... God?"

"Good point," Prost said. "There are many scientists who are converting to the intelligent design principle, and they're using quantum physics to justify their beliefs. Could these memories you've scanned have been dreams?"

As Kanter explained why they weren't, Anderson continued to watch the screen. It was a fascinating and revolutionary discovery, and she was amazed at how young Kanter was. She wondered about his age. The slight grey at his temples suggested he might be at least in his 30s, but his enthusiasm was more like her undergrad assistants. She used to be that way, and tried to recall why she had changed.

"Dr. Anderson?"

Anderson pulled her attention from the monitor and found Kanter staring. The grin was more pronounced.

"Where'd you go?" he asked.

"I think I'm in shock. If these aren't dreams, then these really *are* your past lives?"

He nodded. The grin remained.

Anderson looked back at the screen and watched a scene of what appeared to be a medieval bar. "I'd love to see what a scan would look like from a psychopath or a serial killer."

"Maybe we'll be able to find Jack the Ripper," Prost mused.

Kanter scooted closer. Anderson could smell his aftershave. It reminded her of a guy she had once dated.

"This is when I was an innkeeper. Nobody special. Just a schmo trying to get by in the Dark Ages." Kanter pointed. "Look at the clothes. It's like right out of a movie."

"The clarity is astonishing," Anderson marveled.

"So tell me about this kid," Kanter said. "What's his medical issue? If you can't say, I understand."

"No, it's okay. His name is Eric, and he lives on a farm in southern Wisconsin. He's a darling little boy, but he suffers from a ... condition. The reason Tom asked me along is because he displays some unusual personality changes when he's having an episode."

"What kind of changes?"

The room's quiet was abruptly cut by a digital rendition of Johnny

Be Good. Prost dug his phone out his pants pocket and flipped it open.

"Hi, Kim.... What? ... I can't hear you.... I'm in the basement of a building. Let me get upstairs so I can get a better signal and call you back." Prost folded the phone shut. "It's Kim. Something's wrong." He stood and headed for the path between the computer stacks.

"Do you want me to come along?" Anderson asked.

"No," he said, angling into the path, "I'll be right back."

"Who's Kim?" Kanter asked.

"She's Eric's mother."

"Finish what you were telling me."

Anderson told Kanter about everything that had happened over the last month. He seemed genuinely concerned and was intrigued by the results from the hypnotic regression sessions.

"So you think Eric is manifesting his past lives through his night terrors?" Kanter leaned back, flipped the screwdrivers over each shoulder, and folded his arms.

Anderson hesitated. Something inside her was beginning to crumble, and she suspected it was her skeptical nature. "I don't know if I'm ready to say for sure.... "

"But there's no other logical conclusion, right?"

She nodded.

Kanter rolled closer. "At first, I didn't believe any of this." He motioned to the screen. "I still have to run controls, do some blind tests, you know. But I've got a feeling about this. I think this is the real thing. And if it can help this kid, I'm all over it."

"Thank you, Dr. Kanter."

He made a face. "Please, call me Bill."

“I have to go,” Prost said, rushing into the space. He grabbed his coat off the back of the chair.

“Tom, what happened?” Anderson asked, standing.

Prost zipped up the front of his coat and fished for his gloves. He started to leave, but hesitated. “It’s … ah … Shit, it’s bad.”

“Tom?” Anderson stepped over and took his elbow. “*What* is it?”

Prost glanced at Kanter, then Anderson. “The German just stabbed Scott in his sleep.”

10. You'll get your money.

Phillip Jessel's office was the classic university sanctuary, right down to its cherry-stained shelves crammed with leather-bound books. It smelled of Borkum Riff and academia, and had a bank of tall windows that flooded the room with morning light. Kanter stood at the windowsill and admired the view of the north campus. He hadn't worn a starched shirt since the Medical Design Excellence Award ceremony. The collar dug into his neck, and he resisted the urge to tug at it.

"William, this is Cole Strachan," Jessel said when he entered the room, a distinguished, older black gentleman at his side.

Strachan's suit was so perfectly tailored it looked like a second skin. He extended his hand and summoned a cultivated smile. A dusting of grey lightened his close-cropped hair.

"Dr. Kanter," he said in a rich baritone.

"Hello, Mr. Strachan." Kanter took his hand and felt the alumni ring dig in.

"Please, call me Cole." He joined Kanter at the window. "Beautiful morning." An awkward moment followed as he took in the view. "Phillip has told me that you're about to change the world."

Kanter glanced at Jessel over his shoulder. "I don't know about that," he said, returning to the view. "But if our tests are confirmed, we'll make an impact."

"I've spent most of my adult life positioning myself to be at the right point when the world is about to change." His tone was that of someone accustomed to giving orders and not receiving replies. He faced Kanter. "Am I at the right point, Bill?"

Kanter had dealt with corporates like Strachan. At Genonics, his main contact had been one of those cubical types who wouldn't have thought twice about throwing his own mother under the bus. He had jerked Kanter around several times, which was the primary reason for Kanter's current apprehension with corporate America. Kanter studied the vicious scar that ran under Strachan's right eye and said, "I'm pretty certain you are, Cole."

Strachan's expression hardened. Kanter glimpsed something predatory enter his eyes. "I didn't work my way out of Cabrini-Green to invest in ventures that are 'pretty certain.'"

Kanter tried to swallow but found his throat dry. "Even if we confirm half of what we've discovered, the world will change."

Strachan smiled. "Excellent. Now let's go see this memory

machine of yours."

* * *

"Did you see the look on Strachan's face when he saw that I had been black in a previous life?" Kanter asked.

"I thought it was a deal killer," Jessel said.

"Really? I thought it tipped him over to our side." Kanter accepted his beer from the waitress.

"Thank God you were never a Klansman!"

"No shit. Can you imagine?"

Jessel raised his draft. "Congratulations, William. You're going to be famous. Again."

They clinked glasses. Kanter took a swig and came away with more foam than Heineken. "Thanks, Phillip. But let's wait until we know for sure what we have." He took another drink, mostly beer. "I couldn't read Strachan very well. Do you think he's excited about the project?"

"Are you joking? Didn't you see the way he was taking it all in? I think he was in shock."

"About what? Its profundity or its profit?"

"Don't sell Strachan too short, William. He's given a lot to this university."

"He's like the black Gordon Gecko." Kanter grabbed a couple of pretzels the bar offered as food. "I did some research on Strachan Media," he said, crunching down. "They have a class action pending against them. It has to do with one of their war games. I think it's Mothers Against Violence in Videos."

"That's going to happen in any high-profile business. Why don't you relax and revel in your future?"

"Because the last time I did this, I got screwed to the wall."

"You did it to yourself, William. You should have listened to your lawyer. Do you have someone who can review Strachan's contract and advise you so you don't make the same mistake twice?"

The last lawyer Kanter had used had been a friend of his mother's, and that had created a lot of bad blood between him and his dad. "No, but I'll find one."

"If you need any help, just ask. I know several lawyers who would look out for your best interests."

"Thanks, Phillip. I might take you up on that. By the way, how did you get Strachan to come by your office so quickly?"

"First, I went to a friend of mine on the board and asked her opinion about Strachan, to see if he was in a giving mood. And don't worry. I didn't mention any details about your discovery. Then I contacted Strachan's endowment manager, and I was in luck. Strachan was in town and had an opening in his morning. She put me through, we chatted, and just as I figured, he demanded to see you as soon possible." Jessel sipped from his beer. "The manager called me after lunch, and we've got the wheels turning already."

"So what happens next? When do we get funded?"

"It takes about a month to get through the red tape of the Sponsored Projects Office. Strachan's going to fund a grant, and the majority – damn near a hundred percent – goes to your project. Because of politics, we have to at least show we're spreading the wealth."

"How much? Did you get what I wanted?"

"I still have to work out the details with the dean and Strachan's endowment person. But I have a good feeling, William, you'll get what you asked for."

11. Maybe I did piss someone off.

Anderson glanced at her watch. *Tom, where are you?*

"Sorry!" Prost said as he burst into her office. He opened the door so hard it knocked her doctoral diploma cock-eyed. He was practically dragging Eric.

"We're going to be late," Anderson said. "Hello, Eric."

Prost said, "I know, but the Dan Ryan was insane." He brushed some stray bangs off Eric's forehead. "Can you say hello to Dr. Anderson?"

"Hello, Dr. Anderson." The blue eyes were happy today.

"Where's Kimberly?" Anderson asked.

"At home with Scott. I went and picked up Eric."

"How's Scott doing?" Anderson slipped on her coat.

Prost glanced tentatively at Eric. "He's doing much better."

"My dad cut himself working on the milker," Eric said.

Anderson knelt. "That's what your uncle told me."

"Our farm can be dangerous, but I'm not scared. I've milked the cows before." He kicked at his left foot when he said this.

"You have? I'll bet you're good at it." Anderson straightened. "We better get going," she said to Prost.

* * *

While they walked through the campus to Kanter's lab, Eric told them all about the farm and his own chores. He was in a good mood, considering he had just stabbed his father days earlier. But it was unfair to think that way. Anderson reminded herself that it had been the German guard who stabbed Scott Nelson. Maybe today they would find out who he really was.

They climbed the stairs of the Sciences building and took the elevator to the basement level. The halls were in about the same shape as before, but the odor was definitely better.

"I guess someone complained about the smell," Prost remarked. He squeezed past the crate that previously had grabbed Anderson.

"I don't know how they stand working in this filth," Anderson remarked.

"Researchers are a different breed. All they're focused on is their work."

Eric seemed to enjoy navigating the crates and boxes. When they emerged into Kanter's hall, he broke from Prost's grip and skipped toward the lab door. He stretched and tried the handle.

"It's locked," he said.

"How'd he know which door?" Anderson whispered to Prost.

"Beats me," Prost said.

They walked up to Kanter's door, and Anderson tried the knob. "I thought he lived here."

"He does. Maybe he's running late, too, especially if he's anywhere near the Dan Ryan. God what a mess that was."

"Hi there! Sorry I'm late." Kanter emerged from between the crates and trotted over. Gone was the sweatshirt with screwdrivers. Today, he sported pristine jeans and a turtleneck. The high-tops had been replaced with a pair of tan, slip-on clogs, and his chin was even more pronounced against his clean-shaven face. He swung his backpack off his shoulder.

"I hope you weren't waiting too long," he said, dropping the pack to the floor. He knelt and began rifling through it.

"Stuck in traffic?" Prost asked.

Kanter looked up. "Yeah. What was the deal with that?"

"Big accident on the Dan Ryan. A jack-knifed eighteen-wheeler."

Kanter glanced at Anderson and smiled. "Good to see you, doctor. Where's our little subject?"

"Eric?" Anderson asked. "Come out and say hi to Dr. Kanter."

Eric shuffled from behind Prost's legs and extended his hand. The blue eyes were bright and eager.

"Well, hello there. Such a polite little guy." Kanter shook Eric's hand.

"I've done some thinking about your theory," Prost said.

Kanter produced a set of keys. "Whew. I thought I'd lost these."

He stood and unlocked the door. "So what are your thoughts?"

"There're some theories about dormant genes that I think you'd find interesting," Prost said, and took Eric's hand. "Research has found that some genetically engineered foods are triggering dormant genes into action and producing all kinds of reactions in humans."

The door clicked open, and Kanter walked into the darkness. Prost started to follow, but something stopped him in his tracks. It sounded as if Kanter were walking on plastic Corn Flakes. Then something crashed to the floor.

"Shit!" Kanter exclaimed. "Oh, sorry. Eric, you didn't hear that."

"Are you okay?" Anderson asked from the doorway.

"I don't know." More crunching sounds followed. "This is strange. I didn't turn off the desk lights when I left. I can't see a thing. Let me get the overheads."

Kanter emerged from the blackness and inspected the wall next to the door. "I think the switch is over here. I rarely turn these on. I hate the buzz."

He switched on the overheads and filled the lab with a jarring industrial fluorescence.

"What the *hell*?" Kanter said. "I've been frigging robbed."

Anderson peered in and saw that the lab had been ransacked. The stacks of neatly arranged computer towers had been toppled, and all of the stations looked like they had been worked over with a sledgehammer. She walked to Kanter's side, followed by Prost and Eric. Glass, circuit boards, and paper crunched under their steps.

"Man," Prost said, "they did a number."

Kanter trudged through the debris. His posture indicated his spirit was broken. He kicked aside some papers and inspected a workstation, all the while muttering to himself. He disappeared around the open panel of one of the mini-supercomputers. The name on its panel was *Core 10 Linux Cluster*.

"Damn it!" Kanter exclaimed and punched the panel shut.

"Is there anything we can do?" Anderson asked. "I could call the police."

"No! Don't do that." Kanter came out from behind the Core. He kicked back some trash that had spilled from a waste can and righted a workstation chair. He plopped down and sank his head in his hands.

"Why shouldn't we call the police?" Prost asked.

"This project is too sensitive," Kanter said through his fingers. "I have to think here for a second."

"Am I going to be tested today?" Eric asked.

Kanter looked up and forced a smile. "Not today, pal."

"Who would do this?" Anderson asked.

Kanter shook his head. "I don't know. We've had several break-ins. They've always taken stuff they can fence for drugs. Still," he looked around, "something's weird."

"How's that?" Prost asked.

"Whoever did this knew what they wanted. The fence-able stuff is still here. The memory and logic arrays are gone. Just ripped them out." He gestured to the Cores.

"How would they know what to go for?" Prost asked.

"Good question," Kanter replied.

"Someone knows about your discovery, Bill," Anderson offered.

"I think you're right. But who?"

"And why?" Prost said.

Suddenly, phones rang throughout the lab. Kanter stood and

answered the nearest. As he listened, the color in his face drained. He staggered back against the counter and sat.

"You're kidding me, right? ... Yeah. Yeah ... Okay, thanks Hoop.... Yeah, he was a good man." Kanter, his face vacant, let his arm drop to his side and stared at the floor.

"Bill? What happened? What's wrong?" Anderson walked up and put a hand to his shoulder. Prost followed, towing Eric.

"My assistant's dead."

"I'm so sorry," Prost said. "What happened?"

It was obvious that the weight of grief was pressing on Kanter. He looked up, and a tear rimmed his darker green eye. "He overdosed."

* * *

"You need to eat something," Anderson said.

Kanter apathetically picked up the menu and began reading. After Prost had left with Eric, Anderson felt she better stay with Kanter. He was so distraught he hadn't said a word on the walk over to the sandwich shop. She had tried her best to make conversation, but Kanter seemed lost, like the foundation of his life had been kicked out from under him. It had taken a lot of convincing just to get him to consider eating.

"Are you two ready to order?" a perky waitress asked. The shop's logo was emblazoned in puffy glitter across her t-shirt, which reminded Anderson of the crazy hotrod models her brother had built as a kid. What was that guy's name? Big Daddy-something?

"I think we need a minute," she said.

"I'm ready," Kanter said. "I'll take the turkey with American cheese and fries. No mustard. And a Coke."

Anderson ordered the vegetarian special, while Kanter focused on something out the window. The street was empty. She couldn't see anything of interest.

"Bill?"

He didn't respond.

"Look," Anderson said, "I hardly know you, and it's probably none of my business, but–"

"Something's not right," Kanter said.

"Excuse me?"

"Kelly was a free spirit, but not reckless. He wouldn't have OD'd like that."

"Was he into drugs?"

"Just grass."

"Maybe he had a bigger problem. One he didn't tell you about."

Kanter shrugged. "I doubt it. The guy was brilliant. Had a great future." He leaned back against the booth and resumed searching the street.

When the sandwiches came, Kanter inspected his turkey and cheese like a bomb might be under the lettuce.

"Is it not what you wanted?" Anderson asked.

"No, it's fine." He took a large bite and proceeded to chew. His attention was now focused on the middle of the table.

Anderson's clinical experience had taught her to give grieving people a lot of space. But with Kanter, something else was at play, and she could tell it was eating at him.

"Bill, I know someone who is very good in grief counseling. I could–"

"It doesn't make sense," he said.

"What doesn't?"

"Why did they just take the logic arrays? I know the chips are valuable. I guess they can be erased and sold."

"Did you have everything backed up?"

"Oh yeah, every night Kelly backed up onto the school's server. Plus, I have all my original notes and files in a safe deposit box." He leaned back and wiped his mouth with a napkin. "I can always rebuild, it's just..."

"What?"

"We were about to get new funding. That might be jeopardized now. Plus, it won't be the same without–" Kanter's voice faltered; his faraway demeanor returned; he looked anywhere except at Anderson.

Anderson wanted to comfort him, but she didn't know him well enough to say anything. Her mind kept going back to his assistant's death and the break-in at Kanter's lab. They seemed too coincidental. She began seriously contemplating calling the police, regardless of Kanter's wishes.

"Bill," she said, "who else have you told about your discovery?"

Kanter thought for a second. "Not that many. There was Phillip, and he told someone on the board. You and Tom. And of course Kelly ... and Hoop."

"Who's Hoop?"

"A friend of Kelly's."

"A close friend?"

"I don't know. Maybe."

"Bill, think about it. The break-in and your assistant's death might be coincidental. What if you had been in the lab when they broke in?"

"You mean I could have been killed?"

"You need to call the police."

Kanter shook his head. "I can't do that."

"*Why*?" Anderson asked.

Kanter leaned forward and motioned her close. "Do you know the ramifications of what I've discovered?" he whispered. "This is going to change everything. The legal system, religion, politics. Wait till the government gets hold of this technology. Kind of changes the spy business, right?" Kanter's eyes went to the window again.

"What are you looking at?"

"I don't know.... I think I'm getting paranoid."

Anderson peered around the side of the booth. The street beyond the window seemed relatively quiet. A light-duty truck drove by, and a young couple were laughing and leaning against the window. They were bathed in the harsh orange and green neon of the shop's sign. A gentle rain was wetting the pavement.

"I think there's a guy out there," Kanter said. "There's no bus stop. He's been standing across the street."

Anderson looked again. "Where? I don't see anybody."

"He's gone now, of *course*. Forget it. Come on, let's get out of here." Kanter threw some money on the table and climbed out of the booth. He slung his backpack over his shoulder and charged for the door.

"Bill, wait." Anderson dug a ten out of her wallet and placed it on top of Kanter's money. She grabbed her coat and hurried out of the shop.

Kanter was already on the sidewalk trotting toward the corner. It was raining harder now. Anderson had to run to catch up. She grabbed his shoulder and yanked him around.

"Will you please stop!"

"What?" Kanter asked. A clap of distant thunder reverberated off the buildings.

"Where are you going to go? Back to your lab?"

"Maybe. I don't know."

Anderson stepped closer. "Bill, you can't go back there. Don't you have a friend you can stay with tonight?"

Kanter wiped some rain off his face. "Look, this isn't your affair. You're sweet to show this concern, but this is my mess. I have to figure out what to do. There's no need for you to get involved. Besides, it all might be just a big coincidence."

He had a point, and as Anderson stood there in the cool rain, she thought that letting him tackle it alone might be the best thing. She really didn't know him from Adam, and getting sucked into his drama was the last thing she needed.

"Maybe, you're right," she said. "I'm just being overly dramatic."

"Yeah," Kanter said. "Coincidence does happen."

A rip of thunder cut the awkwardness between them.

"Well," he said, "I'll catch you later."

"Are you going to be okay?" Anderson asked.

"Oh yeah, sure." He was talking and walking backwards. "You in the facility email directory?"

"Yes."

"Cool. I'll email you when I'm back up and running, and we'll hook the kid up." He forced a smile and headed for the corner.

Anderson watched him trot across the street and enter the campus park. "That would be great!" she called out.

He turned and waved and disappeared behind a row of trees.

Anderson fished her cell phone out of her purse and ducked under the awning of the restaurant. She flipped it open and watched a dark gray SUV round the far corner and accelerate down the street. It swerved around a parked car and slowed. She scrolled through her phonebook and dialed her voicemail. Her first voice message started to play when several gunshots cracked the air. Anderson flinched. The SUV had stopped where Kanter had crossed the street. More shots were fired. The sound of a distant trashcan tipping over echoed through the park.

"Bill!" Anderson screamed. She started for the corner, but more gunfire came from across the park. Sparks ricocheted off the hood of the SUV, and she heard glass shattering. The vehicle tried to peel away, but its tires spun on the wet pavement. Its backend fishtailed, then it sped down the street and was gone.

"Oh, God no." Anderson started running towards the park. From her military training, she knew the shots came from small caliber weapons. "Bill, where are you?!"

"Over here," Kanter called out. His hand popped up from behind a toppled U of C newspaper dispenser and waved.

"Are you okay?" Anderson asked, running up.

Kanter stood warily and looked himself over. "Yeah, I think so." He was obviously shaken. "What the hell is going on? Who was shooting at who?"

Anderson surveyed the park. It was a patchwork of lamplight and dark clusters of neatly arranged trees and shrubs. "I don't know."

"Was this some gang thing?"

"I doubt it. Bill, your life's in danger. Do you have a place to stay tonight?"

Kanter's expression went blank. Anderson had seen it before in soldiers when a situation had gone sideways on them. It was dislocation from reality because the mind couldn't process the imminence of death.

Anderson grabbed his arm. "Come on, you can crash at my place." She tugged him forward, but he resisted.

"Wait," he said. "This is getting crazy. You don't have to involve yourself."

"Shut up, come on." She motioned for him to follow. "You have to get off the street."

Anderson pulled again, and Kanter reluctantly acquiesced. Without thinking, she hunched into what Marines called "the creep" and started trotting in quick measured steps. He mimicked her, and she felt his stare. They angled in the direction of the garage where her car was parked. Although several blocks away, they could make it in good time if they kept up their pace. She didn't want whoever had shot at Kanter to get a second chance.

"Were you a cop once?" he asked. They exited the park and stood on the curb as a black Pathfinder drove slowly by.

"No." The Pathfinder sped up, and they crossed. "I was in Iraq."

"What branch?"

"Navy."

"Did you see action?"

Anderson's heel dug into the dirt next to the sidewalk, and she flashed on the first action she encountered after arriving in country. Two months into her deployment, she had been ordered to help set up mental health support at another FOB (Forward Operating Base). Her convoy had taken her through a hostile town north of her base. Insurgents customarily said hello by tossing small IEDs (improvised explosive devices) into Humvees. On the way to the FOB, Anderson had the misfortune to be in one of the older Humvees at the front of the convoy when insurgents had tossed an especially lethal greeting. One of the soldiers stepped on the device and spun it to cause it to detonate out the side. Some of the cruder IEDs had a tendency to explode in one direction, and if you guessed right, you could turn it so it would blow most of its death away from you. Unfortunately, whoever did the turning usually lost a hand or a foot. This device took most of the soldier's leg off. After the IED had detonated, Anderson found herself in the thick of a hellacious firefight. It took her years to get the image of the soldier screaming out of her dreams. Now it was all coming back, and she could feel that icy sensation creeping into her nerves. She instinctively reached for the spot on her thigh where her 9mm pistol would have been strapped.

"Are you okay?" A voice. Maybe a Marine's. Something touched her shoulder. She spun, grabbed the hand, and twisted it into a hold she had been taught in basic.

"Trenna!" Kanter yelled. "My arm, Jesus." He was contorted and grimacing.

Anderson let go. "Oh my God, I-I'm so sorry!"

Kanter rubbed his elbow and glared through the hard falling rain. "What the *hell*?"

Anderson backed away and looked at her hands as if they had acted on their own. It was shocking how quickly it all came rushing back. She shoved her hands into her pockets. "I'm sorry," she said, embarrassed.

"You saw combat, didn't you?"

Anderson nodded. Even saying yes was hard. She stepped away and tried to shake off the feeling.

They were on the other side of the street with the garage in front of them. Something in a newspaper dispenser caught Kanter's attention.

He opened its door and took a paper. "Oh, *shit*," he said, reading.

"What is it?" Anderson asked.

Kanter twisted the paper so she could read the front page. A headline in one of the lead articles made her gasp.

UNIVERSITY OF CHICAGO PROFESSOR, PHILLIP JESSEL, DIES IN CAR ACCIDENT.

12. Happy F'ing Monday.

Kanter woke to something licking his nose. At first he didn't know what was happening. REM sleep had a way of twisting his perception if he was awoken in the middle of it. He tried to focus on the assault to his face.

The dog looked like a Doberman, though tiny, like a Chihuahua. It perched on his chest with a bug-eyed expression, and seemed to be vibrating. It pulled back and looked him over, then resumed its licking mission. Kanter swatted it off. The dog yipped and scampered into the darkness, its nails skittering across the hardwoods. Now he remembered.

He sat up and swung his legs over the side of the couch. Anderson lived in half of a duplex that was far from campus, and by the time they had arrived, Kanter couldn't keep his eyes open. Maybe it had been all the shit that came down last night, or maybe it was his system telling him he needed to cool it and regroup. Whatever it was, he had fallen asleep the second his head had hit the pillow. He checked his watch. *3:34 a.m.*

Now his toes were being assaulted.

"Give it a rest," he scolded.

The licking stopped, and the tapping headed into the kitchen.

"Somebody needs to clip your nails," Kanter said into the room.

"I see you've met Wally."

"Trenna?"

Her slim figure emerged from the shadows. "Who'd you expect?" She tightened her robe's sash and leaned against the doorway. The kitchen nightlight gave her form a soft, backlit glow. Her hair was down, and the lighting made her look like an old movie star from the 1930s. "Couldn't sleep?"

Kanter cleared his throat. "Yeah, and I had the strangest dream about being licked to death."

"I've had *that* one before."

"Nice hair."

"What?" Anderson tried to brush it over her shoulder, but the robe's high collar put a stop to that. She tried to tie it into a ponytail, but gave up and stuffed her hands into the robe's pockets.

"It's longer than I thought," Kanter said.

"I need to get it cut."

More tapping began navigating the living room.

"Wally, go to your bed!" Anderson scolded.

The tapping faded up the stairs.

Kanter realized he was in his briefs and tugged the blanket over his waist. “You couldn’t sleep, either?”

“I couldn’t get the gunfire out of my head.” She settled into an oversized leather club and rested her slippered feet on the coffee table.

Kanter nestled against the cushions and propped his feet on the table. He nudged some magazines that fell to the floor. “Sorry.”

“Don’t worry,” Anderson said. “I’m too tired to care.”

Kanter closed his eyes. Fatigue started dragging him down.

“Bill?”

“Yeah?” he asked, flinching.

“What are you going to do?”

Good question. “Throw myself on the mercy of Cole Strachan.”

“*The* Cole Strachan?”

“I guess. Is there more than one?”

Anderson chuckled. “Let’s hope not. What are you doing hooked up with a megalomaniac like him?”

“Trying to change the world.”

“What?”

“Never mind. Bad joke. He’s going to be my new benefactor. Phillip set it up.” The thought drew his mind to their last meeting, and sadness arced through him.

“Bill?”

“Yeah?”

“Are you okay?”

No. “I’m all right. I was just thinking about the last time I was with Phillip. Anyway, someone on the University’s board recommended Strachan to him." He shifted his feet and more magazines fell. "How are *you* doing?"

She didn't answer. Kanter figured he had stepped over some unspoken boundary. Maybe Anderson's tour in Iraq had done more damage than she let on. Or maybe she just fell asleep. God, he was tired.

"I'll be fine," she said, finally. "How's the couch?"

"It's great, until the licking monster attacks."

She laughed. "Wally's a whore for affection."

"What is he?"

"Miniature Pinscher." Anderson stood. "Hungry? I've made a mean apple pie."

"A la mode?"

"Is there any other way?"

* * *

Anderson had been right about the pie, and as Kanter savored each forkful, they chatted about their careers and families and whatever else came to mind. She was a Marine brat who had followed in her old man's footsteps. Kanter sensed Anderson had been the son her father never had, and they had a special bond that Kanter envied. Anderson gave him a brief overview of her tour in Iraq and the Humvee incident. And she apologized again for laying the Aikido hold on him.

"Don't worry," he said as he eyed the bottle of ibuprofen on the counter. He had already taken four and was contemplating more.

They compared notes about the university and agreed that it was basically a great school, if you could stand the winters. She also related why she had gotten into pediatric psychology, and he felt bad that she couldn't have kids – something about scarring on her fallopian tubes. She thought that it was one of the main reasons why her dating life sucked, but he reassured her that she was pretty, and only a fool wouldn't ask her out. She said that at her age (which he didn't question), people's agendas were different: if you didn't feel a relationship might lead to marriage, then you didn't bother continuing to date. She was surprised by how many men wanted to have kids, which was usually a deal killer after about the fourth or fifth date.

"Really?" Kanter asked incredulously.

Anderson nodded. "Isn't that weird?" she said through her last forkful of pie. "I would have never guessed that guys would be so into having kids."

"Must be a Midwest thing."

"How about you? Do you see yourself having a family someday?" She walked over to an industrial coffee maker that could turn any kitchen into a Starbucks.

"I guess I'm different than Midwest guys." He gathered their plates and delivered them to the sink.

"How so?"

While Kanter washed their dishes, he told her about growing up in Boston under the shadow of the childhood prodigy thing. People had compared him to some old TV show with a genius kid as a doctor. She laughed and called him Doogie, but he didn't know the character and said the show was way before his time. She agreed, which made him wonder how old she really was. If she was over 40, she was the hottest middle-aged woman he had ever seen. Her face looked younger, though. Thirty-five, maybe.

"What was it like winning all those awards?" she asked and poured coffee into a mug bearing the Marine emblem. His cup wore a smiley face, although it looked a bit scared, and the words in the bubble said, "HAPPY F'ING MONDAY."

"Kind of strange. I mean, I was a kid."

"How old were you again?"

"Let's see, I'm twenty-nine now, so I guess nineteen."

"God, that's amazing. Can I ask your I.Q.?"

"That, Dr. Anderson, is a state secret. Can I ask how old you are?"

Anderson smiled. "I'll tell you mine, if you tell me yours."

"One sixtyish."

She choked a little into her coffee. "That's scary."

"And yours?"

"Thirty-four." Anderson wiped her chin with a paper towel. "So what was it like being nominated for the Gates? Did it change your life?" She leaned against the counter. The front of her robe opened slightly. She pulled it together, but not before Kanter caught a glimpse of a breast under a loose t-shirt.

Don't stare. "It did at first." He stepped toward the living room. "Come on, let's sit down."

"But you were all over the news," Anderson said, following. They settled into their respective places and kicked their feet up. "That had to affect you in some way."

"It did," Kanter said and took a sip. "But its not like you're on Entertainment Tonight every day. My kind of fame was a blip on the media radar. Believe me, my fifteen minutes were more like two. The

MDEA award was the one that allowed me to start this latest project. After that, offers started pouring in, and I went with Genonics."

The sound of tapping came down the hall, and Wally jumped into Anderson's lap. He circled twice before he curled up and rested his head on her knee. He let out a sigh.

The living room was a little brighter now, and Kanter could make out Anderson's taste in furnishings: Pottery Barn meets Ikea meets crap left over from grad school. She owned a couple of antiques, which he figured were her family's. The clock on the mantel could have been a knock-off, but then again ...

"You're welcome to stay here as long as you need to," she offered.

Kanter set his coffee down. "Thanks, I might take you up on that." The knock-off clock said 6:57 a.m. "What's today again?"

"It's Monday."

"Right. I knew that." Kanter glanced at his mug's slogan, and his stomach tightened.

13. It's just a thought.

"You're kidding, right?"

"Tom, this is serious." Anderson walked into the living room. "Someone is trying to stop Bill from completing his research." Kanter had folded the blankets into a neat stack on the coffee table, which Wally apparently discovered when they were having breakfast because he was now sleeping quietly in the middle of the pile. The pipes groaned in protest as the shower turned off upstairs.

"It's Bill, eh?" Prost's cell signal broke up a little.

"Oh, please."

"I'm just busting your chops. What makes you think Jessel or Kelly were murdered?"

"Think about it. The lab was trashed; Jessel died in a single car wreck; Kelly died from an overdose; and someone shot at Bill. All within 24 hours. Doesn't that seem suspicious to you?"

"You don't know if they were shooting at him. It could have been random violence. A drive-by. Anything. Have you talked with Kanter about bringing the police in?"

"Yes, but he's adamant about not getting them involved."

"Sounds stupid if you ask me."

"Yes, but I can see his point. If he confirms his discovery, he wants to write it up and get it published. Bringing in the police could delay his research indefinitely. Plus, he doesn't want premature attention on what he's discovered."

"What about Strachan? He's not going to allow Kanter to keep the patents. I'm sure he's got his eye on the gaming rights. I can't say that I blame him. Can you imagine the possibilities?"

"Tom. Focus. We need to help Bill. Besides, think about Eric. The sooner Bill's up and running, the sooner we can get to the bottom of Eric's disorder."

"When's Kanter meeting with Strachan?"

"This afternoon. When he told Strachan what happened, Strachan cleared his schedule."

"Where's he going to set up shop? I doubt he wants to stay on campus. How did the university police handle his lab being trashed?"

"Bill doesn't have any ideas about where to set up. And he's not getting the university police involved. He's just going to lock up his lab and deal with it in the fall. He says he has the room until the end of the year. I'm worried, Tom. I think Bill's life is in danger."

"You don't know that for sure."

"I'm telling you, that wasn't a gang shooting in the park."

"You said there were other shots fired at the SUV, right?"

Anderson hesitated. "Yes."

"Well there you go. Maybe it was a homeboy thing, and they were shooting at each other. Maybe Bill was in the wrong place at the wrong time."

Anderson knew better. She had been around enough small arms fire to know the direction of gunfire, and the shots from the SUV were aimed into the area of the park where Kanter had been. It was the return fire that had her stumped. It had come from across the park, and was definitely aimed at the SUV. Who would be shooting at the shooters, and why?

"Tom, I don't have time to debate this. I have to get to a meeting. How's your brother-in-law doing?"

"He developed a slight infection and went back to the doctor today."

"Give Kim my best and tell her I'm praying for Scott. Is she going to be okay taking care of Eric?"

"I guess she'll have to be."

"Has Eric had any more episodes?"

"No, but it's a crap shoot as to when the German or the whore or whoever might show up again. That scares the hell out of me."

What Kanter needed was a large empty building with plenty of power. "Tom, do Kim and Scott have an extra barn or storage space that's not being used ... something big?"

"I can hear the wheels in your head turning from here. What are you cooking up, Tren?"

"I don't know. It's just a thought."

"Are you thinking that Kanter could set up shop at my family's farm?"

"Maybe. I mean, why not? It's isolated, and we could sneak him out of Chicago so whoever's trying to kill him wouldn't know. It would give him enough time to conclude his research. Once he publishes his findings, he should be home free."

There was some static.

"Tren, did it ever occur to you that getting involved might get you killed? You're also talking about putting my sister's family at risk."

"I thought you said it was just a gang thing."

"Well, yes, but–"

"Tom, this discovery is too important to languish in some police investigation or, even worse, be splashed all over the news. I doubt that whoever is after Bill is anyone of consequence. It's probably some nut job ... a friend of that guy his assistant knew, or someone like that. Maybe you're right about it all being a coincidence. If that's the case, then what's the harm? I'm sure Strachan would fund it all. Bill said Strachan's going to give him five million. Who knows? Maybe he could pay Kim and Scott a usage fee. I bet they could use the money, especially after all the hospital bills."

There was a crackle, and Anderson didn't know if she had lost Prost's signal.

"Okay, Tren. I'll check with them tonight and let you know. Plus, he'd be close to Eric."

"That's right," she agreed. But there was something more than just Eric's well-being driving Anderson. Kanter's discovery could be one of those paradigm shifts, like the invention of electricity or digital media, and she didn't want to see it disappear because of something stupid.

"Hey, Tom?"

"Yes?"

"You realize this could be one of the most important discoveries ever."

There was more static.

"Yeah," he said. "I know."

14. I take that as a yes.

Kanter had been in cool homes before, but Strachan's was one of the coolest. Of course it wasn't like Bill Gates's house. That was just out-of-control cool. When Kanter had gone to the party that honored the Gates' nominees, he had been given a pin that connected him to the home's computer system. As Kanter moved through the house, the music and art changed to match his taste. Even the temperature shifted to accommodate his needs. The creepy thing was, he had never filled out a questionnaire. The house just knew what he liked.

Now he was standing in Strachan's living room, looking at a Rauschenberg painting and wondering if it would switch to some other artist.

Strachan lived in Oakbrook, one of Chicago's wealthiest suburbs. It was home to such megacorps as McDonalds and boasted the first shopping mall built in the U.S. It also had a fashionable mix of modest homes and sprawling mansions. Strachan lived in the latter on manicured acreage that backed up to an equally breath-taking golf course. It had taken Anderson about twice as long to get there because she had insisted that Kanter lay down in the back seat of her car as she "snuck" him out of the city down Ogden Avenue. His protests went unanswered until he had crawled into the front seat somewhere near Cicero. Anderson said she wanted to make sure no one would know where he was, even demanding that he not use his cell phone. The explanation involved some device called a "roving bug," and the only way to defeat it was to remove the cell battery, which she had. Kanter felt naked without his cell. The more he got to know her, the more she was full of surprises, like her hair this morning. It was down and slightly curled.

"Good morning, Bill," Strachan said, walking in. He was dressed as if he was squeezing Kanter in between the front and back nine.

"Morning, Cole.

"Please, sit."

Kanter sat in a curvilinear rattan chair that was apparently the product of an Italian designer's wet dream. Strachan sat in a similar chair opposite him and regarded Kanter with a heavy dose of concern.

"They tried to *kill* you?" he asked.

"I don't really know for sure," Kanter said. "I mean, I was too busy ducking to get an exact take on it all."

"You can't be too sure these days. There are all kinds of crazies out there."

Kanter shrugged. “It could be nothing. Kids looking for crap to fence might have broken into the lab, and the shooting could have been a gang thing. Dr. Anderson thinks all the events are related.”

“Who’s Dr. Anderson? Is she your new assistant?”

Kanter had been ignoring the issue of replacing Kelly. But as Strachan asked the question, something gave way inside, like his pain had been converted into hard-core business reasoning. “Yes,” he said, “she is.”

Strachan nodded. “Good, you’ll need someone. Have you decided where to rebuild?”

Kanter explained about setting up at the Nelson farm. He wasn’t completely sold on the idea but didn’t have a better alternative. He also explained about Eric and Anderson’s involvement. Strachan listened intently.

“What do you think?” Kanter asked.

Strachan leaned back and stared out at the 10th green. A guy dressed like a Tiger Woods clone missed a putt and flung his club into a sand trap.

“We shouldn’t take any chances,” he said. “Given the events of the last few days, there’s a strange logic in the plan. My offices are too high profile for something like this, so being in the middle of nowhere might be the best thing. Just in case, though, we better get some security prepared for you.”

“Let’s hold off. The family that owns the farm is really conservative, and it’s already a stretch for them to allow us onto the property. Let’s take a wait-and-see.”

“Fair enough. I can have a team there in a couple of days, if needed. Do you know this family well?”

"No, but Dr. Anderson does," Kanter said, hoping it was true.

Strachan smiled. "Good. Then we better get started. I'll have my endowment office make the arrangements."

* * *

Kanter watched the Chicago skyline rise before him. Ogden Avenue was a signal-filled, wretched four-laner that Anderson claimed was named after Chicago's first mayor. She also said it ran all the way to Colorado.

"So Strachan bought off on the idea?" Anderson navigated her very used BMW 5-Series around a Jack-In-The-Box semi. It was a moving billboard with two burgers that had thought bubbles. The Jack-In-The-Box burger was touting its new humus and feta cheese flavor, while the McDonalds' burger bitched that it wasn't international enough.

"Hundred percent," Kanter said. "I've already talked with his endowment person. Have you heard back from Tom yet?"

"Yes. He said his brother-in-law was cool to the idea, but left the decision to Kim."

"And?"

"She's okay with it, as long as they get paid rent for the space and it doesn't interfere with their own business. They have a twenty-four hundred square-foot building that's empty. It used to be one of their milking parlors."

"Parlors?"

"Hey, don't ask me. That's what she called it. Anyway, it should have plenty of power for your needs. When you are you going to start?"

"Trenna. There's, ah, something that I should talk to you about."

"What's that?"

"I kind of mentioned to Strachan that you were my new assistant."

There was a long silence as Anderson gunned the BMW through a yellow light. They hit a dip and bounced part of the way down the block. Kanter wondered if he had pissed her off.

"Okay," she said finally.

"Really?"

"Sure, why not? It's a chance of a lifetime, especially if your discovery is substantiated. We're almost through with the semester, and I was thinking of taking the summer off. I know my way around computers, and I'm a quick learner." She glanced over just as she ran another yellow. "I won't be as good as Kelly, but I won't be a hindrance, either."

Kanter saw a sign that indicated they were nearing Cicero. "What about your patients?"

"I don't really have that many, what with my teaching schedule and all. A lot of them take off for the summer. I'll make it work out."

"Okay then. I'll start filling you in on the basics tonight, if you want. I'll need to stop by my bank and get my files."

Another sign mentioning Cicero passed by, and Anderson pointed.

"I know, get in the back." Kanter crawled over the console and lay across the back seat. He had to tuck his legs to get comfortable.

"That sounds good," Anderson said.

Kanter sensed some trepidation in her voice. "Are you okay with this ... really?"

Anderson suddenly slammed the brakes. Kanter flew against the back of the front seats.

"Did the light change too fast for you?" he asked, crawling back into position. His shoulder was hurting a little.

Anderson didn't respond, except to drum the top of the steering wheel with her fingers. The light seemed interminably long.

"Trenna–?"

"Stay down."

"What's the problem?"

"I think that Blazer from the other night is following us."

Kanter's nerves spiked. "Are you sure it's the same one?"

More silence. Kanter looked up through the back window and spied a guy in a delivery truck looking down at him. The guy spit into a foam cup and resumed his conversation on his cell.

"Trenna?"

"Shit!"

"*What?!*"

The BMW lurched and accelerated. There where honks and the screeching of brakes, and Kanter was pressed against the seat. His shoulder dug into one of the seatbelt couplers and pain shot up his neck. As the car swerved through traffic, Kanter was thrown around. He tried to cushion the impacts by grabbing the door's armrest.

"I take that as a yes," he managed between swerves.

"Hell, yes," Anderson said. "The Blazer's hood has three bullet holes in it."

15. Cross that bridge.

Anderson knew the BMW was an agile car for its size, but she never imagined putting it through these kinds of paces.

Kanter kept yelling for her to be careful, and she seriously thought about slamming the brakes just to shut him up. But the Blazer was gaining.

"I thought I left this crap in Iraq," she said under her breath.

"What?" Kanter asked.

The light turned red. "Nothing. Hang on!" Anderson hit the brakes, and the BMW, living up to its slogan, skidded to a perfect stop. The smell of burnt rubber wafted through the vents. Other cars pulled up around them.

"Are you okay?" she asked.

"Yeah," Kanter replied, his voice muffled.

She adjusted the rearview mirror and saw the Blazer was a half-car length off her passenger side. A deep, seizure-inducing bass vibrated the BMW's chassis.

Kanter started chuckling.

Anderson glanced over her shoulder and found him peering out the back window. "Bill, get down!"

"Have you looked at its bullet holes?" he asked.

"What do you mean?"

The light changed, and traffic started to move. Anderson pulled forward, but the Blazer came alongside. It sported a string of bullet-hole decals running from the hood to the side windows and across the rear fender skirt. Its wheel rims were spinning at a nauseating rate. The driver's window was down, and the guy behind the wheel had more bling than hair. He looked over at Anderson, smiling a toothy grin and talking on a cell phone. The base beat Dopplered away as the Blazer passed.

Kanter was sitting up and laughing.

"It's not funny," Anderson said, her attention focused on the traffic.

"Yes it is."

"Get back up here."

"No way. I kind of like this."

"I'm not chauffeuring you around." Anderson jerked the car to the right.

Kanter slid onto his side. "Easy there," he said, straightening.

"I'm not kidding, Bill. Either get up here or get down."

Anderson felt his hands at her shoulders.

"Thanks for taking care of me back there," Kanter said as he began to massage.

Anderson hadn't had a man rub her shoulders, much less whisper something nice into her ear, in a long time. She let him continue for a block before she gunned the BMW through a yellow light.

Kanter flew back against the seat and disappeared from the rearview mirror.

"Thanks," Anderson said, "but I'm your assistant now. It's all business from here on out."

She watched in the mirror as Kanter struggled to right himself. He grinned at her and started rubbing his shoulder.

* * *

"So you see, it's a really simple concept," Kanter said, twirling pasta onto his fork.

He's cute, Anderson thought. She wondered if this was how he might have been as a kid: full of enthusiasm and excitement. But his face belied the thought, shadowed with a day's growth that made him kind of sexy, too. She ripped off a piece of baguette and mopped up the last of her spaghetti sauce.

"Compared to a ... what did you call it?" she asked.

"An MEG?"

"Right. Your design is simple.... I think."

Kanter laughed. "*If* you're a nuclear scientist."

As he explained PETs and MRIs, Anderson tried to grasp the technology. It was hard to understand how an MRI rearranged a person's hydrogen atoms. Even more difficult was the concept of

Kanter's method. It was expensive to build and had to do with the prefrontal cortex and the left tail of the hippocampus. Those were the areas of the brain involved with memory formation, but how his method worked was pure technobabble. Her end of the science dealt with how a person processed information and translated it into behavior. Maybe she could bring a fresh perspective to his work?

"When the atoms are interpolated," Kanter said, "the scanner reconverts them into electrical impulses, which are then processed through what's called a primary cascade emissions channel. Make sense?"

Anderson's head was awash in acronyms. "Kind of."

"Don't worry. I think you'll have a different take on it, since you come from the behavioral side of things."

"That's what I'm hoping. I do have a question."

Kanter sucked down the last of his spaghetti and wiped his mouth. "What's that?"

"What about false memories?"

Kanter leaned back and swirled his Pinot Noir. "That's a damn good question, doctor. Studies have tested whether there are different patterns of brain activity for true and false memory formation, and there's evidence that suggests this. But to answer your question, I have no idea. I can tell you that what I've seen with my scan seems accurate, which suggests that the brain, or at least the parts that I'm tapping into, record what the senses bring in. How it's processed to form a thought or decision is a whole different matter."

"Sounds like that's my area of expertise." Anderson leaned on the table and sipped her wine. "Wouldn't it be fascinating to acquire a scan from someone who has synesthesia?"

"What's that?" Kanter asked.

"A neurological condition where two or more senses are coupled. A person perceives certain numbers as a color, or certain dates evoke a specific location."

"That's bizarre. I can't imagine." Kanter grabbed the bottle of Pinot and refilled his glass. "I'd like to hook up some psycho." He gestured with the bottle.

Anderson shook her head. "What we should do is hook up a psychic."

"Then we'd be able to see future lives."

They both burst out, and Anderson couldn't remember the last time she had laughed so hard. It felt good to let go and relax. Or maybe it was just the Pinot talking. He said it was a good label, but there was something else at play. Being around Kanter made Anderson feel alive, but it also kind of shocked her. What had become of the girl who was going to kick ass and help kids? Had her tour in Iraq damaged her more than she thought? Or maybe it was the years of academic infighting? Her attention settled on Kanter's smile.

"Bill, do you think–" Anderson stopped midthought and focused on a speck of cork floating in her Pinot. She tried to pick it out, but it resisted her repeated attempts. When she looked up, she discovered Kanter had slid his chair beside her.

"Do I think *what*?" he asked.

She hesitated. "That what you've done – that is, if you have developed a way to see past lives – is going to be dangerous?"

This gave Kanter pause. "I think any great invention has that potential," he said. "But if every inventor stopped because they thought only about the bad that might happen, or be caused by what they were creating, we'd still be in the Dark Ages." He stood. "Who knows? Maybe it will change the world for the better."

"Yeah, but I mean you ... Are *you* in danger? Somebody tried to kill you, remember?"

Kanter smiled, though not very convincingly. "You look like you could use a good night of sleep, doctor. Why don't you head to bed? I'll clean up here."

* * *

The house was particularly dark because there was no moon. Plus, the neighbor's mercury vapor lamp had been shot out, much to the relief of Anderson and Mrs. Yenez, who lived in the other half of the duplex. Anderson had lived there for almost four years, but as she stood at the bottom of the stairs, the living room seemed oddly unfamiliar. She peered at the couch and wondered if Kanter was awake.

"Bill?" she whispered.

Silence.

"Bill?" A little louder.

"Yeah?" he asked, his voice raspy. "Is everything all right?"

"Yes."

"What time is it?"

"About three."

Kanter sat up and pulled the blanket around his waist. The top of his head was silhouetted against the windows. He ran his hands through his hair. "What's the matter? More flashbacks?"

"No. I don't have those much anymore." Anderson came over and sat on the arm of the club chair. She couldn't believe what she was about to ask; she had never spoken to anyone about her upbringing. "Can I ask you a question?"

Kanter cleared his throat. "Sure."

"How far back did you go?" Anderson pulled the robe's collar tight to her neck in an attempt to batten her insecurity.

"What? How far to what?"

"In your scan. How far back did you go?"

"Nine lives, as far as we can–"

"No. I mean in this current life ... Bill Kanter's life."

"All the way."

"To your birth?"

"No. It doesn't seem to work like that. Typically the brain doesn't formulate memories until we're about five, but I think if we can calibrate the–"

"Bill?"

"Yeah?"

"Did you see your birth?"

Kanter shook his head. "No. I saw back to when I was about 2 years old. Everything was static after that. If this proves to be the norm in most scans, that would blow the thinking that we don't formulate memories until after four or five. We might create them, but we can't recall them. Who knows, though? Once we start really testing the machine out, we may find something completely different. Why do you ask?"

Anderson hesitated.

"Trenna, what's the matter?"

"I ... well, you see ..."

"Can I ask you a personal question?" Kanter wiped sleep from his eyes.

She felt something heavy pressing against her heart. Nevertheless, she nodded.

"Were you adopted?"

"Yes." The word caught in her throat.

There was silence, interrupted by a dog barking somewhere in the neighborhood.

"When were you adopted?" he asked. "Did you know your birth parents?"

"I was very young. Around four. And no, I don't remember my parents."

"Would it really matter to see what they looked like?"

"I-I don't know."

Kanter stretched and yawned. "It'll take a couple of weeks to get everything squared away in Wisconsin, given the barn we're renting is ready to go. Why don't you take some time and think it through. Once we're up and running, we can cross this bridge again and see if you're still curious."

Anderson nodded. She started to go back upstairs.

"Trenna?"

She stopped at the first stair and looked back. "Yes?"

"Sleep well."

16. Shut up.

Kanter didn't have any predetermined ideas, but as they drove up the long dirt road that served for a driveway, it became obvious that the Nelson dairy farm wasn't Rockwellian at all. The main house was a big, two-story traditional that looked like it hadn't seen a coat of paint since the Depression. It probably had several bedrooms, and its front porch wrapped halfway around the house. The rest of the farm looked more industrial than quaint. As he maneuvered the rental through the deep ruts, Kanter began to wonder if the farm was such a good idea.

"Where's the white picket fence?" Anderson asked, peering out the windshield at two rust-caked silos that towered over the main barn – the only real building that looked like it belonged on a farm.

"Probably in storage, along with the porch swing and the old wheelbarrow filled with flowers," Kanter replied.

"Bill, look out!"

Kanter mashed the brakes, and a large German shepherd leaped onto the hood. It snarled and barked, and spittle hit the windshield. Dust wrapped the car.

"Claudius!" a man yelled from somewhere behind them.

The dog snapped to attention, looked over the top of the car, and leaped from view. Kanter saw in his side mirror a hulk of a man, well over 6 feet, walking toward them. He sported a crew cut right out of boot camp and unnaturally broad shoulders. The expression on his face was all business, and the shovel he carried looked like a toy. He approached the car and stood, squinting in the midday sun.

"Morning," Kanter said through the lowered driver's side window. "I'm Dr. William Kanter. This is Dr. Trenna Anderson. You must be Scott Nelson."

Nelson leaned over and canvassed the car's interior like a soldier at a checkpoint. His scrutiny lingered on the tech cases in the back seat. "Your equipment arrived about an hour ago," he said, straightening. "Your eighteen-wheeler tore the hell out of our road."

Kanter leaned out and noticed the back end of a Strachan Media Group freight truck. It was parked down the road from the main barn, next to a smaller structure that looked about as old as the house. "Sorry about that."

"They're unloading the equipment right now," Nelson said, his face stoic. "We'll have lunch at one. You're welcome to join us."

Before Kanter could offer a thanks, Nelson turned and started toward the main barn. Claudius trotted alongside.

"Charming," Kanter said.

"Looks like he's recovered from the stabbing," Anderson remarked.

"Looks like he could snap me in half. Tom said he was ex-Special Forces."

"That explains a lot."

"How's that?"

Anderson pointed to Nelson as he disappeared around the corner of the main barn. "Either they're totally focused, like him, or they're just a little crazy. Often both."

"How do you know?"

Anderson shot him a "what-a-dumb-question" look.

"Right," Kanter said. "That *was* stupid." He started driving toward the smaller barn. "Lets go see where they're at. With any luck, they'll be finished."

"Don't bet on it," Anderson replied.

"Why?"

"They're probably Teamsters."

Kanter parked the car next to the freight truck, and the apparent supervisor of the loading crew walked up. Part of his gut protruded from under a t-shirt that touted the virtues of a band called *Nighthawk*. It had lots of jagged lightning bolts and chrome type, and Kanter figured it wasn't a light jazz group.

"You Dr. Kanter?" he asked. His name badge labeled him as Hairy.

"Yes." Kanter stepped out and shut the rental's door.

"Sign here." Hairy handed over a metal clipboard.

"Everything arrive intact?" Kanter asked, signing the bottom of the manifest.

Hairy shrugged.

"Did you uncrate the Core 10s?"

Hairy, using the end of a pen, pointed over his shoulder at the building. "Yeah. Those are heavy suckers. We didn't know where you wanted them, so we put 'em near the electrical box."

"Good."

"What's all this for?" Hairy asked. "The job order is straight from Strachan's office. Must be important."

Kanter glanced at his t-shirt. "It is." He handed back the clipboard.

Hairy let out a deafening whistle and started walking toward the four guys milling around the cab of the eighteen-wheeler. "Load up," he yelled.

"Come on," Kanter said to Anderson. "Let's assess the damage."

* * *

Kanter glanced at his watch. *3:34 p.m.*

"We missed lunch," Anderson said from across the space. Her voice echoed off the concrete floor and cinderblock walls.

Kanter glanced around but couldn't see her. "Yeah, and I'm all broken up about it."

The old milking parlor was in better shape inside than it was outside. Its 2400 square feet had just been sprayed with white epoxy, and the row of tall casement windows along its east wall appeared recently scraped. The Teamsters had done a fairly good job of unloading the equipment, and after an hour of shuffling the Cores around, Kanter ended up putting them right back were the freight guys had placed them. Anderson ribbed him for a good 10 minutes.

"Thank God all these servers came pre-stacked," she said, appearing from behind one of the Cores.

"Thank you." Kanter wiped sweat from his eyes with the bottom of his t-shirt. "I staged them at one of Strachan's warehouses before they loaded them on the truck. It makes setting up a hell of a lot easier."

Anderson walked into an open area and surveyed the arrangement. She had her fingers wedged into the pockets of a pair of jeans Kanter could only label "sexy." They weren't like the low-cuts the coeds wore, but pretty close. And her t-shirt clung in all the right ways.

She caught Kanter staring and wagged her finger. "I don't need a scanner to know what you're thinking."

"Hey, what can I say? I'm a red-blooded American heterosexual." Kanter crawled under a secondary workstation and began connecting a small laptop to a printer.

"I hope you know how to hook all this up." Anderson took a seat at the main workstation and started unpacking one of the LCD monitors. Part of her T-back peeked above her jeans.

Kanter could only see her from the waist down. "Do you like pink, Dr. Anderson?" he asked and plugged in one of the printers to a surge tree.

She reached around and yanked her jeans up, but it didn't help much. "Enjoying the view?" She stood and walked away.

"I'm more of a white cotton kind of guy."

Anderson chuckled from somewhere near the Cores.

Kanter crawled to the other workstation, all the while checking connections. He stood and leaned against one of the stacks. Sweat rolled down his ribs as he stared at the cabling.

Anderson walked up. "You okay?"

"I guess." Kanter folded his arms. "I was just thinking about Kelly. He loved setting up. He said there was a Zen to it: the way the cables are arranged, the placement of the computers ... you know, all that *feng shui* crap."

Anderson wiped her brow with the back of her hand. "Why didn't you go to Kelly's or Phillip's funerals?"

"I don't know. I guess I was afraid. After the lab got broken into, you got me thinking. Then the shooting in the park really convinced me. Going to their funerals would only expose me, and I didn't want to take that chance."

"You miss him, don't you?"

Kanter had to admit he would miss Kelly's instincts when it came to solving problems. Even though he had been stoned some of the time, the guy was brilliant, and Kanter had come to enjoy his quirky take on life.

"I sent some flowers with a lame excuse," he said, reflecting on their time in the lab. "Maybe, after I've published my findings and this is out in the open, I'll go visit his mom. He was pretty close to her."

"I'm sure she'd like that very much."

A bead of sweat slid down the side of Anderson's face, and for a second, Kanter mused about catching it with his finger.

"We have to talk with Scott about getting the AC up and running," he said. "The Core clusters are air cooled, so we'll need all the AC we can get."

"No joke." Anderson wiped the side of her face. "I'm burning up." She ran her hand up the side of her jeans to soak up the perspiration.

"You all want some air conditioning?" Nelson asked from the parlor's doorway.

"Yes!" Anderson called out, looking over her shoulder.

Nelson disappeared into the hallway that ran the length of the building. There was a loud clack, and a hum swarmed through the space. The exposed ductwork creaked with contractions as the cool air flowed.

"There you go," Nelson yelled from somewhere down the hallway. A few papers blew off the main workstation.

"Thanks, Scott!" Kanter said.

"Dinner's at six," Nelson said, and the outside door slammed.

"They're into prompt eating around here," Anderson remarked.

"We probably should make that one," Kanter said.

She nodded and began picking up the papers. "I bet they ask you to say grace," she said, straightening.

"I hope not. Tom said they were Charismatics."

Anderson frowned. "You're kidding, right? He told me they were conservative, but ... " She shook her head and started to laugh. "I hope they ask you."

"Shut *up*," Kanter said playfully, but then he noticed the feeds from the Cores were reversed.

17. Downright scary.

Kimberly Nelson scurried around the dining table as if her life might end if the knives weren't perfectly placed. Anderson saw her fork was on the wrong side of her spoon and thought about moving it. The coral rose pattern on the napkins looked to be floating in a sea of eggplants. They matched the table runner in a cheesy retail sort of way.

Anderson hadn't seen such a coordinated setting since two Thanksgivings ago at her department head's home. She had met Phillip Jessel at the party, and he had seemed like such a nice man. A pang of sadness moved through her.

"Come here often?" Kanter said into her ear. His hair was combed and his face shaven. Gone were the faded jeans and torn *X-Files* tee.

In their place was a lightly starched denim shirt and khaki pants.

Anderson had assumed he didn't own anything better than a black U of C sweatshirt, so the look was refreshing. Even the high-tops had been replaced with a pair of work boots, the kind with the yellow stitching along the rim of the sole. She could never remember the brand.

Kanter pulled her chair out.

"I hear the veal is excellent," she whispered, taking her seat.

"I'm trying the sea bass," Kanter replied. "Her glaze reduction is *superb*."

"I hope you like chicken casserole," Kimberly announced as she followed Eric into the dining room. She carried a large serving dish, and Eric held a wooden bowl filled with mixed greens.

"Bringing out the good silver tonight," Nelson said.

Anderson watched him descend the stairs. He grabbed the banister, and she flashed on Eric's video. At one point, the camera caught Kimberly jumping from the stairs into frame. Anderson tried to imagine her panic and recalled how Kimberly vaulted off the last step and landed at the threshold of the living room.

"We have special guests," Kimberly said and smiled – this time genuinely. "And I thought I'd bring out grandmother's china."

Eric set the salad bowl down next to Anderson. He stared at her for a second before he smiled.

Kimberly placed the casserole in the middle of the table and took her seat at one end. Nelson sat at the head of the table, and Eric took a chair across from Anderson and Kanter. He folded his hands, and his parents followed.

"Dr. Anderson-" Nelson's voice sounded a little weak, and

Anderson wondered if he had fully recovered from the infection. "-would you do us the honor and say grace?"

Kanter nudged her foot under the table.

* * *

Anderson stepped onto the upstairs landing.

"That was a fairly nondenominational blessing," Kanter said coming alongside.

"It was my grandmother's. I thought it wouldn't offend the Nelsons, but I doubt it convinced them that I'm God fearing."

"I thought it was very nice," Kanter said through a yawn. "Now get some sleep. We've got a busy day tomorrow."

"Good night, Bill."

"Good night," he said and headed to his room.

Kimberly Nelson, Anderson noted, apparently liked to decorate her bedrooms in themes: Kanter's theme was cowboys, and Anderson's was dolls. She got the sense that the room might have been meant for a little girl, but Tom had never mentioned that his sister was thinking of having another child. Hopeful decorating, maybe?

The bathroom had a large claw tub that was calling Anderson's name. Kimberly had adorned the bath with an assortment of toiletries, and Anderson poured a generous portion of something called "Lemon Sunrise" into the running water. An inviting mound of bubbles soon beckoned. She lit a candle from a local shop called Hillary's Closet and opened a bottle of Merlot she had snuck inside her suitcase. The water felt heavenly, and the wine was a welcomed finish to the busy day.

Anderson closed her eyes and granted herself permission to relax. It had been a long time since she had been away from Chicago, and the thought of spending the next three months on a farm in rural Wisconsin was intoxicating. She imagined discovering amazing things with Kanter's new invention. She hadn't felt this excited about anything since grad school, when her career was just a vague promise that resided somewhere in the future. The smell of lemon and vanilla hung in the air. She could feel the tension in her shoulders melt away.

A knock at the bathroom door caused her to flinch. The bottle of Lemon Surprise fell to the tile floor and clattered around.

"Hello, is anyone home?"

It sounded like Eric, but his voice had an adult quality. Something in the cadence and inflection. And there was an accent. She sensed he was having an episode, but it didn't sound like anyone she had met. "Who is it?" she asked.

"Arthur W. Wellington, madam. I hope I'm not intruding. I can come back."

Amazing. "What can I do for you, Mr. Wellington?"

"I sell ladies undergarments -- corsets and the like. I'm staying in the room down the hall, and I wanted introduce myself. Your bedroom door was ajar and I, well ... took the liberty."

Anderson was intrigued. "It's all right. Please-"

Before she could finish, Eric pulled the door aside and stepped into the bathroom. His eyes were partially rolled back, and he was wearing a matching pair of Star Wars pajamas. The juxtaposition was bizarre.

"My dear woman!" He quickly covered his eyes and retreated into the bedroom. "Why didn't you say you were in the altogether?"

"You didn't give me a chance to finish my sentence." Anderson sunk below the bubbles as much as she could. Eric's accent and vocabulary were definitely British, possibly from the turn of the last century.

"I'm terribly sorry," he said. "I shouldn't have been so forward."

"It's all right," Anderson said. "I'm not shy. You can come back in."

Eric slowly came out from behind the door. His eyes weren't as rolled back, and he was moving a wooden toothpick across his teeth. He smiled, then flicked the toothpick like a pro. It landed somewhere near the wastebasket.

"To tell you the truth, madam, I'm as queer as the day is long. You have no fear in that department. I was just looking for an honest sale. And who am I having the pleasure to talk with?"

"Dr. Trenna Anderson. Do you always burst unannounced into a woman's room in the middle of the night?"

"Again, please forgive me, but I was absolutely taken by you at dinner tonight." Eric sat on the stepstool next to the sink and crossed his legs. "A doctor, eh? I didn't know the Royal College allowed women to become doctors, let alone practice medicine."

"I'm the first," Anderson said. "What do you sell again, Mr. Wellington?"

"Ladies unmentionables. I have a fetching collection of nightwear that I think will complement a woman of your beauty."

"Well, Mr. Wellington, I'll have to set up a showing with you."

Eric clapped his hands demurely. "That would be splendid!"

"Tell me, where are you from?"

There was a knock at the bedroom door. "Trenna?"

"In here, Bill."

Eric's eyes grew big, and considering they were partially rolled back, the look was unnerving. "Oh dear," he said. "The husband?"

Anderson hesitated, then nodded.

"Are you decent?" Kanter asked.

"Well-"

Kanter poked his head in and his eyes darted from Anderson to Eric. "Jesus," he said and recoiled behind the door.

"It's alright, *honey*. Come in and meet my new friend."

Kanter sheepishly peered around the door.

Eric stood and extended his hand. "Arthur W. Wellington," he declared.

Kanter stooped and shook Eric's hand. He shot a questioning sideways glance at Anderson.

"Dear," Anderson said, "Mr. Wellington is a salesman and wants to show me his collection of *corsets* and nightwear. I was about to tell him I'd have to get my *husband's* opinion before I set up a showing."

Kanter did a double take. "Right, yeah. Um ..." He looked at Eric, who was still smiling as if his presence was totally normal. "What are you doing in our boudoir, sir?"

"As I told your wife, I was merely looking for an honest sale. My interest in women is strictly business, if you get my meaning." He winked.

Kanter looked at Anderson in confusion, then his eyebrows arched. "Oh, yes. I *see*."

Eric smiled. "*Precisely*." He bowed slightly to Anderson. "I shall take my leave. I've intruded, and I deeply apologize. If you wish to view my collection, I can schedule a showing when it's convenient." He tipped an imaginary hat and strutted from the bathroom.

Kanter stepped aside and watched Eric walk through the bedroom.

"What the hell was that?" he said, turning back. His eyes were naturally drawn to the water, although he quickly averted his glance.

"Please," she said, "get real."

"Hey, you're naked."

"There're plenty of bubbles."

Kanter slowly turned, his eyes never wavering from hers.

Anderson guided more bubbles over her chest.

"Who was that? I mean, is that what he's like when he's reliving a past life?" Kanter sat on the floor across from Anderson and leaned against the wall. He was now slightly lower than the top of the claw tub, and Anderson sensed he was more comfortable just seeing her head.

"Arthur W. Wellington is a turn-of-the-century, gay British salesman of ladies unmentionables. This was a new person." She took a sip of wine.

"Hey, did you sneak that in?"

Anderson grinned slyly. "You want a glass?"

"Hell yes. After that, I could use a drink." Kanter crawled over and grabbed the bottle and a glass from the sink.

Anderson waved her empty glass at him.

He laughed and filled it before he emptied the last of the bottle into his.

"Oh, Dr. Kanter. We could get into a lot of trouble with the Nelsons."

"Let 'em sue us."

Anderson settled back and inspected her glass. "I've got to figure out what's causing Eric's past lives."

Kanter took a sip of wine. "I did some research into Tom's comment," he said. "He's right about the theories that suggest altered foods might be triggering dormant genes. One study showed genetically modified soybeans were causing children to develop things like allergies when they never had any before. Maybe that's what's happening with Eric."

"But how could a gene, even a dormant one, carry old memories?"

"This is going to sound real new-agey, but there are theories that postulate human DNA might carry ancestral codes."

"Do you mean something like instincts?"

"Sort of," Kanter said, swirling his wine. "Maybe Eric's manifesting past lives because some prehistoric code is being triggered. Maybe the code allows him to retrieve his past-life memories by tapping into a higher source."

It was hard for Anderson to take this concept seriously. She made a face and finished the last of her wine. "The mind is capable of some amazing things," she said, "but I doubt it can tap into God. You're beginning to sound like Tom. He thinks Eric might be one of those Indigo children."

"I've heard of them ... something to do with having purple auras. What's your take on it?"

"There're some amazing children out there, but I don't think they're a more evolved human. And I certainly don't believe they're paranormal. It pisses me off that people can't give credit where credit's due. A gifted child is just that. And labeling a disruptive child as an Indigo can delay proper diagnosis and treatment."

"Yeah, but Eric is more than gifted. He's downright scary."

"You want scary? Come into the inner city with me, and I'll show you scary."

"Even if we prove that the hooker and the German were past lives," Kanter said, "we may never understand why Eric manifests them."

"One thing's for sure..." Anderson gathered up what was left of a bubble burg and guided it up around her neck.

"What's that?"

"Whatever Eric turns out to be, I'll bet you there's nobody else like him."

18. Don't worry, mon.

It had taken Kanter the better part of three days to set up all the equipment. Anderson had frittered about for most of it, and it was becoming increasingly apparent that the loss of Kelly was going to impact the success of the project. Even though Anderson was very enthusiastic, the technology seemed lost on her. Kanter knew her insight would be invaluable, but what he needed now was someone who knew hardware *and* software. He flipped open his cell phone and headed for the front door of the lab.

"Where're you going?" Anderson asked from one of the workstations. She didn't bother to look up.

"I have to make a call. The best reception is next to the house,"

Kanter said, "near the doors to the storm cellar."

"Really? I've found if I stand about halfway down the driveway, I get great reception."

"Thanks, I'll try it."

It was a stunning morning. The sky was a shade of blue Kanter had fallen in love with on a trip to Santa Fe. It had a richness you didn't get in Chicago. The driveway's gravel crunched under his boots as he searched for Anderson's sweet spot. When his cell's signal strength shot to full, he stopped. Something rubbed against his calf.

"Hey, boy." Kanter scratched behind Claudius's ear, and the shepherd sat. The air was as cool as it had been since they had arrived, which caused Kanter to reconsider the shorts he was wearing. He could feel Claudius's panting breath across his shins. The number he dialed rang forever.

"Yeah?" a woman finally asked. Her voice sounded Jamaican and carried a lot of attitude. A baby wailed in the background.

"Hello, is Hoop there?"

"Hold on." The woman scolded the child, and the crying shifted to whimpering. After a long pause, during which Kanter thought he heard dishes jangling in a sink, it sounded like the phone fell to the floor. The clatter was piercing, and Kanter jerked his head away.

"Damn, woman," a voice said from the phone. "Yeah?"

"Hello, Hoop?"

"Maybe."

"This is Bill Kanter. We met at your party about a month ago. You called me about Kelly's death."

"I remember."

There was a long silence. Kanter checked his signal strength.

"You didn't come to the wake," Hoop said.

"I know." A large crow flew low across the road about 20 yards away. It glided into a grove of elms and disappeared among the branches. "I'm sorry I didn't make it. To be honest, some things have happened that made going out in public a little hard for me."

"Really? You okay?"

"Yeah. I just can't talk about it."

"No worries, mon. You'll find the right time to pay your respects. Now, you didn't call ol' Hoopy just to chat."

"Remember that project we talked about at the party?"

"You still trying to catch souls?"

"Well, it's not really catching ... more like documenting."

Hoop grunted. Kanter didn't know if he was pissed or what.

"Kelly said you were pretty good with platform integration."

Another grunt. "In a prior life."

"I was wondering if you'd be interested in helping me with the project."

Hoop made a sound that resembled a laugh. "I thought you might call."

* * *

Kanter learned that Hoop was a freelance consultant whose summer was open. When he arrived two days later, the big Rastafarian threw himself into the work. Hoop knew more about system integration than Kelly had let on. His knowledge of platforms was extensive, and he had an instinctive way of solving problems. Kanter immediately took to him but sensed Anderson was intimidated by Hoop's presence. Ever since he had told her that Hoop was going to join their team, her enthusiasm had waned. She had become reticent and went about her work with a detached ambivalence.

Kanter knew his decision might tick her off a little, but he sensed that something else was going on. The day after Hoop had arrived, he practically rewrote the code for the data stream buffers and asked Anderson to back-up the data onto the Cores. She had struggled with the sequencing, and it took every ounce of Kanter's willpower not to intervene and take over. Hoop had ended up helping her, but it was obvious that the whole thing had punched a mean hole in her ego. She had excused herself early to catch up on some email, claiming she'd probably miss dinner because of the Nelsons' slow Internet service.

All through the meal, Kanter kept thinking about the whole situation, eventually concluding that after he had done his dishes, he'd go upstairs and see what was bugging her before it festered. He set his bowl into the sink's soapy water and began scrubbing.

Anderson entered the kitchen and froze. She acted as if she might back out slowly, but didn't.

"There's some soup left," Kanter said, trying to sound normal. He motioned with the scrub brush to the large pot on the stove.

"Thanks, but I'm not that hungry," Anderson said as she opened the refrigerator.

Kanter dried his hands and hooked the dishrag over a drawer pull. He leaned against the counter. They were alone. "Tren, we need to talk."

"I'm kind of in the middle of something," she said, rummaging through one of the lower shelves.

Kanter was growing frustrated. "Just for a second."

"Can it wait?"

"Tren, come on. I know you're boogered about Hoop coming onboard."

She straightened and stared like she was daring him to figure her out.

"Tren?–"

"*Boogered?*"

"Yeah, boogered. Upset. To be uneasy with a situation."

"Is this Webster's definition?"

Hell. "No, it's a Carol Kanter term. My mom uses it when I get mad about stupid things."

"I'll have to remember it next time I'm upset about something stupid." Anderson pulled the tab of a ginger ale and took a sip.

"Having a pity party upstairs?" Kanter asked, though he immediately regretted it.

Anderson slowly lifted her eyes over the can and swallowed. "No," she said, her brow furrowed. "I'm paying bills. Some of us still have to deal with the real world."

Any sympathy Kanter had for her situation dissolved. "You're getting paid pretty damn well for this assignment."

Anderson's jaw muscles flexed. "I know." She set the ginger ale down and leaned against the counter.

"Look," he said, folding his arms, "I know Hoop can be intimidating–"

"That's an understatement."

"But he knows his stuff."

"And I don't, right?"

"Okay, so the tech part of this is a little lost on you. But you bring a lot more than tech knowledge to the table."

"Really? Like what?"

Kanter had to think. "How people process memories, for one."

"Bill, I'm not a scientist or a techie. I'm a behaviorist, and I'm beginning to feel like a third wheel here."

"That's crap. You're an important asset to this project. If I didn't think so, I wouldn't have asked you to be part of it."

"If I'm so important, why didn't you discuss bringing Hoop on with me?" Anderson's tone was accusatory.

Kanter was pissed. He raked his fingers through his hair. "Tren, Hoop is just more experienced in certain areas. I guess I should have talked with you, but I didn't see the need. This is my project, and I have the right to bring on whoever I think has the expertise I need. Plus, he already knew about it, so he was the natural choice."

Anderson angrily grabbed the ginger ale off the counter and started to leave.

"*Tren!*" To her back.

She turned, and Kanter realized what the expression "*if looks could kill*" really meant.

"I thought you were more..." She bit off her words and slammed the ginger ale onto the counter. Foam hissed out of its top.

"More *what*?"

Anderson leaned in. "Understanding."

Kanter lost it. "Well excuse the *hell* out of me if I'm not Mr. Sensitive! Last time I checked, this was all on my shoulders!"

Anderson took his arm. "Bill," she said sternly, "calm down."

Kanter jerked away. "Don't tell me to calm down. I'm on, no ... *we're* on the brink of something incredible!"

Anderson gestured for him to lower his voice.

"I won't shut up! You're not the one being shot at, or-or getting people killed!"

Anderson said something, but all Kanter could hear were the words *people killed* looping in his mind.

"Bill, what's the matter?"

Kanter tried to focus, but his mind couldn't put her words into the correct syntax. An overwhelming emotion clouded his ability to answer. He felt like his soul was shredding, and he had no way to stop it. It must have showed on his face, because Anderson's expression grew serious.

"My, God, Bill, you're turning white."

Kanter looked into Anderson's eyes, and the guilt, which he had kept at bay for the last several weeks, came crashing down. He sank into a kitchen chair and put his face into his hands.

Anderson knelt and put a hand to his shoulder. "Bill, listen to me," she said calmly. "You didn't kill them."

"Yes, I did," he said, pulling away. "Don't you get it? It was my discovery! I'm responsible!"

"No," she said and grabbed him by the shoulders. "You can't think like that. It's not fair to you, or to the memories of Kelly and Phillip. Kelly wouldn't have blamed you, right?"

Kanter's mind was swimming in guilt. "I-I don't know."

"Bill, think. You can't run this kind of judgment on yourself."

Hoop suddenly stepped into the kitchen and swept the room with his eyes. He regarded Kanter and Anderson, then nodded to himself and walked to the refrigerator. The gold chains on his wrist clinked as he reached in.

Anderson stood and started sipping from her ginger ale.

Kanter wiped his eyes.

"Don't worry, mon," Hoop said and pulled a Diet Coke out. He closed the refrigerator and pulled the tab.

"Don't worry about what?" Kanter tried to sound normal, but the words were coated with emotion. He wiped some hair off his forehead.

Hoop took a swig and stared at the floor. "Kelly wouldn't have blamed you," he said before he strolled from the kitchen.

19. The rest of your lives.

Kanter hadn't said a word all day. At first, his minor meltdown surprised Anderson, but Kanter had been a prodigy, and studies had shown that gifted people often suppressed emotions – sometimes to an unhealthy point and with dangerous consequences. People under stress, especially when their lives were threatened, could do things they normally wouldn't. Anderson had seen a lot of that in Iraq.

Once, about halfway through her tour, she was treating a wounded solider who had been suffering from post-traumatic stress disorder (PTSD). Anderson thought their sessions were going well until she received word that he had almost beaten an Iraqi orderly to death for bumping into him. She didn't think that Kanter would ever go postal

... he just wasn't the type. Then again.

"Shit!" Kanter began wildly shaking his hand. He looked at Anderson over the large crate he was working on and rolled his eyes.

"Are you okay?" she asked.

"*Yes*," he said, rubbing. "I just smashed the hell out of my finger." He threw his hammer across the top of the crate.

Today they were uncrating the equipment that did the actual scanning: a ramped-up version of Kanter's famous MedBed. Anderson couldn't wait for him to hook it up. She had seen pictures of it in a magazine. The article had been mostly about Kanter and featured the MedBed photographed like a sports car. He told her that an industrial design firm called Chaos had developed the initials, whatever that meant. Who would name their company Chaos, anyway?

"You need any help?" Hoop held a crowbar in one hand and coffee in the other.

"Yeah." Kanter grabbed another crowbar off the floor. "Let's get after it."

Kanter and Hoop disassembled the crate and stacked the pieces against the wall near the Cores. Anderson could barely make out the MedBed's shape through all the foam inserts and bubble wrap. She started removing one of the cardboard wedges from the bed's frame.

"Watch how you pull those off," Kanter said. "Especially the one that protects the control panel."

Anderson peeled away the last of the bubble wrap and stuffed it into a large industrial trashcan that had a U of C logo on it, along with several gang symbols markered in metallic silver. Kanter had brought everything from the old lab, including the trash.

"Now that's a damn work of art," Hoop said.

In the late afternoon light, the MedBed looked even edgier than it had in the magazine. Its shape reminded Anderson of a chrome letter opener she had seen in the gift shop of the Museum of Modern Art. It was about the size and shape of a surfboard. The middle was contoured to fit a person lying down, with deep indentations for the head, back, and legs. A dozen tiny holes semi-circled the head indent, and the control panel was merged so seamlessly along the edge it was hardly noticeable. The bed balanced delicately on six spider legs that articulated from two center points under the frame. The legs were of a metal that mimicked snakeskin, and the whole thing had an organic energy, like at any moment it could shake off the last bits of foam and scurry out of the lab.

"What do you think?" Kanter asked Anderson.

"It's beautiful," she said. "What are the holes for?"

"Those are for the coolest part." Kanter walked over to a small crate and slid it up to the bed. He crowbarred the top panel off and lifted out a foam square about the size of an old 20-inch tube TV. Gingerly, he pulled off the upper half of the square and laid it aside. Nestled in the bottom half was something that resembled a Chihuly glass sculpture. As Kanter moved the square around, it reflected little color spectrums throughout the lab.

"What is that?" Anderson asked.

"The heart of the scanner," he proudly replied. "Hoop, can you give me a hand here, please?"

Kanter and Hoop lifted the device out of the foam square and walked it over to the bed. It looked like they were carrying a giant, upside-down glass insect. Its underbelly was flat; its legs arrayed in a semi-circle and folded in.

"Its base slips into these connector holes," Kanter instructed.

Hoop knelt and eyed the holes around the head indent.

"You'll feel it when it slides into place," Kanter said.

Hoop moved the insect's body with the tips of his fingers until there was an audible "click."

"There," Kanter said, straightening. He looked at Anderson and smiled. "Bitchin', isn't it?"

Sometimes, Kanter's language reflected his age. "That's a word for it," she said.

Hoop laughed.

Anderson circled the bed and noted that the insect's belly was actually where a person placed his or her head. She pointed at the 12 spindly glass legs. "What do these do?"

Kanter leaned close and eyed his invention. "These are the targeting scanner arms. This part," he gestured toward the area where a person's head would go, "reads your head's shape and instructs the arms into position."

Anderson leaned closer. They weren't glass, as she had first thought, but were instead a pliable translucent material, somewhat like plastic yet more fluid, if that were possible. Each one featured a needle connector at its tip along with a fiber-optic thread that ran inside the length of the arm. The base was a darker material than the arms and wasn't translucent.

"Can I touch one?" she asked.

Kanter grinned like a kid. "Sure."

Anderson reached and was an inch from the closest arm when all 12 suddenly came alive and tentacled around her hand.

"Shit!" She jumped back and slammed into Hoop, and both

stumbled into a workstation. She lost her footing, but Hoop grabbed her before she could fall.

"What the hell *is* that?!" she demanded and tucked part of her work shirt back into her jeans.

Kanter was laughing so hard he couldn't answer.

"Mon, that's crazy shit," Hoop said.

"No," Kanter managed, "it's artificial intelligence."

"It's *alive*?" Anderson asked.

"In a way. I turned it on before we positioned the scanner module. The head unit is programmed to read anything that comes into its field."

Hoop started looking around. "Where's its power come from?"

"Reserve battery system," Kanter said. "In case you're in the middle of a scan and the power goes off."

Anderson rubbed her hand, even though there wasn't any pain. "That was mean."

"Aw, come on. I was just playing with you. It doesn't think, and it won't bite." Kanter glanced at it and smiled devilishly. "At least it's not supposed to."

* * *

"That should do it," Kanter said, stepping out from behind one of the Cores. He wiped his hands down the front of his shirt and went to the main workstation.

He and Hoop had crawled over the equipment all afternoon; their technospeak had reached a point where they practically finished each other's sentences. The sound of three beers being opened brought Anderson's attention around.

"Ah, Red Stripe," Hoop said. "God's drink!" He was standing by the refrigerator Kanter had brought from Chicago and holding the bottles up in both hands. His gold-laced smile radiated against his dark skin.

"No shit," Kanter said, focused on the large screen at the main control interface for the system.

Hoop passed out the beers, and Anderson eagerly took a drink.

"Are we almost ready?" Hoop asked Kanter.

Kanter typed in a few commands and leaned back. "As ready as we'll ever be. Who wants to go first?"

A sharp tingle danced through Anderson's nerves. She glanced at the scanner arms and felt their phantom touch across her knuckles.

Kanter spun in his chair and faced her. "You don't have to, you know."

She hesitated. "I'm not–"

"I'll go." Hoop set his beer down and approached the bed.

"Okay," Kanter said, standing. "Since you're kind of a big guy, let me adjust the base."

Hoop let out a laugh. "Ol' Hoopy's gonna crush that delicate bed of yours, Doc."

Kanter paused at the MedBed's control panel and regarded Hoop like he had just insulted him. He entered a few keystrokes into the panel, and the bed shifted its position like a horse taking a piss. Its legs spread with an almost dancerlike grace, and the platform tilted down. The body indentations on its surface rippled, which appeared to Anderson as if the bed's surface had changed to accommodate Hoop's large frame.

"I thought you said it wasn't alive," she said.

Hoop took a step back. "I-I'm not getting on that thing."

"Don't worry, you're not going to crush it," Kanter said. "It can accept up to a thousand pounds." Its legs spread wider, and the platform dropped about a foot.

"You've lowered its center of gravity," Anderson said.

"I haven't done a thing," Kanter replied. "The bed reads its patient and adjusts accordingly."

Anderson folded her arms. "Now wait a minute. Hoop is at least five feet away, and he hasn't even touched it."

"Yeah," Hoop said, "it can't determine my size ... can it?"

"It uses an Interactive Proximal Accessor," Kanter said. "It scans whoever's nearest, determines the correct height and weight distribution, then resets the legs to adjust for the next patient."

"Why didn't it read *you* and adjust accordingly?" Anderson asked.

"It's already taken my scan. I'm in its database. Plus I'm at the control panel. It uses fingerprint recognition. Since I'm inputting the commands, it's doubtful I'll be the next patient. It's not foolproof, just logical."

Hoop whistled. "I don't have a good feeling about this."

"Bill, this is amazing," Anderson said. "I've never seen anything like this."

"No one has," Kanter said, "except the Defense Department. The commercial version was redesigned for hospital use."

"You're kidding."

"Who do you think funded the first MedBed?"

"But I thought it was a private investment."

Kanter shook his head. "No. The DoD had it a year before any of it was made public. The leg design was a bonus. They said it would revolutionize battlefield triage."

As Kanter explained how the DoD had set him up behind a false grant, Anderson couldn't help but be amazed. He was truly a genius, and what made him charming was that he didn't seem to know it. If he did, he was the most humble genius she had ever met, and his boyish, *aw-shucks* routine made him all the more endearing. Anderson leaned against the counter of the back-up workstation and watched him help Hoop climb onto the MedBed. Kanter took great care to make Hoop feel comfortable, and while he explained that there would be no pain involved, he glanced at her. It was a fleeting look, but something passed across Anderson's heart that she hadn't felt in a long time.

Kanter leaned onto the MedBed and regarded Hoop like a close friend might just before an important surgery.

"You see," he said, "there's no chance of any feedback or looping of the data. You'll feel a little pinprick at the points of contact. Ever had acupuncture?"

Hoop nodded.

"It's just like that." Kanter patted Hoop's shoulder. "Now relax. You're about to discover the rest of your lives."

20. This is getting very spooky.

"Are you sure it won't hurt?" Hoop asked.

"The only thing you'll feel," Kanter said, "are the pinpricks from the connectors. Now hold still while it scans the shape of your head."

Kanter checked the reserve battery to see whether he had enough power in case of any electrical issues. There was plenty. He hadn't bothered to review the breaker situation when Anderson plugged the bed into the same box as the Cores. Now, however, he was eyeing the power cord suspiciously.

"Trenna," he said. "Do me a favor and connect the bed into that plug over there."

"Are you afraid of throwing a breaker?" she asked.

"I don't want to take any chances."

Anderson dragged the heavy-duty extension cord to an outlet on the far wall and plugged in the bed. "You should be okay," she said upon her return. "Scott said this building was wired for industrial use."

"Hey!" Hoop said.

"What's up?" Kanter asked.

"Is it going to scan *everything*?"

"It should, why?"

"I don't want you two to see *all* of my current life, know what I mean?"

"Have you been a bad boy?" Anderson asked.

"I've done my share of things to get by."

"I'll let you screen your current life alone," Kanter said, "so you can tag anything that's questionable, and we can edit it out later. I don't care about your sex life, and you haven't done anything really bad, have you?"

Hoop hesitated. "Define bad."

"Anything violent."

Hoop looked over. "Hell no, mon! Hoopy's a decent guy. I'm talking about the *ganj*."

Kanter laughed. "You're going to feel a little tingling at the points of contact. It goes away after a couple of seconds. The scan takes about twenty minutes. Can you hold still for that long?"

Hoop grunted.

"I'll take that as a yes. Okay, try and relax while the arms get into position."

Hoop clenched his fists as the 12 translucent scanner arms closed around his head. "This is too weird," he declared.

"Hang in there," Kanter said. "One more adjustment."

The last arm positioned itself between Hoop's eyes and slowly moved in.

"I *can't*, mon."

"Close your eyes and think of something peaceful."

The last arm pressed into place, and Hoop groaned.

"There," Kanter said. "That wasn't too bad, was it?"

"Twenty minutes?"

"Nineteen minutes and forty-three seconds, to be exact. Now if for any reason you want to stop the procedure, there's a shut-off button just below your right hand."

Hoop felt for the button. "This one?"

"Yes. All you have to do is press it, and the bed shuts down and lets you off." Kanter turned to Anderson. "Want to check out the sunset?"

"Don't you stay and monitor the scan?" she asked.

"I've only scanned three people, and two of them squirmed so much, their scans never took. I think people get fidgety when I hang around, and you can't be fidgety with this equipment. Besides, there's nothing really to monitor. The bed does it all. It'll disengage when it's done and tilt down to let him off." He called to Hoop, "You cool with us leaving you alone, big guy?"

"Sure. You two go have fun. Hoopy'll be right here."

"Don't move!"

Another grunt.

Kanter grabbed two more Red Stripes from the fridge. "Come on, doctor, let's go watch the cows come home."

The Nelson farm, Kimberly had informed them, was a small

operation by industry standards. Their new milking parlor was state of the art, which set them back quite a bit. The farm had been in her family for two generations, and the building that was now the lab had been the second parlor, which explained all the retrofitting for the HVAC and electrical.

"I need to check the breakers tomorrow," Kanter said as they walked up the driveway. The sound of the dry gravel under their shoes reminded Kanter of lazy days at his grandfather's cottage in upstate New York. The late afternoon sun just crested the treetops, and the air smelled of the approaching summer. The melodic whine of cicadas rose and fell across the late afternoon wind.

"I could get used to this," Anderson commented, taking in the view. "Couldn't you?"

Kanter was running ahead of his grandfather down the road that led to the lake where he had swum and played and tried to be a normal kid. He could feel the fishing pole bounce in rhythm with each step.

"Bill?"

"Yeah?"

"Where'd you go?"

Heaven. "Just thinking."

Anderson's hair blew across her angular face and shielded one of her eyes. "About what?" she asked, more out of the side of her mouth. She did this when she was being professional. A kind of tension reflex, Kanter figured, that she had unconsciously developed.

He studied the striations of auburn the sun embossed in her hair. "Sorry about last night."

"It's okay," she said, her mouth normal. "You don't have to be. You're under a lot of stress."

The sound of someone approaching from behind made Kanter turn.

"Hey!" Hoop called. "Your machine released me."

"Right," Kanter said. "When it's done scanning, it automatically disengages. Sorry, that was faster than I thought. I would have come back in and helped you."

Hoop already had Red Stripe in hand. "That ain't no acupuncture, mon."

Kanter grinned. "Are you okay?"

Hoop nodded and took a gulp. "The bed actually lowered so I could get off." He walked up to Kanter's side and let out a small belch.

The wind had kicked up. In the distance, Kanter watched a red dually cruise the main road.

"I've changed my mind," Hoop said finally.

"About what?" Anderson asked.

"You two can watch my life, I guess."

Kanter laughed. "Don't worry," he said and patted Hoop's back. "We can cut out the naughty parts."

* * *

The upgraded software Kanter had installed, along with Hoop's reconfigurations, allowed them to tag and manually edit certain elements of the scan. He and Hoop were working on a program that would automatically remove and back-up the functional and routine parts of a person's life, such as going to the bathroom or having sex, but they hadn't finished it yet.

Hoop's life was surprisingly dull, and Kanter, although he would never admit it, was slightly disappointed. It wasn't like he expected a gangsta's life. Something a little more sinister than recreational drug use would've been interesting, though.

"Hmm," Kanter said. "So you went Rasta *after* your stint at Oracle."

"I embraced the faith on a vacation to Jamaica. When I heard the mon's music, that was that." Hoop sat back and folded his arms. He had set the scan to rewind at its maximum speed. Kanter wanted to protest, but it was Hoop's life, and he could view it anyway he wanted.

"Are you sure you didn't just embrace the smoke?" Anderson asked.

Hoop, his eyes locked on the screen, cracked a slight smile.

"Ah-ha. That's what I thought."

"You two keep watching," Kanter said. "I have to hit the little inventor's room." He headed for the bathroom, which, unfortunately, hadn't been upgraded like the HVAC. When he got back, Hoop and Anderson were still crowded in front of the monitor.

"We thought you'd fallen in," she remarked.

"Very funny." Kanter pulled up a chair. "So what life are we on?"

"This is unbelievable, Doc." Hoop looked at Kanter and pointed to the screen. "Is this real?"

"That's what we're here to find out."

"Damn."

"We're on his second life back," Anderson said. "We blasted through his current one and most of this one."

"I wanted to get an overview, in case I was someone bad," Hoop said. "Now we're going back and checking out the cool parts."

"So what were you?" Kanter asked.

"I was a barber and a musician," Hoop said, "and I was white!"

"But it was a short life," Anderson countered.

"Why?" Kanter asked.

"I cheated on my wife, and she shot me," Hoop said. "I was in my 30s."

"Really?" Kanter asked. "That's harsh."

"No shit."

Anderson gave them both a look. "I think we're proving the law of karma here."

They continued watching Hoop's second life as a New Orleans barber when something caught Kanter's attention.

"Hold it!" he said.

Hoop paused the frame.

"Go back a few months."

Hoop tried but overshot the date Kanter wanted.

"What is it?" Anderson asked.

"Let me slide in there." Kanter exchanged places with Hoop and toggled to the scene that had grabbed his attention. He called up his scan and split the screen into two.

"Bill?"

"Hold on." Kanter flew through his current life and part of the one prior. After they had reconfigured the playback filters, he had gone back and begun the process of building case files for as many of his lives as he could. He had discovered, buried in the data stream, a life right before his current one in which he had been white, lived in New Orleans during the early 1950s, and worked a ghastly job as a typewriter salesman. It seemed that past lives didn't follow one right after another, and Kanter wondered what happened to the soul between lives.

"Maybe if you tell us what you're looking for, we could help," Anderson offered.

The scene Kanter was searching for flashed by.

"Found it," he said and stopped the rewind.

"Found what?" Hoop asked.

Kanter toggled back, tagged the scene, and aligned it next to the paused image from Hoop's past life.

Anderson sucked in a breath.

"I'll be damned," Hoop said.

On the left, Hoop had paused in mid-sentence, presenting a finished haircut to a young businessman. He was looking into a large mirror that ran the length of the small shop. The young man had a classic 50s cut, complete with a pronounced part and combed over wave. He was smiling, and his hand was smoothing the hair on the side of his head. On the right, Kanter's paused image was almost identical to Hoop's, except the perspective was clearly from the young businessman.

For the next five hours, they reviewed Hoop's past lives and discovered six instances of crossover with Kanter's. Each time was unique. Sometimes it was fleeting, such as the visit to the barber. Other times, they were friends or rivals. There was even a moment when they might have fought each other in a 17th-century bar. Hoop's lives were in fragments, like Kanter's, but they could easily piece together most of the scenarios. Hoop had never been anyone of importance except in the 1400s, when he appeared to have been some kind of royalty in France.

"This is amazing." Kanter was looking at two scenes: one was of him as an 11th century Asian peasant, and the other was Hoop as his brother -- or so they thought. Because they had been moving back in time so quickly, it was like rewinding a very long silent movie and trying to figure out the plot. The only way to decipher a life was by reading anything that appeared, and if they didn't know the language, it was nearly impossible to fully grasp what was occurring. But Kanter wasn't interested in what Hoop had been, he just wanted to see when their past lives had intersected.

"This is getting weird," Hoop said.

"What do you think it means?" Anderson asked.

Kanter leaned back in his chair and wondered. "I read a theory once that suggested souls travel in groups. New Age crap, or so I thought."

"Yeah," Hoop said. "I saw a show on that. Very cool."

"But this could be an isolated occurrence," Anderson said. "There's no way to prove any of it."

"Yes there is," Kanter said.

Anderson turned and eyed the MedBed. "Right," she said. "I was afraid of that."

21. Crap.

Anderson woke to the patter of rain hitting the roof. A similar sound had awoken her during her first week at U of C, but that had turned out to be hundreds of marathoners running past her old apartment. Any other morning, she would have welcomed the sound of rain and embraced the chance to stay in bed, if only for an extra hour. Today, however, something else kept Anderson under the covers.

Kanter had attempted to be considerate the previous night. He had walked her to her room and assured her that she didn't have to be scanned to test the soul group hypothesis.

"The chances of seeing your birth parents are remote," he had said. "The images around my birth were very fractured. Short-term memory doesn't seem to imprint, or if it does, it's spotty at best. And we didn't see any of Hoop's first moments. Besides, since you were given up at the hospital, I doubt you ever saw them."

Anderson reminded him that Hoop's parents had been druggies, and his first images were of his mom's sister. Child Services had taken Anderson from her parents around the age of two or three, and she had never learned why. The thought of seeing her birth parents was both frightening and intriguing. She had once entertained the thought of hunting them down, but a friend in grad school had convinced her not to. Now, though, there was more at stake than just her need to know. If Kanter's machine could really prove reincarnation, and if her scan could have some sort of relevance, then who was she to let her ego stand in the way of the next paradigm shift?

There was a knock at her door.

"Tren?" It was Kanter.

"Come on in," she said.

He cautiously opened the door. "How are you doing?"

Kanter entered and stopped at the foot of the bed, which Anderson took as his way of keeping a respectful distance. She wanted something else. She wanted him to sit down and reassure her that being adopted didn't really matter. A little part of her also wanted him to crawl under the covers and hold her, but that part was losing out.

"I'm fine," she said.

He nodded and nervously looked at the floor.

"Bill?"

"Yeah?" he asked, glancing up.

"You were very good with Hoop yesterday."

Kanter sat on the bed next to her. For a second, she thought he had read her mind, but he did nothing more than sit there and look at her with polite concern.

"You know," he said finally, "the images of your birth parents will be only about one billionth of the total data we collect. I have a feeling you're an old soul, Dr. Anderson, and there's a lot more to you than just this life."

* * *

"Does it hurt?" Anderson asked Hoop. She eyed the MedBed and rubbed her wrist. With a clap of thunder, the rain began pounding the metal roof even harder, and she practically had to yell to be heard.

He grunted a laugh. "Nah, it's over before you know it."

"Okay," Kanter said from behind the monitor, "hop up."

As Anderson walked toward the MedBed, it bowed to her. She froze in midstep.

"It doesn't bite," Kanter reassured.

Anderson glanced back. "I don't know about this."

Kanter looked over the monitor with the same expression he had displayed at her bedside. He motioned for her to get on.

Anderson cautiously climbed up and settled in. Even though the MedBed's surface appeared metallic, it actually was a grid of tightly compressed, rubberlike sensors. These undulated up and down her back as the bed conformed to her body's contour.

"If this doesn't work, you can always sell this thing as a massage table," she said, wriggling.

"Already in the works," Kanter replied. "Now hold still while the targeting arms get into position."

The arms enclosed Anderson's head like a 12-fingered hand. The sensation was like acupuncture, and when the last arm pricked the center of her forehead, a heads-up display appeared in her vision.

She gasped.

"Sorry," Kanter said. "I forgot to tell you about the virtual interface."

"No shit," Hoop said.

"These look like medical stats." Anderson recognized some of them, but there were others that didn't make any sense.

"You're seeing what I'm seeing over here. Sorry, I haven't had time to cut the feed to the patient yet. Many of the readouts are your vitals, along with some system stats."

"I see an EEG."

"Correct," Kanter said. "Plus a few diagnostics on brain function, nervous system. You know."

"How long will this take?"

"That depends."

"On what?"

"How many lives you've had, I guess."

Great. "Then if I'm an old soul, I could be here for hours?"

"No, I don't think so."

"I've been told I'm an old soul," Hoop said, "and my scan took about 20 minutes."

"Okay," Kanter said, "I'm going to start the procedure. There'll be a little tingling at the points of contact, so just relax and clear your mind. Are you ready?"

Anderson sighed. "I guess."

"Good. Now try and relax, but don't fall asleep. Hoop and I can stay, or we can step out and give you some privacy."

"I think I want privacy."

"If you want to stop the scan, the button's by your left hand. Just press it, and the bed will release you."

"Is it scanning yet?"

"Yes, so stay still."

"What if it–" A hand touched Anderson's shoulder. She tried to turn her head, but the targeting arms prevented her.

"You sure you want us to leave?" Kanter leaned over so she could see his face.

"I'll be fine. But what if I have to, you know, go to the bathroom or something?"

"Try and hold it. We'd have to start all over again. You comfortable?"

"Yes."

"Good." He patted her shoulder. "Hoop and I will be back in about a half hour."

The slap of the screen door shutting was barely audible above the noise of the rain. The tingling Kanter referenced was more like biting, as if a dozen little bugs were stinging Anderson's head. After a couple of minutes, the urge to scratch was driving her nuts. She tried counting the bolts in the cross beams above her.

"Hey," she called out, "is it supposed to itch like this?"

The rain was now pelting the roof in waves.

"Guys? Are you there?"

Another rumble of thunder.

"Crap."

The readouts cascaded down the edge of Anderson's vision; the effect was a bit nauseating. She tried to read some of the data, but it was sequencing too fast for her to pick anything out. When she closed her eyes, the displays only dimmed. She tried to relax and let her mind empty, but thoughts of her adopted parents and how wonderful they had been filled her mind. Her friend back in grad school *had* been right: the only thing that really mattered was that loving people had raised her. Anderson began chastising herself for being so selfish. Simultaneously, the sensation at the contact points shifted. Warmth now accompanied the tingling.

For a couple of minutes, the sensation wasn't that painful. It sort of reminded her of the time, as a kid, when her older cousin had shown her the joke about how a match burned twice. He had lit a match, blown it out, and then pressed the still hot, burnt end to her arm. He had laughed his guts out while she cried to her mother.

Anderson didn't think much of the sensation. She figured it was part of the scanning process. Probably another thing Kanter had forgotten to mention. But the temperature kept increasing until it came close to burning.

"Bill?!" Anderson couldn't move her head. "This is getting a little uncomfortable. Is it supposed to get hot? Hel-*lo*?"

A flash of lightning filled the long row of window by the ceiling. The lights in the lab flickered. She heard a cracking sound somewhere behind her, and a burnt smell drifted up from the floor. A stabbing sensation replaced the tingling heat, as if the connector tips had dug in deeper.

"Guys? I think we better–"

Anderson's words were eclipsed as her life abruptly exploded across her field of vision. Whole sections of her life fractured into chaotic images that tumbled through her consciousness like bright balls of emphatic light. She groped for the shut-off switch but couldn't find the button. The stream of readouts and her life now raced across her vision.

"Bill, please! Get me out of this–"

Through the image's pellucid veil, lightning again filled the upper windows, and there was another crackle. Then something primordial, a scream, emerged from Anderson's throat, and everything went black.

* * *

Anderson opened her eyes to the same cross beams, but the lab was darkened, and the light from the monitors cast the ceiling in a harsh patchwork of shadows. Haze rimmed her vision, and a faint drumming sound emanated from the floor. The readouts were gone, as well as the heat, and when she blinked, her eyelashes stuck together like she had been crying. Anderson tried to move her head, which caused a stinging as the targeting arms tightened around her. A drop of sweat stung as it rolled into her eye. Panic was filling her when she heard someone speak softly near the edge of her hearing.

"Tren?" The voice repeated. A shadowy figure came into her periphery, and then Kanter's smile came into focus.

"Welcome back," he said.

She tried to speak, but her throat was raw and dry.

Kanter put a finger to her lips. "Don't. You're dehydrated." He placed a straw near her lips, and she eagerly sipped the cool water.

"Better?" he asked.

"Yes," Anderson managed. "What happened?"

"I'm not sure, but I think there was a feedback loop. Something to do with the storm. We're on back-up generators."

"Why am I still connected?"

Kanter hesitated, and she didn't buy his reassuring look.

"I can't just yank you from the system," he said. "I have to disengage you in the correct sequence."

"Am I hurt?"

Kanter's smile returned. "No, Tren. You're not. There's not enough juice running through the bed to cause any permanent damage."

Permanent damage? "I felt the connectors heat up, then there was a cracking sound, and I smelled smoke."

"Yeah, there was a power surge, which caused the loop. It tripped a breaker. I think lightning struck one of the barns and maybe jumped a roof."

"Bill?"

Kanter leaned closer and reprised the look from her bedside. "Yes?"

"I saw–" Fragments of the images flashed in Anderson's mind, but the words caught in her throat.

"What, Tren? What did you see?"

"I saw it, Bill ... my life, all at once, like what people say they see before they die. And there was more. It was like–"

"Living your life again?"

"*Yes*." Their eyes met, and something jumped between them: a common bond, like she imaged people who had gone through a trauma might feel. She had seen it in the soldiers she had treated but could never really understand it like they did.

"Pretty amazing, isn't it?" Kanter took her hand.

Anderson thought about pulling away, but his touch was comforting.

"So, Dr. Anderson," he said while rubbing her fingers, "are you ready to get out of this thing and view your soul?"

22. It's in the past.

It took Kanter almost 30 minutes to disengage Anderson from the MedBed. The sequencing went well, but the final power-down was a little rough. He realized he was going to have to check every damn element before he even thought about scanning again.

Anderson looked drained, as if someone had tapped her veins and extracted every bit of enthusiasm. As Kanter helped her from the MedBed, it seemed like her mind wasn't in sync with her body. She took a step and nearly collapsed into his arms.

"You need to sit down," he said and gave a nod to the old Eames chair and ottoman. He had told her that the Eames had been his dad's and was now a kind of good luck charm. He'd explained it one night over the last bottle of wine Anderson had snuck into the house. They both had gotten pretty toasted and had lingered a little too long for a simple "goodnight." She had leaned in like she expected to kiss him ... but angled for a hug instead. He had almost planted one for the hell of it, but lost his nerve in spite of the Merlot buzz.

"Whoa." Anderson grabbed his shoulder.

Kanter steadied her. "Easy there. Are you all right?"

She rubbed her forehead and coughed. "Just some bad vertigo."

"That's to be expected. There's always a little residual effect from the virtual connection. I've got to work that issue out." He poured Anderson into the Ames, then went over to the main workstation and began reviewing the system logs to see where the failure had occurred.

"Hey," Hoop said to Anderson, acting like he needed to leave. "I promised Eric I'd show him Tai Chi. Are you okay on your own?"

"I'll be all right," she said. "I just need a minute."

"Thanks. I've canceled on him twice now, you know?" Hoop excused himself and left.

Anderson sat on the edge of the Eames and sipped from the straw. "It's so nice that Hoop has been spending time with Eric," she said after a minute.

"He's a natural father type." Kanter glanced over his shoulder at her. "How are you feeling?"

"Better, thanks." Anderson climbed out of the Ames and gingerly walked to the main workstation. She sat and stared at the morphing solar system screen saver.

Kanter rolled over in his chair and joined her.

"Are you sure you want to view your scan?" he asked. "Maybe you should get some rest first."

"I'll be all right, really."

Kanter didn't believe her smile. "Let me show you how this works," he said and scooted closer. "This command starts the data flow." He pointed at the TAB key. "And you toggle up and down the linear time line with this interface panel." He dragged the interface to the lower right corner of the screen. "It works like a DVD player, but it runs *very* fast. You can track the years here." He pointed to timeline bar at the bottom of the screen.

"How fast does it go?"

"If you want, you can burn through 20 years in about five minutes."

Anderson seemed to understand but still looked a bit out of it. Kanter stood and slid the chair back to the other workstation.

"You're not staying?" she asked, her brow knitted.

"I think you should do this alone. It's kind of personal, you know?"

Anderson looked to the monitor and back. She started to say something, but caught herself.

"How about if I park myself over there?" Kanter gestured to the large sofa by the Cores.

Anderson nodded with an absent smile and faced the monitor.

Kanter grabbed his laptop. He could link up with the Cores and figure out what happened during Anderson's scan. He glanced at his watch. *6:20. This is going to take all night*, he thought.

For the next four hours, Anderson reviewed her life and, for the most part, sat perfectly still. Kanter counted only three times when she sort of laughed, which confirmed to him that Anderson's over-achieving mantra had done a number on her happiness.

Kanter's eyes grew heavy. He had been fighting to stay awake for the better part of the last hour but felt himself slipping. When

Anderson began to cry, though, it snapped him back. He jumped to his feet, rolled a chair to her side, and sat.

"Tren, what is it?" Kanter put an arm around her, and she leaned in.

On the screen was a staticky image of a small, wood-paneled living room. It was crowded with tattered boxes, strewn clothes, and a few beat-up baby toys. It could have been any of the shitty mobile homes Kanter had seen in South Chicago. The point of view seemed to be a child held by an adult. Two bodies, a man and a woman probably in their twenties, were slumped in death throes on a torn, green vinyl couch. Two distinct sprays of blood painted the wall behind them. A section of the man's forehead was missing, and the woman had a vicious wound just below her sternum. Her lifeless eyes stared forward, blood splattered across her face.

Anderson's agony was now coming in waves. Kanter quickly docked the image and took her into both arms.

"It's okay, Tren," he said, stroking her hair. "Let it out."

"My real parents were *murdered*." Her face was awash in tears.

Kanter wiped at her cheeks with the cuff of his sleeve. "It's in the past," he said, then kissed the top of her head.

Anderson pulled back. "No, it's not!"

"What do you mean?"

Anderson turned to the monitor and brought up the living room image. She sequenced back a few days, then paused on a scene of the same room from a different position. The point of view was from the floor, looking up. The couch loomed in the left of the frame, and the same man and woman were standing with their backs to the couch. A young teen-ager in a wife-beater and jeans was holding a shotgun on them. He was frozen in an angry gesture, the shotgun jabbing the woman in the chest. They looked in the middle of a nasty argument, and the woman, her mouth contorted like she was swearing, was pointing at the kid. Kanter could make out a fair amount of detail, yet he couldn't take his eyes off of the dragon tattoo spread across the kid's upper shoulder and neck.

"I witnessed it, as a child," Anderson said, her face tight with pain. "I saw *everything*."

The whole scene was too heinous to process. Kanter didn't know what to say. "Tren," he said, finally, "for all you know, this guy might have been caught. You can't let it mess with you."

Anderson swiveled from the image to him. She pointed at the screen. Her finger was shaking. "I-I *know* him."

Kanter was lost. "The kid with the shotgun?"

Anderson wagged her finger in frustration but couldn't choke the words out. She buried her face in her hands.

Kanter took her by the shoulders, but she didn't look up.

"Tren, please, don't worry. I won't say—"

"You don't understand," she said through her fingers. "The kid with the gun ... he's my uncle."

23. Won't you join us?

Anderson stopped short of the lab's main door. It had been over a day since she had viewed her scan. She had stayed in her room for most of that time – either reading, catching up on email, or sleeping. Anderson had taken her meals there too, although she hadn't felt much like eating. She wasn't depressed, at least not in the clinical sense. Rather, it was like her life had gone through an emotional earthquake, its foundation now webbed with stress fractures.

Kanter had been sweet to her after she had broken down watching her current life. He had walked her to her room and stayed up with her most of the night, discussing the scan and its ramifications.

Anderson had always felt that she was a strong woman, but nothing

– not even Iraq – had prepared her for what she had seen. And it wasn't so much the gruesomeness of the images – she had seen her share of terrible things – it was more what *hadn't* been captured. According to the scan, her adoptive father had arrived at her birth parents' mobile home two days after they had been shot and had taken her home with him. There were no images of police, social workers, or her adoptive dad and uncle ever meeting after the killing.

Her birth parents must have been related to her dad. Otherwise, how could they have taken a 4 year old from a murder scene and never dealt with the Chicago social system?

Kanter, however, had speculated that the murdered couple might not have been her birth parents. He suggested that watching the rest of her current life and finding out the truth might help her heal.

The psychologist in Anderson agreed, but the child in her – the one who had crawled into her dead mother's lap and wiped the blood from father's lifeless face – wanted no part of it.

"It won't matter," Anderson had said to Kanter. Whatever happened in her first few years of life wouldn't change the love she had for her adoptive parents.

"You need to find out the truth," Kanter had argued. "All you have to do is call your dad."

Anderson knew it wouldn't be that easy. Her adoptive father always claimed her birth parents had been heroin addicts who had given Anderson up at the hospital, and her uncle had been a Marine in Somalia who suffered from post-traumatic stress syndrome. Her dad had said his brother had been institutionalized, but after what she witnessed on her scan, Anderson suspected the "institution" was prison. The thought of broaching the subject with her adoptive father, much less explaining how she acquired the information, made Anderson sick to her stomach.

Now, standing at the outer door to the lab, she had to remind herself that she was a woman of science who needed to put aside any emotions that might interfere with the success of the project.

Heal thyself, she thought and twisted the knob.

The squeak of the inner screen door echoed across the structure's hard surfaces. Hoop and Kanter were hunkered around the main monitor, which seemed odd because Anderson thought they'd have the Cores halfway torn down by now.

Hoop stood and lumbered toward her. He bear-hugged her and said, "You hang in there, sista. God gives you only what you can handle." He waved at Kanter and headed for the door, mumbling something about a call he had to make to his lawyer.

Anderson wasn't sure what God gave humans to handle, but Hoop's words were a sweet gesture. As she approached, Kanter stood and dug his hands into his pockets.

"How are you doing?" he asked.

Anderson flashed on his kiss to her head. At the time, she had been so overcome with grief that he could have been naked and she wouldn't have noticed. But now, remembering what he did, she couldn't think of anything that could possibly express how grateful she was. Kanter started to say something, but she leaned in and kissed him on the cheek.

"You're welcome," he said, surprised. He guided a stray lock of hair off her face. His fingers lingered at her cheek, before he gestured to the monitor. "I have something to show you, if you're up for it." His voice was full of enthusiasm.

The monitor was blank, but Anderson could see the image of her parents again. Her legs felt weak, and she cautiously sat. "Bill, I don't want to see the rest of my–"

"I didn't watch the rest of your current life's scan," Kanter said. "But I took the liberty of viewing some of your more recent past lives." He smiled. "I just wanted to confirm our soul group theory."

Anderson felt a little violated and started to protest, but Kanter stopped her.

"Before you get mad, doctor," he said, "you should check out what we found. It's really quite remarkable."

Kanter reached past her and called up an image that could have been from the 1800s. It was a street scene in a large city, and people were paused in various blurs of motion. A man's bearded face filled much of the frame. He was tall, possibly in his 30s, and wore a dark blue uniform with gold epaulettes on the shoulders. The point of view was looking up slightly, and the man was paused mid-sentence. Anderson studied his eyes, which had something familiar about them.

"Boo," Kanter said, behind her ear.

"Is this you?" she asked.

"In the digital."

"And this is from *my* scan?"

"That's correct. This is at the start of the Civil War, about 1861-ish, I think."

Anderson was astonished. The pain from the other night would have to wait. This was too important. *I can't control the past*, she thought, and reached to start the stream sequencing.

"Hold on," Kanter said.

Anderson, her finger poised above the play tab, froze. "What's the matter?"

Kanter hesitated. "This is a little weird."

"Bill, please. It's my soul, remember?"

He reluctantly nodded and motioned for her to continue.

Anderson clicked the tab, and the image sequenced forward. The man finished whatever he had been saying, then leaned in and filled the screen with his face. The point of view tilted, and flashes of the street appeared in different corners of the screen. There were glimpses of people's reactions, which varied from disgust to women covering their smiles.

"Wait a minute." She paused the image. The man had pulled back, but his eyes were closed. "Is he kissing her ... I mean me, I mean ... you're kissing *me*?"

"My dear Miss Anderson," Kanter said in a phony southern drawl. "I do believe we were having relations." He sat and put his arm across the back of her chair.

Anderson was amazed. She looked at the image, then Kanter. "Is there more?"

A devilish smile grew across his face.

"You're kidding. Did we–"

"Screw like porn stars?"

"Y-yes."

He laughed. "Every time we could."

Anderson clicked the image away.

"Hey, wait–"

She stood and blocked the monitor. "I think I'd like to view this myself."

"Too late, doctor. Hoop and I have seen it all, unedited."

"*Hoop*? Where's your professional ethics?"

"Come on, you're a doctor. I'm sure you can understand the thirst for knowledge." Kanter couldn't contain himself anymore and started laughing. Anderson punched him, but he raised his arm and took the blow on his shoulder.

"You guys are assholes!" She stifled a laugh and reared back for another strike.

Kanter slapped her swing away. "Don't worry, we didn't watch anymore of your lives. Besides, you're no angel in this life. You were married, and I wasn't."

Anderson stopped attacking. "I was having an affair?"

"A very hot one, I might add."

"So what happened?"

Kanter's smile faded. He brushed some hair off his forehead.

"Bill, what is it?"

"I was killed in some big battle," he said. "I was a Union officer, low ranking. I think infantry from New York."

"Oh, God, Bill. I'm so sorry."

He shrugged. "It's not like I remember any of it. Something exploded near me, and I saw my arm fly away from my body."

Anderson gasped.

Kanter forced a smile. "At least I got some before I died."

The joke didn't work on Anderson. She looked into Kanter's face and wondered about the soldier in the scan. What had she felt for him? Had she been in love, or had he been a passing fling?

"God*damn* lawyers!" Hoop declared and slammed the screen door.

"What's the matter?" Kanter asked.

Hoop shook his head and sent his dreads flapping. "My old lady hauled off and cold-cocked someone in a bar. And now the bitch is going to sue us." He glanced at Anderson. "Sorry."

"I've heard it before," she said.

Hoop noticed what was on the screen. "I hope you don't mind us taking a peek."

"It's okay. I have a thick skin."

"Did he show you the good parts?" Hoop asked.

"Not yet," Kanter said.

"Maybe we should put it on a DVD and sell it. Call it *Civil War Ho*." Hoop made a sweeping motion with his hand.

"Hey, don't forget your little tryst with that farmer." Kanter made a similar gesture. "We'll call yours *Medieval Gay Boys*."

"Fuck you, mon."

Anderson knew they were trying to keep things light. She appreciated their effort. "So," she said, "does my scan confirm souls travel in groups?"

"We need to do about a thousand more scans to confirm," Kanter said. "But I'm going to go out on a limb here and say yes."

"Then this deserves a little celebration," Anderson announced. "Let's go into town for lunch."

Kanter frowned. "Don't you want to stay and view your other lives?"

The thought of sitting in front of a computer for hours didn't appeal to Anderson at all. Besides, she had sequestered herself in her room for the previous 24 hours; she needed to get out.

"Frankly," she said while she docked her scan, "I've had my fill of surprises. I'm starving. Come on, my treat."

* * *

The town of River Point was not, as its population sign declared, worth writing home about. It was quaint, but Anderson had never been a fan of quilts and ruffles, so the side of River Point that catered to the occasional tourist held no appeal for her. They had never gone farther than the local Wal-Mart, so going into town was somewhat of an adventure.

Kanter steered the rental onto Main Street. "This place sure is schizophrenic," he said, looking out the driver's side window.

"How's that?" Anderson asked.

"Well, you have Torturous Tattoos on one side of the street," he pointed, "and Mother's Café on the other."

"Meth Nation," Hoop said from the back seat.

Kanter had rented a midsized car, which had served fine for Anderson and him. But Hoop was the size of a bull and had to sit sideways just to fit.

"Yeah," Kanter said. "Welcome to Middle America."

"What's it going to be, boys?" Anderson asked. "Mother's or Jake's?"

Jake's boasted the biggest hamburger in the county – so big you could cut it into fourths and feed your entire family. And if you had any room left, you could also down one of their "world famous" shakes. Jake's sign had an image of an old-fashioned soda jerk holding a milkshake upside down. The significance of this was lost on Anderson. Kanter caught her staring.

"Am I dense?" she asked. "I don't get it."

Kanter leaned across to look out her window at the sign. "I think it means their shakes are so thick, doctor, they can be served upside down." He slowed to a crawl, and a car behind honked. "My vote is for Mother's."

"I'm there," Hoop said.

"Great," Kanter said and eased the rental into a parking space about half a block down.

The sign hanging on the door to Mother's declared: *No shirt. No service. No bull.* A perky red-headed hostess, probably a cheerleader at the local high school, promptly greeted them and asked how many were in their party. Her eyes almost popped out of her head when she saw Hoop.

"Three," Kanter said.

The hostess led them to a four-top at the back of the café. She kept glancing at Hoop every few steps, while some patrons stared them down from under the bills of their mesh backs. When she presented the table, Anderson noticed her feet were in Fifth position.

"Excuse me," the hostess asked Hoop, placing their menus down on the table. "Are you Damien Ray?"

Hoop grinned appreciatively. "No, but I'd sure love to have his bank account."

"Too bad. You look so much like him. My boyfriend would be so stoked if you were." She spun and scampered back to the front.

"Who's Damien Ray?" Anderson asked.

"Ex-famous defensive end," Kanter said, settling into his chair. "Chicago Bears."

"I get that all the time," Hoop said. "One night in college, I was bouncing this club, and Ray walks up with a babe on each arm. He and I did a stare down, then he fell out. Damnedest thing."

A waitress, who could have been the hostess's older, cuter sister, took their orders. She didn't seem to care if Hoop was Damien Ray or about her job; her attention was glued to her cell phone and the stream of messages she was receiving.

"You're staring," Kanter said to Anderson.

"It's just so rude to do that," she said.

"Boyfriend," Hoop said. "My daughter's way into Gatewaying. I think I'm going to have to get her into rehab."

"You have a daughter? And what's Gatewaying?"

Hoop smiled. "She's 17 going on 30."

"And a hottie," Kanter added.

"When'd you meet her?" Hoop asked.

"At your party. And Gatewaying is like the old texting, but it uses iconic graphics."

"Where *have* I been?" Anderson mused.

"I'm starving," Hoop said as he snapped open his menu. "I wonder how their pork–"

A tall, broad-shouldered man approached their table and stole Hoop's attention. The man looked like he was in his late 20s, and his posture was perfect. He removed his Ole Miss ball cap and nervously twisted it with his hands.

Hoop scooted his chair out as if to say he was ready to pounce on the guy.

"Hello," the man said.

"Hello," Kanter replied cautiously. "Can we help you?"

"Maybe." The man shifted his gaze onto Anderson and flashed an unnerving smile. His haircut was what Marines called "high and tight," and his whole demeanor smacked of ex-military. "This is going to sound crazy," he said, "but is your name Dr. Anderson?"

Anderson's nerves spiked. *Who the hell would know me up here?* She straightened. "Yes."

"Well, damn, this *is* a small world." The man slapped his thigh with his hat. "Ma'am, you won't remember me, but I sure remember you." His accent sounded Southern, but not Deep Southern.

"I'm sorry, you have me at a disadvantage, Mr....?"

He stuck out his hand. "Sergeant Gerald Park, 5th Reg. You helped me after my MRAP took an EFP ... back in the zone."

Anderson stood and shook Park's hand. She desperately racked her brain but couldn't register his name or face. "Forgive me, Mr. Park, but I don't recall our time together."

"You probably wouldn't," Park said. "Most of my face was bandaged. That EFP damn near took it off. I think they did a pretty decent job for Army doctors." He stuck his chin out and rubbed it. "Still got a little shrapnel left. A keepsake from the war."

Anderson had treated many soldiers whose faces had been heavily bandaged. "Won't you join us?" she asked, feeling the need to be polite.

"Thank you," Park said. "I'd like that very much."

24. For Christ's sake.

Before Kanter could protest, Park yanked out a chair and sat. Kanter thought about reaching over the table and dragging Anderson outside to ask what the hell she was doing.

"Oh," he said and flipped open his cell as if it had vibrated, "I have to take this."

Anderson glanced at him and went back to small talk with Park.

Kanter flashed the hostess a cursory smile and marched into Mother's parking lot. He punched in a text message to Anderson and demanded she come out.

A moment later, Anderson burst from Mother's and stormed up to Kanter.

"What *is* your problem?" she asked.

"What *are* you doing?"

She put her hands on her hips and mouthed the word *Huh?*

Kanter was beyond pissed. "What the hell are you going to tell Sergeant Haircut about why you're up here?"

Anderson hesitated.

"See, I knew it. Tren, this is serious shit here. Too many people know about my discovery already. I don't need to complicate matters with one of your ex-army patients."

"Bill, give me more credit. I know I can't say anything. I was going to make something up."

"Like what?"

"I don't know. But you have to understand. These people were badly injured, both physically *and* mentally. Sometimes reconnecting with someone who helped them through a tough situation can be very therapeutic. What would you like me to do? Tell him to *fuck off*?"

Kanter had never heard Anderson swear like that and figured he had hit a nerve. Maybe she was right ... maybe he was overreacting.

"Okay," he said, calming. "But this is your problem."

"Who goes in first?"

"You go. I'll be along in a minute."

Anderson rolled her eyes and went back in.

Kanter watched a couple of America's Most Wanted roll up on some righteous choppers and walk into Mother's. He followed in their wake and discovered they hadn't showered in months.

"Bill!" Anderson said as he walked up to the table. She was all bright-eyed and big smile. "Hoop just finished telling Gerald about your discovery." Her eyebrows went up. "He thinks it would be a good test of our soul group theory to scan Gerald."

What the fuck? Kanter slowly sat and gave Hoop his best death stare.

*   *   *

The drive back to the Nelson farm was a huge test of Kanter's patience, and the silence in the rental was as thick as the stench in the feed barn. Since Hoop had let it slip about their work, the lunch conversation had centered mostly on Kanter and his discovery. Park hadn't said much, except to ask some basic questions about the technology. He had nodded like he understood it all, but Kanter was skeptical. How could a Madison High School social studies teacher who was born in the same town as Elvis grasp the intricacies of particle wave scanning? Yet, his training in the military might have taught him something. Park's tour had taken him through the final two years of the Iraq conflict, though his last three months had been spent in a U.S. hospital in Landatuhl. Whatever had happened to his face, the military had repaired it with remarkable precision and virtually no visible scarring.

Hoop grunted, and Kanter glanced at him in the rearview mirror. Hoop was sitting across the seats and looking out the back of the rental. He turned back and caught Kanter's stare. A large dreadlock dropped across his face.

"Why the hell did you tell him?" Kanter asked.

Hoop looked out the back window again. "You two were gone," he said. "It was me and him and the table. We were talking and, I don't know ... it just came out."

"You know how important secrecy is to this project. We have no idea who this guy is." Kanter's anger boiled over, and he smacked the top of the steering wheel with his fist.

"I wasn't thinking."

"No shit."

"What's done is done," Anderson said. "And I *do* know who this guy is, kind of."

Kanter shot Anderson a look. "You do?"

"Park knew far too many things about my FOB in Iraq. Only someone who had been there would know. He's the real deal, all right."

For the last three miles, Kanter had been following a huge combine – the kind probably tricked out with satellite TV and a wet bar. It finally turned onto a farm road, and he gunned the rental.

"I'm sorry for gator-mouthing back there," Hoop said.

Kanter met Hoop's eyes in the mirror again.

"Gator-mouthing?" Anderson asked.

Hoop brought both hands up to his face and mimicked an alligator's jaw.

Anderson turned around, and he playfully snapped at her.

"Hoopy's running his mouth off again," he said.

Kanter wanted to say, "No shit," but held his tongue.

They now followed an old primer-grey pickup. Two young kids sat in the truck's bed facing backwards. Each held a fishing pole straight up, and the rods were bent in the wind. Kanter waved and smiled at them. The kid on the left flipped him the bird.

"Is it weird that Park doesn't want to be scanned?" Hoop asked.

"I don't think so," Anderson said.

"Why's that?" Kanter asked.

"Because. If he saw action, he probably doesn't want to relive any of it. Believe me, a lot of these Marines saw things they'd rather forget. I spent most of my time helping them deal with it." She wiped at something on the glass. "Looking back, I think I only helped them forget."

Kanter's frustration was ebbing. He pulled onto the dirt road that led to the Nelson farm. "New rule," he said. "If we run into any more of Dr. Anderson's old patients, let's just talk about the weather, okay?"

Anderson nodded, and Hoop gave a thumbs-up.

"Now," Kanter said, "since *someone* invited the good sergeant to dinner …"

"I didn't see you trying to stop me," Anderson retorted.

Kanter shook his head.

Anderson threw her hands up. "I'm sorry. It's the healer in me."

"Okay, Mother Theresa, how are we going to handle tonight?"

"Keep it light," she said. "Let Kim and Scott make the conversation. I'll coach Kim on what to say."

"Are you going to show him the lab?" Hoop asked.

"Why not?" Kanter replied. "He practically knows everything already. Hell, I might even give him a copy of *Civil War Ho*."

Anderson punched him in the shoulder.

Kanter veered off the driveway and almost clipped the fence. "Jesus!" He yanked the wheel, and the car swerved back. "I was joking," he said and rubbed his shoulder.

Anderson folded her arms and gave him an angry sideways look. A half smile grew at the edge of her mouth.

*   *   *

"Eric, it's time for bed," Kimberly said.

The boy reluctantly took his mother's hand and followed her out of the dining room.

Dinner had been pleasant. Midwestern. Kimberly had prepared her signature chicken casserole, which was beginning to wear on Kanter, although it did make killer leftovers. Park and Nelson had found common ground in their military backgrounds, and Hoop had entertained Eric when the subject had gotten heavy. Mostly, though, the evening featured Anderson playing catch-up with her former patient.

Park explained that he was camping outside of River Point for much of the summer. He loved to hunt and fish, and the forests around the area had great hiking trails. It was the first summer in years that he hadn't taught school. He had followed a girl to Milwaukee, but it hadn't worked out. He liked the energy of the city, though, and had decided to stay.

Kimberly insisted on clearing the dishes, which left Kanter, Anderson, Park, and Nelson relaxing around the table and sipping pedestrian coffee. Folgers, if Kanter had to guess.

"He's a bright young boy," Park said to Nelson. "You should be proud."

Nelson lifted his eyes from his cup. "Eric's interesting," he said while he stirred in some Sweet'N Low.

Interesting? Kanter thought. What a weird thing to say – as if his kid were some kind of experiment he and Kimberly had concocted.

Anderson's expression suggested she was thinking the same

thing and was holding back something that wasn't complimentary.

"Tell me, Dr. Kanter," Park said. "Aren't memories stored in various parts of the brain?"

"I'm not an expert in memories," Kanter replied. "But I've been doing a lot of research lately. The model that seems to be generally accepted is that memories are recorded and stored somewhere deep in the brain."

"Even though this contradicts what is known about memory construction," Anderson added.

"That's correct," Kanter said. "It's the recall that's up for debate. Current studies support the notion that memories are a set of encoded neural connections and that encoding happens throughout the brain."

"Think of memories as jigsaw pieces that are reassembled by a neural network," Anderson said to Park.

"This might explain why the images we retrieve are so fragmented," Kanter said. "Not to mention brain damage, neurological disorders–"

"And don't forget drinking," Hoop offered. "That kills a lot of brain cells."

Nelson looked up, but it was hard to tell if Hoop's joke had registered.

"But you said your data streams run in a linear fashion, which supports the idea that everything gets imprinted, right?" Park asked.

"Yes," Kanter said, "but nobody knows for sure what memories are or how they're formed. It's all theory."

"One thing is pretty certain," Anderson said. "Whether you believe the behaviorist model, where thinking is a set of behaviors, or the cognitive model, where the brain is a computer, how memories are recalled is the part of the equation that interests people the most. Especially the police and lawyers."

"Until now," Park said.

"That's right," Kanter said. "Kind of makes you think, doesn't it?"

"Makes my head hurt." Nelson pushed back from the table and stood. "I have a farm to run in the morning. If you'll excuse me." He turned and headed for the stairs.

There were "good nights" all around. Park leaned forward and stared into his coffee.

"Gonna be an early one tomorrow," Hoop said through a yawn. "I'm getting' these bones to bed, too." He made his way to the stairs.

"Tell me," Park said, still focused on his mug. "Aren't you a little concerned?"

Kanter wasn't sure who the question was directed toward. He glanced at Anderson, but she folded her arms in a gesture that said, *"Go ahead, smart boy."*

"About what?" Kanter asked.

Park looked up, and something peculiar in his expression suggested this topic was of particular importance. "The impact of this kind of discovery."

"Which one?" Anderson asked.

"Religion?"

"I don't really know," Kanter said.

That apparently didn't sit well with Park. "Isn't it a bit reckless to tamper with a person's life?"

"Which *one*?" Anderson asked again.

Park's smile looked a bit forced.

"Science is in the business of tampering, I guess," Kanter said.

"That's my *point*," Park said before he resumed analyzing his coffee.

"Tampering probably isn't the right word," Anderson offered. "But science has been advancing into areas that were taboo for decades. It can't be helped."

Park reacted with annoyance, but the look quickly vanished. He pushed away from the table. "I think I'll follow Hoop's lead and get my bones back to the campsite."

Kanter and Anderson walked Park to his truck, exchanged polite good nights, and watched him drive to the main road. As they stood under the cupola of glittering stars, a dog yipped in the distance.

"I don't trust him," Kanter said.

"He's harmless," Anderson replied.

They started back up the gravel path, and Anderson stumbled.

Kanter caught her by the arm and helped her straighten. "Have a nice trip?"

Anderson chuckled. "That's so high school."

Kanter felt his gaze caught in hers: hazel eyes, nestled in soft, high-set cheekbones. "You seem to be holding up."

"I am."

They started along the path again.

"It's weird," Anderson said.

"What is?" Kanter asked.

"That I don't remember any of it. I mean, I know all about repressed memories. It's just weird when it happens to you."

"I guess it's a natural reaction," Kanter said. "Are you going to call your dad?"

Anderson walked in silence for a few steps. "I'm working up the nerve," she said. The dog now barked frantically like something had spooked it. "Once I go there, there's no turning back, you know?"

Kanter was never good in these kinds of conversations. He hesitated to answer. A woman began scolding the dog down near the road, her voice barely overcoming the wind. The dog's name was Rex, or was it Tex?

Something cracked off to Kanter's left, like a dry branch being stepped on. The sound appeared to come from the large bushes near the path, but the high clouds didn't allow the moon to illuminate the area. The land around the house was filled with large shrubs and old trees, and it was hard to make out any detail in the patchwork of shadows. There were two more snaps.

"Did you hear that?" Kanter asked.

Anderson stopped and put an ear to the wind. "Could be Claudius."

"He's inside."

They stood and listened. The wind whipped Kanter's shirt.

"Probably a raccoon," Anderson said finally. She started walking.

"Think you'll be up for watching the rest of your lives tomorrow?" Kanter asked.

"Maybe." A touch of melancholy tinged her voice.

"I'd be surprised if the rest of your lives are as traumatic as–"

Kanter was blindsided in the ribs, which knocked the rest of his words right out of him. He landed on his back and was pushed through the path's pea gravel until the back of his head slammed into a large stone. The pain was excruciating. He heard Anderson scream, though it sounded more like a karate yell. A man swore and went tumbling past.

Hands were grabbing at his limbs, and suddenly Kanter was being carried away from the path toward the grove of trees that edged the land around the house. He heard the sound of duct tape being ripped, and his mouth was covered, which blocked one of his nostrils and rendered it hard to breath. Panic surged through him. He broke free from the person holding his right arm. A bearded man tried to pull a black hood over his head. Kanter connected with the guy's nose and thought he felt two of his fingers go out of joint. The men carrying him began barking at each other in some Middle Eastern language. The bearded man's nose was bleeding. He grabbed Kanter by the hair and yanked the hood over his head. It reeked of gasoline and dirt, and Kanter's adrenaline was ebbing, giving way to fatigue. Someone grabbed his right arm and twisted it beyond pain.

"Hey!" a man yelled, distant and dreamlike. It sounded like Nelson. Three cracks echoed. Gunfire. The men started running with Kanter. More shots rang, closer now, and muffled. A van door opened, and Kanter felt he was floating. He landed on his side and skidded across what felt like Astroturf. His ribs, where he had been tackled, ached as if someone had slammed him with a baseball bat. A man said something about Allah, and the van door slammed shut.

"For Christ's sake, don't hurt him!" a voice said. It was high-pitched and without accent. It sounded oddly like a lesbian grad student he had known. The engine revved, and the van lurched forward. It bounced and swayed and didn't feel at all like it was on the driveway. With his head covered, the motion was nauseating.

"We haven't dropped him yet," a man scolded. Another Middle Eastern accent.

Kanter came up kicking and swinging, but the hands returned

and held him down. His sleeve was rolled up.

"Come on!" the androgynous voice said.

Something was jammed into Kanter's arm. A needle that felt like it was the size of a chopstick. There was an impact, and the van's left side reared up. When it crashed back down, Kanter's head hit a metal edge in the same spot that the rock had. His vision filled with shooting flecks of light, and the back of his collar felt wet.

Part of the duct tape had worked loose, and Kanter took in a couple of gulps of air.

"Who are–?!" he screamed, but the word *you* didn't come out; it drifted across an old blackboard filled with equations and scribbling, then swirled into a prismatic dot and disappeared.

25. Deeper than deep.

Kanter's mind seemed tethered past the edge of his dreams when something sharp pricked his neck. He tried to lift his head, but the act felt remote, unnatural, as if his body were struggling to catch up to his mind's commands. Then he realized his head was dangling with his chin against his chest.

A distant voice crossed his consciousness and lodged somewhere behind the pain. It repeated. *Bill?*

"He's coming around." Another voice, maybe the lesbian's.

Kanter found opening his eyes difficult; they didn't seem to be adjusting well to the light. He was in a motel room. The muffled sounds of a highway hovered in the background. The room was warm and smelled of cigarettes and equipment cases and cheap cleaning products. He was perched on the edge of a twin bed, the lamp beside him the room's only light. It must have been adjusted somehow because it dropped off just past the foot of the bed.

A man leaned against a low dresser. Instead of a TV, black cases of the kind photographers used were stacked behind him. Someone was tapping on a laptop, but Kanter couldn't discern the direction of the sound. He tried to look around, but the muscles in his neck resisted.

"Hello, Bill." The man's tone was flat, and there was a clipped measure to the word "hello," as if the "e" wasn't important enough to utter.

Kanter's eyes adjusted. He perceived that the man was tall, and the suit he wore had once been expensive and fit loosely on his frame. The man's face was stretched across sharp features. Maybe he had a drawstring he pulled to tighten up his appearance.

"What the hell is going on?" Kanter managed. "Who are you people?"

The words didn't sound like they had come from his throat. Someone handed him a glass of water; the arm emerged into the light in a disembodied way. The water tasted rural but did the job.

"Better?" The man lit a cigarette. The glow from the lighter revealed skin speckled with acne scars below deep-set eyes. Kanter caught a glimpse of a pronounced brow and flashed on an article he had read about the effects of steroids. The head wasn't shaped well for a bald man. It came to sort of a ridge that started where his scalp line would have been. The man exhaled, and there was a slight delay before the smoke drifted into the light.

Menthol.

“Yes, thank you,” Kanter replied, his voice back from the dead.

The distant rumble of an 18-wheeler downshifting vibrated the room’s windows.

“How are you feeling?” the man asked.

“I’ve felt better,” Kanter said.

The man exhaled again. The area around the bed was getting hazy. “NT-45,” he said. “Blocks glutamate receptors. Knocks you out instantly. Lowers your voice pitch, too. Trenna might think it’s sexy, but it’ll wear off long before *that* ever happens.”

There were soft laughs around the room.

It was hard for Kanter to process what was happening. “Why have you–?”

“How’s the project coming?”

“What?” Kanter started to feel the back of his head, but lifting his arm sent a vicious stinging across his shoulder, like a pressure bandage was attached to his scalp, and there was a weird sensation at the point of contact. He tried reaching again, but gave up.

“Sorry about that.” The man pointed with the cigarette. “We got a little sloppy. What you’re feeling is an organic wound cream. I’d explain how it works, but hell, I don’t even know. Something to do with active enzyme cultures.”

He shifted his weight to his other foot and crushed out what was left of his cigarette in an old-fashioned, plaid beanbag ashtray.

“Bill, I don’t want to waste your time.” He folded his arms. “Keep working on your discovery. Play it out to its conclusion. When you think you’re ready to publish your findings, we’ll take it from there.”

“Who’s we?”

The man extracted another cigarette from the pack and ritually lit it. As he drew on it, the tip glowed, and Kanter noticed a nasty dent above his left eye.

"We're not like those DoD boys who funded the MedBed. I'm happy letting Strachan pay for this one." The man took another drag and regarded Kanter like a piece of fine art. "Finish your study. We get first usage for two years, and then you can publish."

Kanter wasn't going to get his answer. "What if I don't?"

"Don't what?"

"Find anything."

"I got faith in you."

"But Strachan has first–"

The man crushed out the cigarette and entered the circle of light around the bed. He leaned down, fully revealing the leathery details of his face. A small scar line ran across the rim of the dent.

"I'm surprised, Bill." His breath was hideous. "A smart young man like yourself, thinking like that. I thought you'd learned your lesson with DoD."

"What if I don't go with you?"

The corners of the man's mouth turned up slightly. He leaned next to Kanter's ear and whispered, "That's what Phillip and Kelly asked."

It felt, for a second, like the temperature in the room dropped below freezing.

The man straightened and resumed his position against the cases.

"That's big of you to let me have it after two years," Kanter said.

The man's eyes narrowed, and Kanter figured sarcasm wasn't a good approach.

"Bill, we're not the Evil Empire, but we are in a war, and there's nothing we won't do to save our troops. Besides, it's in our best interest to have you continue with your research.... Maybe you'll discover something else. Who knows, we might be working together again."

It was hard for Kanter to wrap his head around it all, but he obviously didn't have a say in the matter. "So what's next?" he asked.

"We'll dump you about a mile from the Nelson farm."

"W-what should I say?"

"You were abducted by radical militants who wanted to stop your experiment. You know, Allah's great, death to America, the usual bullshit. But when they stopped for gas, you had to take a piss. The local cops stumbled on them. Found weapons. You hid in the woods. They got hauled off. You hiked it back. Say they were a small cell. Amateurs. Don't allude to any major Middle East affiliations."

"You're kidding, right?"

Again the smirk. The computer tapping started up again.

"What about my team? The Nelsons?" Kanter asked. "They're probably freaking out right now. It could all fall apart."

"Let me tell you about Scott Nelson. He's a real American hero. Naval Academy, Special Forces, Iraq, and Iran. Why do you think we used the people we did to kidnap you?"

"I don't know."

"Leverage."

"Excuse me?"

"Don't let all that Arab Spring crap fool you. Al-Qaeda are still the worst of the worst, *believe* me. But when you need to create a little disinformation, they can be very useful."

"You've lost me." But as soon as he said it, Kanter remembered the men who carried him. Weren't they speaking in Arabic? "Why didn't you just approach me? Why the big scene at the farm?" He felt for the bruise on his side. Touching it made him gasp.

"There's nothing a guy like Nelson wouldn't do to protect his family," the man said. "Our little scene will resonate with him ... redefine how important your project is."

"You don't understand," Kanter said. "He's ultra conservative. He might kick us out, and then where would we be?"

"He won't. You're family now."

"But his wife ... she's a real–"

"Don't let Kimberly Nelson's 'I'm the timid wife' routine fool you. She wears the pants, and I'm sure she wants that kid of hers cured."

"Hers?"

"She had Eric before she met Scott."

"But I thought they were–"

"She's the one who got religion, then pulled him in. Nelson can't have kids. You might say he gave the ultimate sacrifice for his country. Are you with me now?"

Kanter tried to nod, but it hurt too much.

"So ... what do you think?" The man pulled out another cigarette, inspected it, and returned the pack to the inside pocket of his coat.

"Do I have a choice?" Kanter knew he didn't.

The man lit up again and exhaled.

The tapping on the laptop stopped just as the highway noise subsided. Kanter looked down at his hands. He had dirt under his nails and dried blood across his knuckles.

"Bill?"

Kanter lifted his eyes. "Yeah?"

"When you go back, try and act the part, will you please?"

"I will."

"You better, because I don't want this assignment to get physical."

More laughs.

"Now." The man sighed a large amount of smoke, like what he was about to say was difficult for him. "This is where you have to toughen up."

"What do you mean?"

"Appearances. Your *team* needs to believe you were in something bad."

"Am I?"

The man smiled for the first time. "You've heard the expression 'in deep shit'?"

Kanter nodded, and another sharp pain shot down his neck.

"This is deeper than deep, Bill."

The man gestured, and someone punched Kanter in the jaw.

26. Embrace the suck.

Scott Nelson laid the shotgun on the dining table like it was his firstborn. Anderson recognized it as a Mossberg. Her dad had a similar model, but this one appeared more tactical. Twelve-gauge, if she had to guess. Nelson had assembled two shotguns, three pistols, an assortment of hunting knives, and a high-tech compound bow that could have come out of a black-ops department. He arranged them as if setting up for a gun show – the barrels flush together along an imaginary line, the knives splayed out in a fan.

"Is all this necessary?" Hoop asked.

Nelson passed his fingers down the Mossberg's matte grey barrel, and something hardened behind his eyes. He glanced at Hoop, and

Anderson recognized the look. She had seen it on the face of the young Marine who had sacrificed his leg to kick the IED out of the Humvee. A tough-assed matter-of-factness – burned in after years of war – that made the act of risking life and limb easier.

"You ever used one of these?" Nelson asked, pointing to an M9 semiautomatic handgun.

"Hell no!" Hoop replied.

Nelson shifted his gaze to Anderson. "I know *you* have." He picked up the weapon and handed it to her.

"It's been a long time," Anderson said, wrapping her fingers around it. It felt dense in her hand, as if death itself resided somewhere inside the chamber. She checked to see if it was loaded, and the actions instantly came back. She slid the magazine back in, clicked the safety, and placed it next to a vintage Colt .45 revolver.

"To answer your question," Nelson said to Hoop. "This *is* necessary. Whether you want to believe it or not, we're under attack. Dr. Kanter has been kidnapped, and I'll be damned if they'll get my family."

Hoop folded his arms. "Who's *they*?"

"The man I threw, well ... he smelled," Anderson said and rubbed her left hip. The guy hadn't been much bigger than her, but throwing him had wrenched the shit out of her back.

"Like a *haji*?" Nelson asked.

Haji was soldier speak for any person of Middle Eastern descent. It was a title of respect that a Muslim gained after completing the pilgrimage to Mecca. How the U.S. military had bastardized it was beyond Anderson. "Yes," she said.

Nelson shook his head, as if this confirmed his worst fears.

"Are you two talking Al-Qaeda?" Hoop asked.

"An outer fringe, maybe," Nelson said. "The men I saw from the porch looked tough. Probably some small cell."

"Why would they take Dr. Kanter?"

"Who knows? Most of these guys are basically mobsters, tribal gangs looking to extort money to fund their operations."

Hoop made a face. "In *Wisconsin*?"

"You'd be surprised," Nelson replied.

"Bill isn't rich," Anderson said. "And Hoop's right, they wouldn't come all this way just to kidnap him. They're after his discovery."

"How could they know about his–?" The sound of the front door opening cut Nelson off. He had the Mossberg in his hands as quickly as it would've taken for him to finish his sentence.

Anderson watched Kanter stumble through the doorway. "Bill!"

Kanter, favoring his right shoulder, leaned against the hallway table. He forced a smiled but flinched like the act had hit a nerve. His left cheek was swollen, and a patch of dried blood clung under his nose.

Anderson ran up and took him by the arm. Hoop took his other arm, and they helped him to the couch. Nelson had positioned himself against the wall by the large picture window in the living room. The sight of Kanter must have flipped a switch, because he was now in full commando mode. Kimberly appeared at the bottom of the stairs, but he shooed her back up with a warning to keep an eye on Eric.

"There's nobody out there," Kanter said, easing onto the cushions.

"We don't know that," Nelson said, focused on something out the window.

"They were all arrested."

This got Nelson's attention. He lowered the Mossberg.

"They were?" Anderson asked.

Hoop had gone to the kitchen and come back with a blue ice pack. He gave it to Kanter, who pressed it against his right side and told them how the men had hooded him and thrown him into a van. They had spoken in some Middle Eastern language, so he never knew what they were saying until a guy told him in broken English that he was going back to Chicago. They never said why they had kidnapped him and had hit him repeatedly to shut him up. Finally Kanter had pleaded with them to let him take a piss. They stopped at an old gas station, pulled around back, and escorted Kanter, hooded, to the bathroom.

"They sound like dumb-asses," Nelson remarked.

"No doubt." Kanter shifted the blue ice to his jaw and leaned back against the pillows.

"So why did they get arrested?" Hoop asked.

"I don't know," Kanter said. "I was in the men's when I heard a car pull up. I could hear the police radio, and the officers telling the Middle Eastern guys to get on the ground."

"Local cops score big for Homeland Security," Nelson said. "They probably stole the van. The cops ran the plates, found the weapons, and 'bingo.'"

"After a few minutes, I heard another car pull up and another." Kanter shifted the ice pack to the other side of his jaw. "I snuck out and hid in the woods behind the station. All I could hear was the police radios."

"What did they do with the terrorists?" Hoop asked.

"I didn't stick around. We were off 18, so I walked to the on-ramp and got a ride back to River Point in the back of a pick-up. I hiked it the rest of the way."

"Did you ever learn why they took you?" Anderson asked.

"No."

Anderson noticed a large bandage at the back of Kanter's head. "Bill, what happened here? My God, your collar is soaked in blood."

"Yeah," Kanter said and leaned forward. "They slapped that on me. I must have hit my head in thc van. Bled like a sonofabitch."

Anderson started to inspect the dressing, but Kanter jerked away. "It hurts like hell," he said. "Let's look at it later."

"I doubt we'll ever see those guys again." Nelson walked away from the window, the Mossberg draped over one arm. "I'll bet my farm they never make the news."

"Why's that?" Anderson asked.

"If they're a cell from Chicago, I can guarantee you the Feds are all over this by now. Those guys will disappear and America will never know."

"There's more where they came from," Hoop said.

"You got that right." Nelson fixed a look on Kanter and let it settle there. "My family comes first, Dr. Kanter," he said finally.

Kanter shifted the ice pack to the back of his neck. "I'm sorry, Scott. I never intended to bring all this down on your family. If you want us to leave, I'd understand."

Nelson squatted in the center of the living room's circular rug, like he had reverted to an old position he used to take in his Special Forces days. He stared at the rug, and Anderson figured he was back there now, hunkered down in some godforsaken desert hellhole. His hand went down the Mossberg's stock and rested near the trigger.

"I don't know much about what your machine does," he said in a low tone. "But Dr. Anderson says it could change the world for the better."

"I think it will," Kanter replied.

Nelson glanced at Anderson. "Will it help Eric?"

"We hope so," she said.

His attention went to the rug again.

"What do we do if more of those guys come back?" Hoop's voice was rimmed with fear.

Nelson looked up, and Anderson wondered if she had ever seen him grin before.

"Embrace the suck," he said.

* * *

Anderson and Hoop helped Kanter to his room. He reeked of sweat and blood and refused to undress, saying he just wanted to crash and deal with it all in the morning. The kidnapping must have profoundly scared him, because when Anderson helped him up the stairs, he was shaking.

She watched Kanter settle onto the bed like her grandfather had during the last year of his life. "Bill, are you really okay? You're not moving well at all."

He smiled half-heartedly and gave a thumbs-up. "Just living the dream here in America's dairy land."

Hoop shut the door and walked up to the bed. "Look, I don't want to be a jerk, but what the *hell* are we going to do? I didn't sign on for all this." He spread his arms to the room.

Anderson cajoled Kanter into getting undressed. She pulled his shirt over his head; he could barely lift his right arm. "You need to call Strachan and get some protection up here," she said and tossed his shirt into a corner.

"You mean like Blackwater guys?" Kanter asked.

"Yes."

"Hell yes!" Hoop agreed.

"I don't think we're in that much dan–"

"Bill!" Anderson folded her arms. "Hoop's right. Our lives are in danger."

A large spot of dried blood was smeared across the left shoulder of Kanter's undershirt, and there was a dark blue bruise under his right arm.

"How's my head look?" he asked.

She hesitated.

"That bad, eh?"

"Whatever's in that bandage seems to be working because I swear it looks smaller than it did downstairs. So what do you think?"

Kanter didn't respond. He just sat there like he was struggling to comprehend the situation.

"Bill?"

"Yeah, sorry. I zoned out for a second. What did you say?"

"What do you *think* about going to Strachan?"

Kanter sucked in a ragged breath and tried to pull his shoulders back. He grimaced and slumped back down. "Bringing in the troops will only call attention to the farm." He rubbed his eyes. "Plus, it means more people will know about the machine. We can't take that risk."

Anderson knelt and took Kanter's face into her hands, being careful not to touch his bruised cheek. "Bill, think."

His eyes seemed to focus on her, and his mouth was partially open.

Either he was having trouble breathing, or he was truly in a state of shock. Sadness etched his face, like he had finally realized just how far down the rabbit hole he had traveled. It wasn't the look Anderson imagined from someone who was going to change the world, but the more she thought about it, the more it made sense. Most inventors had greatness thrust on them; Kanter was going to have his cracked over his head. Unexpectedly, she noticed that the eye she had thought was a darker green wasn't green at all, but grayish blue. She wiped at the dried blood under his nose, and their eyes met.

"If you're killed," she continued, "then all of your work ... all this *hope*, will be in vain. This project is bigger than you now, Bill, and you owe it to the world. Give the deaths of Kelly and Phillip some meaning. Remember, you have Hoop and me and the Nelson's to consider. Our lives are at stake, too. You don't have a choice. You *have* to call Strachan."

Anderson wasn't sure if her words had registered. She sat next to Kanter and took his hand. There were crusty patches of dark blood across his knuckles.

"She's right, Doc," Hoop agreed. "If you think this machine is that important, then you need to protect it. Who knows what other nut jobs are gunning for you."

"Us," Kanter said under his breath, staring.

"What's that?" Hoop asked.

Kanter looked at Anderson and squeezed her hand. "They're gunning for *us*."

27. State-of-the-art.

Nearly two days had passed since Kanter had made the call to Strachan. The conversation went well, considering he was potentially involving his benefactor with national security. Oddly, Strachan didn't seem too concerned about the incident. He simply assured Kanter that he would keep a tight lid on everything and send up the "best of the best." *Best what?* Kanter wondered. The thought of dozens of professional soldiers storming the Nelson farm didn't sit well. But Anderson had been right – Kanter didn't have a choice. If anything happened to the Nelsons or Anderson and Hoop, he would never forgive himself. Even though the agent – or whatever he was – hadn't mentioned it, Kanter was sure that a big reason they had staged such an elaborate stunt was to make Nelson think there might be others coming for Kanter and his invention. And if the CIA was thinking like that, then hell, it might be true.

Over the last day, the weight of the situation had settled around Kanter like a thick fog. If Anderson hadn't been such a saint, he might have gone nuts. She had brought him his meals and even offered to feed him when he couldn't lift his arm because his shoulder felt like shit. Her doting was comforting, but now he was feeling better, and much remained to be done.

Kanter scooped another spoonful of Kimberly Nelson's chicken soup when the floorboards in his bedroom began vibrating. He went to the window and watched a large freight truck rumble up the drive, followed by a nondescript step-van and a white Suburban. All the vehicles' windows were blacked out, and Claudius was barking madly at the Suburban's tires. It pulled in behind the step-van, and four casually dressed ex-military types piled out. Scott Nelson approached the eldest and shook his hand.

Kanter threw on some shoes and hustled downstairs. It seemed that Nelson was briefing the older guy, and as Kanter walked up, all the military types turned and scrutinized him.

"And this is Dr. William Kanter," Nelson said.

The older man's face was like carved wood, and his dark mustache didn't match his grey hair. "Sam Claymore. Primus Security." He took off his ball cap and extended his hand. His demeanor was all business. He didn't introduce his team.

Kanter shook Claymore's hand and felt the ridges of small scars across his palm.

"Mr. Nelson was good enough to give us a quick overview of the situation." Claymore eyed Kanter's bruised cheek. "Looks like they busted you up a little."

Kanter started to reach for his cheek, but stopped. "You could say that."

"That won't happen again. After we're through unpacking, I want a full rundown of what happened."

"What has Strachan told you about what we're doing up here?" Kanter asked.

"Frankly, not much. And to be honest, it's not a Primus concern. We're contracted to protect you and your team, Dr. Kanter. I'm more interested in who's coming after you, not why." Claymore surveyed the farm. "How many acres are we talking about here, Mr. Nelson?"

"The main home and production facilities are on 80, but we can farm 300 if you count the outlying fields. We have 120 milking cows and 5 bulls."

"That's a lot of bullshit," one of the Primus guys said, then spit.

"Actually, it's a lot of cowshit." Nelson flipped the pitchfork he was holding and stabbed it into the ground. "It powers our two generators." He glanced at their trucks.

"We thought it would be best to come in as some type of delivery service. Like you're getting a new piece of equipment," Claymore said. "That way we don't arouse suspicion with the locals or the police. We were told that this operation has to be very covert, and we plan to keep it that way."

The two other drivers joined them and exchanged expressionless nods with their comrades.

"We're going to set up an invisible perimeter around your acreage, Mr. Nelson, and lock this farm down tight. We won't interfere with your day-to-day chores, but I will have to secure an area for staging our equipment."

Nelson pointed to the main barn. "Behind those two silos should be out of the way. You can park your trucks and set up there."

Claymore pulled on his cap and gave a nod to Kanter and Nelson. "Webber!" he yelled.

A lean, athletic woman with sharply galvanized features and a crown of cropped red hair stepped up to Claymore's side. She reminded Kanter of a praying mantis, which he suddenly recalled ate the heads off their mates once they had copulated.

"Sir?" she asked.

"I want eight screamers, the Sentry 58s, set up right now around the main farm. Once we have the sat intel, we'll move them to the outer perimeter."

The mantis woman gave a crisp nod and trotted to the step-van. Everyone else began walking away.

"Excuse me," Kanter said to Claymore's back.

Claymore opened the Suburban's driver-side door and tilted his head in a way that asked, *"What the hell do you want?"*

Kanter walked up. "I know it's none of my business, but there's only six of you." He could see his reflection in Claymore's sunglasses. They distorted Kanter's face and made him look like a 12 year old. He wondered if this was how Claymore thought of him. "There were at least eight guys who took me."

Claymore made a sucking sound, like he was trying to get a horse to move. He pointed to the larger freight truck. "There's over ten million dollars worth of advanced ISR equipment in there. State-of-the-art. I think we can handle a dozen rag-heads, doctor." Claymore climbed into the Suburban and disappeared behind its smoked glass.

28. Maybe it will.

Kanter had been unusually quiet for the past two days. Anderson didn't want to bug him about how he was feeling, though. The last time, he'd been polite but made it abundantly clear she didn't need to ask anymore. He was now intent on scanning the Nelsons to further verify the soul group theory and had asked Anderson to broach the idea with them.

"Scott, Kim ... can I talk with you for a second?" Anderson stepped into the kitchen and approached the table. Nelson looked up mid-bite from his roast beef sandwich. A large drop of mustard fell onto his chips.

"Does this have to do with Eric?" Kimberly asked.

"No," Anderson said.

"Is the Primus team getting in the way?" Nelson asked.

"Oh, no. They're not bothering us. We hardly notice them. I'm here because Dr. Kanter would like to scan you both."

"Doing his dirty work?" Nelson went back to his sandwich.

The statement dug at Anderson. "No. He's busy with a filtering program for the scanner. He knows about your religious views and wanted to make sure he wasn't overstepping any boundaries."

"If we didn't need the money so badly, I wouldn't have any of this on my farm." Kimberly pushed away from her lunch and folded her arms across her chest. She glanced out the window. "And now we have an army guarding us."

"I know this whole situation must very trying for you both," Anderson said. "But please understand, we're very grateful for you letting us use your farm's facilities, and I know Dr. Kanter is upset about what happened the other night, and about Primus being here."

"Not half as much as me," Nelson said.

"He's working hard to complete his tests as soon as he can," Anderson said, "so we can leave, and you can get your farm back to normal."

"Why does he need to scan us? I thought you were going to scan Eric." Nelson asked before he crunched down on a chip.

Here we go, Anderson thought. "We still want to scan Eric, but we've discovered that, in addition to the past lives that have been imaged, there's reason to believe that groups of us might all be connected somehow."

"Through Jesus!" Kimberly's conviction was set like concrete.

"Well, yes," Anderson said. "If that's your belief, which I know is yours and Scott's. Which is fine ... I mean, it's your right–"

"Get to the point, Doctor." Nelson wiped his mouth and leaned back in his chair. "I have cows to feed."

Anderson took a deep breath. "We've discovered that, in our scans – I mean Dr. Kanter's, Hoop's, and mine – our past lives have crossed paths."

One of the Nelson's roosters crowed somewhere near the main barn. Kimberly's look hardened. "We won't be part of anything like that," she said sternly.

"You don't have to believe in what Dr. Kanter's machine shows in order to be scanned." Anderson tried to sound as sweet as possible. "All you have to do is lie still for about twenty minutes. It's totally safe." *Unless there's an electrical storm.* Even though Kanter had fixed the MedBed's electrical issues, Anderson wasn't sure if she would ever get on it again herself.

"I most certainly will not lie down on that devilish bed. The only ghost I believe in is the Holy One."

Anderson sat in the chair next to Kimberly. "Couldn't you, just for a moment, open your mind to the possibility that–"

Kimberly slapped the top of the table. "Science is one of the biggest reasons our world is so screwed up. Psalm 40:4 says that–"

"I'll do it," Nelson said.

"Scott Michael Nelson!" Kimberly stood. "You will not submit to this kind of test. It's blasphemy."

Nelson looked up. "Kimberly," he said as if addressing Claudius, "sit *down*."

Kimberly slowly sat and began folding her napkin.

Nelson leaned forward on his elbows and knitted his hands

together. He regarded Anderson like he was about to divulge some deep, personal secret. "I believe in the Lord Jesus Christ as my savior, Dr. Anderson. I know there are some things in this world that our Christian viewpoint can't justify. There's some science that I think is just plain wrong, but I'll admit, it has done a lot of good."

"Scott–?"

"Kim, *please*."

She stared at the neatly folded napkin.

"We also want to scan Eric," Anderson said.

"That's always been on the table," Nelson replied. "We're at our wit's end with that boy, and if there's anything you can do to help him, we'd be grateful." He reached across the table and took Kimberly's hand.

It seemed at times that Kimberly Nelson's conservative beliefs were genetically written into her own DNA. But when it came to Eric, she had shown signs of relaxing. She took her husband's hand with both of hers and forced a smile.

"I love that boy with all my heart," she said and wiped at her eyes. "I don't know what to do anymore."

Anderson began to reach for Kimberly's shoulder, but thought better. "I respect your beliefs, I really do. And I've come to like Eric a lot. I think he's a wonderful little boy. We're going to try our best to find out what's causing his episodes. I promise."

Kimberly broke from her husband's grip and took one of Anderson's hands. "Thank you," she said and wiped back another tear.

"Well," Nelson said, standing, "I guess the cows can wait another hour. Let's get this over with."

* * *

After the scanning arms disengaged from Nelson's head, the MedBed tilted forward, and Nelson slid off onto his feet. He required a second to get his balance.

"Maybe you should sit down," Hoop said, taking his arm.

Anderson flashed on the Chicago VA hospital where she worked after returning from Iraq. She had treated many young vets there, but she could never get over the sight of imposing Marines reduced to a state of invalidism. Now, Nelson was staggering a bit, just like those soldiers.

"I think I will," Nelson replied. He shuffled to a workstation and collapsed into one of the chairs. Hoop passed him a bottle of water that he gulped down.

Anderson joined Kanter at the main workstation to wait for Nelson's scan to be compiled. He and Hoop had developed some sort of filtering program. Kanter had explained it, although most of it went over Anderson's head: something to do with data separation to disregard what he called "back life" – the parts of a scan that weren't of interest, such as going to the bathroom, eating, or sex. Hoop had been able to tag certain definitions of information, whatever that meant. The result, in theory, was a shorter scan, but it worked only on a current life. There was some sort of conflict with the transition buffers that wouldn't allow the program to work on past lives.

"You aren't going to like what you see," Nelson said while he polished off his water. He stood and trudged toward the front door.

"Aren't you going to watch?" Hoop asked.

Nelson stopped, but didn't turn. "I've been to hell before," he said into the empty expanse that was the north corner of the lab. "I didn't like it much." He opened the screen door and left.

After about 30 minutes the main console chimed, signaling that the filtering program had finished. Kanter reviewed the scan's specifications.

"Something's off," he said.

"Why do you say that?" Anderson asked.

"Most of our scans have been running between five and six million hours. Scott's is only about two and a half million."

"Maybe he's a young soul."

"Only one way to find out."

The three of them gathered at the monitor to watch Nelson's current life.

"I hope this filtering program works," Hoop said. "I don't want to watch those two doing the funky monkey."

"I think it has." Kanter rechecked the time code. "How old would you say Scott is?"

"Maybe thirty-four," Anderson said. "Eight tops."

"That's what I thought, too. The count on this time code suggests the program did filter something out. Let's hope it caught more than just his funky monkey."

The new filter also made it possible to identify the beginning of a person's current life, which allowed them to watch it chronologically from birth, rather than working backwards to that point. As they skimmed through Nelson's early life, it became evident that his domineering father, who seemed to have lived vicariously through his only son, choreographed much of it. He was a hyper-intense kid who ROTC'd his way through much of high school. As an undergrad at the Naval Academy, he had been an above average student and rarely partied. So far, they had seen no instances of crossover.

"I think we're coming up to his service years," Kanter said, stretching.

Anderson hardly noticed that four hours had passed. Watching another person's life was fascinating but, at the same time, extremely awkward. She had never considered herself a voyeur and had never liked reality shows, but here she was, totally enthralled by Scott Nelson's early life. Now, though, they were near the part of his scan where he went to Iraq, and his life, she feared, was about to turn ugly.

"I don't know if I can watch some of this," she said.

Kanter faced her. "We can blast through this pretty quickly. I can have it slow every two months, so we can keep track."

"Thank you."

Nelson's life radically changed after he entered active service. After a few years, he applied for and received admittance into the Marines Special Forces. Anderson had heard stories about their grueling training, but they paled in comparison to what she saw through Nelson's eyes.

After he had landed in Iraq, Nelson's unit had been dispatched almost immediately on a routine mission that had thrust the 23-year-old into the depths of war. The mission began routinely, going door-to-door and asking Iraqi civilians basic questions about an insurgent they were hunting. But an intense firefight boke out after they had left a house, and a member of Nelson's unit was horribly killed before his eyes by an RPG (rocket-propelled grenade).

"Oh God," Anderson said and turned away.

Kanter paused the streaming. The image caught Nelson dragging the upper half of his comrade's body back to their Humvee, his left hand gripping the collar of the kid's body armor. In the lower right of the frame, the dead soldier's entrails were visible. Kanter quickly clicked the frame into the dock.

"Hey, you don't look so good," Hoop said to her.

Anderson picked up the workstation's trashcan and held it under her chin.

"Tren?" Kanter asked.

"Hold on–"

Try as she might, she couldn't escape the scene: the lower half of the soldier's body rolling to a stop, intestines spilled across the pale sand in a crimson trail. Worse yet was the soldier's silent scream once he realized he had only seconds of life left. It had all streamed by so fast, yet...

Anderson felt a heavy feeling in her stomach, and a weight at the back of her throat. The trashcan seemed too small.

Suddenly, Kanter was there, steadying her and taking the trashcan out of her hands. The smell of vomit lingered.

"Here." Hoop handed her a bottle of water and a paper towel.

She sat in one of the workstation chairs and held the cold plastic bottle to her forehead and wiped her mouth.

The sound of the screen door's rusted metal hinges brought Anderson back.

"Hello?" Kimberly said, stepping in. She had Eric in tow.

"H-hey, Kim," Hoop said and jumped up. He trotted over and knelt in front of Eric. "Hey dude. Give me five!"

While Hoop high-fived Eric, Kanter clicked Nelson's scan off the screen. He waved. "Hi, Kim. Can we help you?"

"I was just wondering how Scott's scan went. He won't tell me anything about it."

Anderson scooted the trashcan under the workstation with her foot. "It went great, Kim!" she said with forced enthusiasm. She stepped forward, and her stomach lurched.

Kimberly and Eric didn't venture any farther into the lab. "Did it help you find what you were looking for?" she asked.

"Not yet," Kanter said. "But we should know something in a day or two."

Kimberly pulled Eric close to her legs. Her eyes went to the MedBed. "Is that it?"

Kanter glanced at it over his shoulder. "Yes," he said. "Do you want to see it?"

This was the first time Kimberly and Eric had been in the lab, and Anderson didn't want to take any chances. She stepped up to Kanter. "Don't have it walk to her," she whispered out of the side of her mouth.

Kimberly, with Eric in tow, stepped cautiously toward the MedBed. "It's kind of creepy looking," she said.

In the late afternoon light, the MedBed appeared to be an industrial-sized deep-water crustacean, and Anderson couldn't blame Kimberly for thinking that way.

"It won *ID* magazine's New and Notable award," Kanter remarked.

Anderson could tell the comment was lost on Kimberly. She kicked Kanter's foot.

Kimberly took a few steps closer to the MedBed when Eric grabbed her leg. His yell shrilled through the ceiling's metal trusswork.

"Honey?" she asked. "What is it?"

Eric frantically tugged at Kimberly's jeans and tried to pull her away from the MedBed. "I don't want to be *scanned*!" The word scanned came out more as a scream.

Kimberly tried to pick Eric up, but he broke from her grasp and sprinted for the front door.

"Eric Nelson, what's the matter with you?"

"We aren't going to scan you," Anderson called out.

"Don't be scared, dude." Eric sidestepped to elude Hoop, who snagged him by the arm and spun him around. Eric tried to wriggle free, but Hoop held him tightly against his leg.

"Come on, honey," Kimberly said, walking up to Hoop. She took Eric by the hand. "You don't have to stay if you don't want to."

Eric buried his face in Kimberly's leg and sobbed.

She looked at Anderson. "Maybe this isn't good time."

"It's probably all the equipment," Anderson said. "Kids hate anything medical. I can come up later and tell you what we found, if you'd like."

Kimberly gave a worried glance to the MedBed. "All right," she said and hurried Eric out of the lab.

Anderson approached Kanter. "It won an *award*?"

Kanter shrugged. "Well, it did. Why did Eric freak like that?"

"I'm not that surprised. Medical stuff can set a lot of children off. It could have been the equipment. From his point-of-view, all this might look very intimidating."

Kanter nodded and turned to the monitor.

"Are you two going to watch the rest of Scott's scan?" Anderson asked.

"Might as well, because I doubt now we'll ever get Eric onto the bed." Kanter had called up Nelson's scan and had it on the screen.

"If Eric's an old soul, like you think," Hoop said, "maybe there's something else going on."

"Such as?" Anderson caught a glimpse of the paused image. "Bill, could you not watch that yet?"

Kanter docked the scan and spun in his chair. "Hoop, what are you suggesting?"

Hoop leaned against one of the workstations and brushed a dreadlock off his face. "Mon, what if Eric's something special? Maybe he senses what the bed can do and doesn't want to reveal his lives."

Kanter snickered. "What, are you thinking Eric's the next Dalai Lama?"

"No, but he might be like that. Maybe he's divine, or something."

"Or something," Anderson said.

"First, we have to find out if Eric is really manifesting his past lives," Kanter said, "then we'll tackle if he's divine or not."

"You may not get a chance," Anderson said. "That was a full-on panic attack. I think it's going to take an act of God to get him on the bed."

"Maybe it will," Hoop said.

29. My God.

After Anderson left, Kanter and Hoop had watched the rest of Nelson's current life, although Kanter did turn away more than he thought he would. The military had required Nelson and his unit to do some nasty shit, and it almost seemed at times like a war video game. But in this case the death was very real.

"This guy is a one bad motherfucker," Hoop declared and stood to go. "No wonder he's so cold."

"You had enough, too?" Kanter looked at his watch. *5:37 p.m.*

Hoop nodded. "If you don't mind, I need to do some Tai Chi and get my head in a better place."

Kanter docked the scan. "Sounds like a good idea. I think I'll get in a workout before I start the back-ups."

*   *   *

Late at night, when the farm was asleep, the old milking parlor reminded Kanter a little of his lab back at U of C. It was dark and cool and quiet, and the hum from the Cores always had been a comforting backdrop. He'd even started sleeping on the lab's couch rather than the cowboy bedroom because it felt more like home.

Once Kanter had finally gotten used to being under guard, he tried to chum it up with the mantis woman. He learned from Claymore that her first name was Mira, but just getting that little bit of info had been a bitch. She had been assigned to guard the lab at night and was very tight lipped. He could get a hello out of her, but that was about it. Tonight, he greeted her as Mantis, but the joke bounced off her exoskeleton.

Kanter returned to the lab after dinner to see what kind of past lives a guy like Nelson had lived. Mostly, though, he wondered why Nelson's scan was shorter than everybody else's. Surprisingly, Nelson's lives were about as boring as Kanter's, and after four hours of viewing, Kanter concluded that he wouldn't find any crossovers with the other scans. Maybe Anderson was right. Maybe Nelson was a young soul. Kanter wondered if submitting all young souls to war was one of God's cruel jokes.

Nelson's past lives seemed to end around the 1700s, but the scan was so fragmented that it was hard to tell. He would have to talk to Hoop in the morning about possibly cleaning up the targeting parameters. If they were going to get any clear results, they'd have to–

"Hello, William."

"Jesus!" Kanter spun so quickly in his chair that he rammed his leg into the edge of the workstation. He doubled over and desperately rubbed his kneecap.

"I'm sorry I startled you."

Kanter looked up to find Eric standing at the perimeter of the workstation's light. His voice sounded lower. And how the hell did he get past Mantis?

"Ah, hi Eric." The stabbing pain from Kanter's kneecap was subsiding, and he stopped rubbing so hard. "What are you doing here?" He glanced at the time on the monitor. *11:47 p.m.* "Shouldn't you be in bed?"

The boy just stood there, his eyes fluttering between all whites and a hint of pupils. The light cast him in angular contrasts and revealed the same Star Wars pajamas from the night he had walked in on Anderson's bath.

Something shivered through Kanter, but he didn't feel afraid – only curious. "Who am I talking to?" he asked.

Eric didn't respond, and his fluttering eyes slowed considerably.

Kanter scooted closer and studied the boy. He seemed to be in a kind of trance, although Kanter sensed a distinct personality present, as if Eric were possessed like the kid in those old Damian movies. *Creepy.*

"Eric, can you tell me who I'm talking–?"

"I'd like to be scanned, William," Eric said, his voice now rich in timbre.

Kanter hesitated. Eric was a minor and performing a test without parental consent was unethical. But he was pretty sure Kim and Scott were cool with it, plus the opportunity to scan him during an episode was too tempting. Sure, Anderson might rip him a new one, but this could be his only chance.

Eric tilted his head questioningly. His eyes were now normal and stared at Kanter with a sense of intelligence far beyond his eight years.

Kanter didn't know who – or what – he was talking to. He glanced at the MedBed and back. "Are you sure you want to be scanned?"

"Yes, William, I am."

Kanter began to second-guess what he was about to do. "Look, I don't know if this is such a good idea."

Eric brushed past Kanter and approached the MedBed.

"Hey, wait a minute!"

The MedBed tilted down, and Eric climbed on. He scooted his head into the nest of targeting arms and folded his hands across his chest.

"Look, Eric – or whoever you are – I don't think this is such a good–"

Eric turned his head, and his look sent a cold rush down Kanter's spine. He suddenly felt vulnerable in the dark expanse of the lab.

"All right, then." Kanter backed up to the main workstation and sat. "The man wants to be scanned." He cued the scanning program and waited as the bed calculated the contour of Eric's head.

The boy didn't squirm.

"There'll be a little pin prick when each arm sets into position on your head and neck," Kanter called out. "You have to remain very still, or it won't work." Kanter said those last words to himself because Eric seemed oblivious to his directions. The arms closed in and nestled into position.

"Okay," Kanter said, "I'm going to start the scan, so keep very still. This might take a few minutes."

More than two hours later, the Cores, their LED lights dancing in rhythm, were still processing.

Eric had remained motionless thc entire time, and Kanter thought that he hadn't blinked, but was that possible? He had checked on the kid many times, but everything seemed normal – except those eyes. They just stared up at the rafters. *Weird.*

Another hour passed before the monitor finally signaled the end of the scan. Kanter was well past concerned: every other session had taken no more than 30 minutes. Eric's scan was sitting on three and half hours, and it was close to three-thirty in the morning. His dad would be up in an hour, and Kanter didn't want to deal with Nelson's wrath.

"Eric, are you okay?" he asked, approaching the bed.

The targeting arms released their grip, and Eric's head rolled to one side. His eyelids were clenched tightly, and a bit of drool trickled from his half-opened mouth.

Kanter freaked.

"*Eric?!*" He jiggled the boy's arm, but received no response. "Shit." Kanter felt for a pulse. *Thank God!* Then he noticed Eric's head and arms were slick with sweat.

Kanter threw open the parlor's main door and ran toward the path to the main house.

"Dr. Kanter," Mantis called out. "Is everything all right?"

Kanter looked over his shoulder and gave an animated okay sign. He quietly entered the house and took the stairs two at a time. Anderson's bedroom door was ajar, and he didn't bother to knock.

"Tren, wake up," he whispered, slipping into the room.

Anderson was balled around one of her pillows, and her face was mashed into another. She had kicked off most of the covers, and Kanter had to creep around to the other side of the bed to face her. He knelt.

"Hey, Tren?" A little louder this time.

Anderson raised her head. "Bill?" she asked sleepily. "What's the matter?"

"You've got to come down to the lab," Kanter whispered. He tried to sound calm, but it didn't come out that way.

Anderson sat up and brushed a strand of hair off her face. She glanced at her watch. "It's almost four in the morning."

"Trenna, I need you in the lab right *f'ing* now."

Anderson's eyes went big. "Bill, what's going on?"

"I'll tell you on the way."

Anderson pulled on her robe, slipped on a pair of flip-flops, and hurried down the stairs with Kanter. As they turned onto the landing, he noticed light under the door of the upstairs hallway bathroom.

"We've got to hurry." Kanter took Anderson's arm and practically dragged her down the front porch stairs.

"Are you going to tell me what's going on?" Anderson asked, yanking her arm free. "And what are you doing working so late?" They were now trotting along the path that led to the lab.

"I scanned Eric."

Anderson stopped. "*You what?!*"

"He asked. No wait, he *demanded*."

"Bullshit."

"The little fucker marched into the lab, past the guard – God knows how – and *demanded* to be scanned. Tren, he gave me a look that was the scariest thing I've ever seen."

Anderson shook her head. "Bill, this is totally unethical. And I can't believe you left him alone in the lab." She took off running.

Kanter ran and caught up. "The opportunity presented itself–"

Anderson cut him off with a disgusted sideways glance.

Mantis stepped aside and opened the door, as if running into the lab at four in the morning was a matter of routine.

Anderson hurried around the stacks and came up to the MedBed's side.

Eric was sitting up, his legs crossed.

"Honey," she asked softly. "Are you all right?"

Eric moaned a little, his blue eyes sleepy and innocent.

Anderson placed the back of her hand to his forehead and neck. "His temperature feels normal." She wiped some sweat from his arm. "Why is he sweating so much?"

"I don't know," Kanter said. "Maybe it's a reaction to the scan."

"How did that go?" she asked, feeling the lymph glands in Eric's neck. "Were there any incidents?"

"Tren, his scan took over three hours to complete."

"What?!"

Eric wrapped his arms around Anderson's neck and hugged her.

"I want to go to bed," he said and coughed.

Anderson helped Eric off the MedBed. "Okay, honey, I'll take you back to your room." She took his hand and headed for the door.

Kanter walked with them. "Maybe I should join you."

"No," Anderson said sternly. "I'll take him back. If Scott's up, I'll think of some excuse."

"Say he was sleepwalking. Maybe I should come along."

Anderson raised her hand. "Don't push it, Bill. We'll talk in the morning."

The lab's inner screen door shut with a crack. Kanter mulled his decision to scan Eric.

"I had my chance, and I went for it," he said into the darkness. "The opportunity presented itself. I weighed the outcomes and chose the side of science. He's a tough kid."

Despite it all, something tugged at Kanter, and it sure resembled guilt. What if the scanning *had* damaged Eric somehow? As Kanter walked back to the main workstation, he couldn't escape the conclusion that he probably had screwed up, and Anderson wouldn't let him forget it. He sat and checked the filtering program. By the looks of it, it might take a while.

"There's nothing I can do about it now," he said, pushing the guilt down.

The filtering program's beep snapped Kanter awake. He glanced at his watch and saw he'd only dozed off for 20 minutes.

"That's weird," he said. "How can the filtering be finished when it took so long to scan Eric?" He sat and started inspecting the scan's primary components. There were no components, fragmentation, or back life to be edited out. Just one, continuous scan. Kanter checked again, but the results were unchanged: nearly 26 million hours recorded.

Astonished, Kanter did a quick calculation and concluded that was close to 3000 years of life. He glanced at the clock on the monitor. *4:52 a.m.*

What the hell? Sleep was overrated. He clicked the scan into sequence and leaned back against the chair's mesh.

At first, there was just the staticky white noise he and Kelly had gotten back when the machine wouldn't register anything. This continued for several years, which caused Kanter to wonder if the MedBed had malfunctioned. Then something strange and astonishing began to emerge from the noise. Kanter unconsciously leaned forward while he watched.

"My God," he whispered, and the hum from the computers grew around him.

30. It's funny.

Anderson had stopped carrying her cell phone, but always checked it at least once a day for messages. There usually weren't any in the mornings, although occasionally her mother would send a text insisting she call home regarding whatever new drama was happening with Anderson's sister. She was involved with a man who was, as her mother put it, of a "different persuasion." Anderson didn't understand why being Jewish was such a big deal, but her mother was old school and couldn't be swayed. This morning, a text from Kanter caught her attention. All it said was for Anderson to skip breakfast and get her butt down to the lab ASAP.

"Good morning to you, too ... jerk," She plugged the phone back into its charger and headed downstairs.

"Trenna?" Kimberly called from the kitchen.

Anderson stopped just shy of the front door. "Yes?"

"I'm making eggs. Do you want some?"

"No, thanks. I've got to get to the lab early." She reached for the doorknob, but hesitated. "Hey Kim?"

"Yes?"

"How's Eric doing this morning?"

"Good. He's helping his father. Why?"

"Nothing. Just wondering. See you at lunch." She yanked the screen door open and hurried for the lab.

Anderson found Kanter and Hoop at the main workstation, focused intently on the monitor. Hoop turned and grinned.

"I see you got the same text I did," Hoop remarked upon her entrance.

"So, what's going on?" Anderson asked as she pulled up a chair.

Kanter didn't acknowledge her as she sat.

"This is some whacked-out shit," Hoop said.

"What is?" Anderson asked and scooted between them.

The monitor contained a bird's-eye view of a large urban city, although she couldn't tell which one. There was something odd about its perspective, however. It didn't appear to have been taken from an airplane, yet the detail was amazing.

"Is this from Google Maps?" she asked.

Hoop stifled a laugh.

Kanter looked like he hadn't slept all night, and smelled it, too. "Guess again, doctor."

Anderson leaned closer to scrutinize the image. "I don't know. One of Primus's satellite photos?"

"This is Eric's scan," Hoop said giddily. "The whole thing is full of this kind of stuff."

The scan began sequencing, and the city's perspective morphed into a closer viewpoint. Anderson could now make out horses and carriages. Still, it all looked vaguely familiar.

"Is that the Water Tower?" she asked, catching a glimpse of it in the lower right of the screen.

"So," Kanter asked leadingly, "how did little Eric see Chicago from so high up? Especially when planes hadn't been *invented* yet?"

Anderson wanted to slap the smugness off his face. She looked back at the screen when the view pulled back to reveal a much smaller Chicago. "Now wait," she said. "This is Chicago from the 1800s?" The images quickly sequenced into farmland before they shifted to a blur. "Bill, wait. Slow it down. I want to go–"

The image refocused. They were now high up and looking down on a black undulating mass that rolled like an enormous wave across a vast open plain prairie. On the horizon, the sun was cresting distant foothills. While Anderson tried to discern the nature of the mass, the viewpoint zoomed nearer.

"Buffalo," she whispered.

"Thousands of them," Kanter said.

Closer still, and they were tracking alongside the herd as it churned over the grassland. It appeared to be winter; steam billowed from their hides and nostrils like lacy fog. A horse and rider entered the frame, and Anderson recognized it as an American Indian. The warrior was at full gallop, his bow and arrow drawn.

"Did we just move back in time?" she asked.

Kanter continued calibrating. Hoop shrugged.

Anderson looked back at the screen. "What is this?" she whispered.

Kanter grinned. "God's view."

"You haven't *even* seen the best part," Hoop said excitedly.

Kanter increased the sequencing until it came to a view from space. The curve of the earth was pronounced; the atmosphere appeared as a soft blue ring; lightning arced across the tops of gigantic thunderheads over South America.

Kanter faced her for the first time. "Look, I'm really sorry for what I did last night. I know it was unethical, and I don't have an excuse. I just went for it. I mean, he kind of forced the issue."

"Ah, cut the drama," Hoop interjected. "This kid *is* the Dalai Lama! So you scanned him, so what? He's young. He'll get over it." Hoop leaned on the counter and stared at the screen. "This is just *too* cool."

Even though Anderson was still pissed at Kanter, she had to admit that Eric's scan was amazing. "Well, Kim did say Eric was doing okay this morning."

"See," Hoop said. "The kid'll be all right."

Anderson watched the tip of Florida break the corner of the earth's horizon, and her anger toward Kanter waned. "Is it all like this?" she asked.

Kanter nodded.

"But where's the English salesman or the crack whore?"

Kanter shrugged. "Hell if I know. We are way out of known science here."

"How far back does the scan go?"

"Hard to tell. I'm guessing by the time code the early Roman Empire? There's close to twenty-six million hours in the scan." He glanced at Hoop.

"Beats me," Hoop said.

"Twenty-six *million*?" Anderson was astonished.

"It'll take weeks," Kanter said, "maybe months, to watch it all, even as fast as we can."

"What kind of state was Eric in when you scanned him? Was he having an episode?"

"Yeah, but what's weird is he wasn't doing the eye thing. I mean, at first he was, but then he sort of came out of it. I think."

"What do you mean, *you think*?"

"Trenna, I don't know. He talked to me like an adult, used my formal name. And when he looked at me, it was as if he knew everything about me. It was creepy, like he could see right into my soul. It's hard to describe."

"You sure you're not reading back into things? He said he wanted to be scanned?"

Kanter nodded. "Once I agreed, he marched right over to the bed and hopped up. I think we should scan him again, when he's not having an episode. I bet that's when we'll see the salesman and the crack whore."

"Are you saying this scan is a *not* a past-life?" Anderson asked.

Kanter started to say something, but stopped. He thought for a second. "Maybe ... I guess." He raised his hands in frustration. "Hell, I have no idea."

"Should we tell his parents?" Hoop asked.

"No," Anderson said, "we don't know what we're dealing with

here. They're hyper-religious, and they might freak out. I want to have a better grasp on all this before I go tell them something crazy like their son is channeling God."

"Okay," Hoop said as he went back to the scan.

"Maybe we could ask the Nelsons if we could scan Eric this afternoon, after his nap," Kanter said.

"I wouldn't do it so soon," Anderson said. "Let's give Eric some time. He really broke down before. Plus, I want to see how he does over the next couple of days. See if he has any reactions from his scan."

"Fair enough," Kanter said. "We have other scans we can do before we try Eric again."

Hoop laughed under his breath.

"What's so funny?" Anderson asked, unable to pry her attention from the monitor. The sun bathed an ocean, and the cloud's shadows danced across the glittering water. It was hard for her to accept that this was Eric's scan.

Hoop paused it. "It's funny, that's all," he said.

"What is?" Kanter asked.

"That God needs a nap."

31. You be careful now.

Since they had decided to postpone scanning Eric again, Kanter was anxious to move on to the next test. He was curious to scan a blind person, preferably congenitally blind. He wanted to see what would appear, if anything, for the current life. The test also would help validate the machine's accuracy, although after Eric's scan, Kanter wasn't so sure.

"So you see," Kanter said around a forkful of mustard potato salad, "scanning a blind person would yield fascinating data."

Kimberly didn't seem to care what Kanter thought, which wasn't surprising, but Nelson appeared mildly interested.

"I know of an old black guy who's a greeter at Wal-Mart," Nelson said. "He's blind as a bat. I think from birth." He stirred a bag of Sweet N' Low into a tall glass of tea.

"Perfect," Kanter said. "Let's go this afternoon."

"Claymore's not going to like that," Anderson said.

"He works for us."

"No. He works for Strachan, who *owns* us."

Nelson laughed into his tea.

Kanter wasn't sure if Anderson had forgiven him, or not. She hadn't read him the riot act, but in light of Eric's scan, who could have? She actually had been fairly nice for most of the morning, so maybe his apology had done the trick.

"What if we went and talked with Claymore *en masse*?" Kanter suggested. "You, me, and Hoop?"

"I don't think ganging up will persuade a guy like Claymore," Nelson said.

"I think it's worth at least a try."

Anderson stood. "Come on, tough guy." She patted Kanter's shoulder. "Let's go talk with our keeper."

* * *

Claymore, his jaw grinding away, stared for a second. "No way," he said finally.

Kanter saw his own reflection in the sunglasses. He still looked like a kid. "I don't think you have a say in this."

"The hell I don't!" Claymore stepped away and pulled out his cell phone. He fingered a speed dial number. "Mary, is Mr. Strachan in?"

Kanter glanced at Anderson. She grinned and crossed her fingers.

"Mr. Strachan, it's Tom Claymore from Primus… Yes, everything is going well. Sir, I called because Dr. Kanter and his team want to go offsite.... Wal-Mart ... What are my options?... No, not at the present time.... Yes, I think there's a significant risk factor. But what if ... yes ... I don't believe this is a good idea.... Yes *sir*!" He stuffed the phone into his front pocket. His jaw was in overdrive.

"Well?" Kanter asked.

Claymore looked away, then back. "Meet at the Suburban at," he glanced at his watch, "fourteen-hundred. I'm sending Webber and Gibson with you." He walked away shaking his head.

Anderson saluted his back. "That guys needs to learn to relax."

"Seems I rate a little more than I thought." Kanter said.

"Don't get your hopes up," Anderson said. "Claymore is just keeping Strachan's investment happy."

*　　*　　*

Webber, Kanter remembered, was Mantis, and Gibson was an imposing linebacker of a man who Hoop thought looked like an old sparring partner of his. Kanter had never met him up close, but the guy cut quite a figure, even from a distance. Now, standing next to the Suburban, Kanter imagined Gibson could give Nelson a run for his money in a knockdown, drag-out.

Kanter and Anderson walked up, and there were sirs and ma'ams from Mantis and Gibson. Kanter thought about cracking wise to Mantis, something like, "We have to stop meeting like this," but her demeanor snuffed the impulse.

"Do you know where we're going?" Kanter asked.

"Yes, sir," Gibson said. "Got the Wal-Mart's coordinates off of sat nav." He held up what looked like an iPhone, more military than consumer, a map app filling most of its screen. "We're ready to move out."

Fortunately, Wal-Mart wasn't as far as Mother's Café because the ride was excruciatingly quiet. Primus might be great at security, Kanter concluded, but they were lousy at client relations. He tried to strike up a conversation only to be met with what Anderson had dubbed "the Primus grunt." Gibson was driving like it was his first driver's test. Smooth, efficient stops. Even accelerations. Always at the speed limit. Definitely no reasons to be pulled over.

After they went inside Wal-Mart, they could have been anywhere in America. The whole building seemed air lifted and dropped into place. Kind of like a giant boot that stamped out mom and pop stores, Kanter mused. They roamed around looking for the blind man until Anderson finally approached a greeter and asked where they could find him.

The woman's name was Betty, and she informed them the blind man was on break, but he would be back to replace her in a couple of minutes. She also gave his name as Terence and said he was "a right-fine gentleman."

Kanter observed a 5-year-old pull a sale rack of sweaters over and wondered how many Chinese laborers Wal-Mart kept employed when someone tapped his shoulder.

"You looking for me?" The voice sounded like it lived at the bottom of a roadhouse ashtray.

The weathered face of the blind greeter smiled back at Kanter. He wore a vintage pair of Ray Bans and a Porkpie hat, the kind Kanter had seen on street tap dancers in New Orleans. His aged, dark skin clung to his bones like burnt leather.

"Terence?" he asked.

"That's what my momma called me." His smiley face badge labeled him as Toothie, and judging by the fact that he had maybe five in his head, the title fit.

"My name is Dr. William Kanter. This is my assistant, Dr. Trenna Anderson."

Terence shook Kanter's hand like he saw it, but when he shook Anderson's, he felt for her wrist with his left hand before grasping with his right. Anderson didn't pull away, but Kanter could tell the action unnerved her.

"Dark hair, green eyes," Terence said, and he felt around her forearm like a piece of fruit. "Slim ... and not too bosomy." He leaned over to Kanter, his head swimming between the ceiling and the watch counter, "That's the way I likes them!"

Anderson shied away from his grip. "Hazel, actually."

"They look green to me." Terence faced Kanter as if he could see. "Betty tells me you all were wanting me for some kind of medical test?"

"Kind of," Kanter said. "We're from the University of Chicago, and we're conducting tests on people who have been blind from birth."

"Are you all trying to make this old Negro see?"

"Not exactly," Anderson said.

Terence's attention shifted to her. He grinned.

"We want to learn how you've processed navigating through your environment," Kanter said.

"You mean, how I see?"

"Yes, that's right. It's totally safe and will only take a couple of hours of your time." Kanter caught Mantis out of the corner of his eye. She was standing by a self-serve checkout line and motioning that they needed to hurry up. Kanter raised his hand to signal her to hold on. Terence seemed to perceive the exchange.

"We're willing to pay you for your trouble," Anderson said. "When can we schedule you?"

"Hell, if you're going to pay me, we can go right now! I'm just a volunteer." Terence slipped his arm through hers. "Come on, let's go see what's inside this old noggin of mine."

"Trenna," Kanter said, "why don't you clear things with his manager. I have to use the restroom."

"That guy wouldn't know if I was here or not," Terrance said. "I don't need his permission. I'm eighty-nine years old. I come and go as I please."

"That's cool, Terrance, but I don't want Wal-Mart to send the cops out looking for you. If you could please go with Dr. Anderson and make sure it's okay for you to leave, that would be great. She'll explain to you what the test is about." Kanter glanced at Anderson, and she mouthed a sarcastic, "*Thanks*."

"Now," Kanter said, stepping back, "will you excuse me for a minute?"

"They're by the outdoor furniture," Terrance said. "Against the wall."

Kanter headed for the back of the store, which must have sent

Mantis into a tailspin. She intercepted him near a display of Martha Stewart cookbooks.

Mantis grabbed him by the elbow and spun him around. "Where are you going?" she asked not too politely.

Kanter pulled his arm away. "To the restroom. Is that allowed?"

"Mike will escort you to the lavatory." She pulled her cell phone out and called Gibson in from the Suburban.

The bathrooms were actually near the tires. Gibson took a position across the hall beside a water fountain while Kanter took care of his business.

A young Hispanic kid who worked for Wal-Mart looked up from washing his hands. His vest was so littered with promotional flare it was hard to tell what color it was. Kanter chose the center urinal, mostly because it was the only one that had been flushed. The kid left, and someone else entered. He picked the urinal next to Kanter.

"Bill, why don't guys flush after they piss? Can you answer me that?"

The bald agent from the motel. His breath hadn't changed, but the dark suit had been swapped for jeans, cross-trainers, and a long-sleeved Nike warm-up. The dent in his head was hidden under a long billed black ball cap. Its white embroidery asked "Got Cojones?"

Kanter was so startled he missed his mark, spraying piss on the edge of the urinal.

"Watch your aim, my friend," the agent said out of the side of his mouth.

Kanter gathered himself. "What do you want?" he asked, desperately pushing his bladder to finish.

"Thought I'd check in on my favorite boy genius. How's it going?"

If he could buy more time, Kanter thought, he might be able to figure a way out of dealing with the CIA. "We're having trouble creating a solid imaging field," he lied. "Hoop and I are working on a new program to fix the problem."

"I don't like the word *trouble*, Bill. Makes me twitchy. I go off and do irrational things when I'm twitchy."

"I'm sure we'll fix it," Kanter said, almost done.

"How do like Strachan's little army?"

"They're okay."

"They're amateurs, Bill. People who can't cut it with groups like ours. Companies like Primus are building armies of losers all over the world." He zipped up and walked over to the far sink.

Kanter finished and buttoned his jeans. He approached the sinks.

The agent, washing his hands, regarded Kanter in the mirror. "This isn't a game, Bill." He rubbed his yellow teeth with his forefinger, then inspected his smile.

Kanter twisted on the cold and rinsed his hands. "I know."

"Good. That's what I like to hear." The agent started to leave, but stopped. "Should be interesting to see what you get with the old blind man," he said over his shoulder. "Don't you think?"

"You'll be the first to know."

The agent looked at Kanter like he might kill him right there. "You got *that* right." The door shut with a loud thwack.

Kanter waited a minute before leaving the men's room. Gibson was still standing guard across the hall.

"Ready to go, sir?" he asked.

"Yeah." The word stuck in Kanter's throat. He sucked a couple of deep breaths and tried to shake off his nerves while he followed

Gibson to the front.

"We cleared everything with Terence's boss," Anderson said as they approached.

"Let's get out of here," Kanter replied flatly.

Anderson and Kanter walked Terence to the Suburban. At one point, Terence asked Anderson who the muscle was following them. She tried to explain that Mantis and Gibson were part of the team, but Terence didn't seem to buy it.

* * *

The ride back to the farm proved to be a trip down Terence's memory lane. He had been everything from a shoe shiner in Grand Central Station to a bartender for Burlington Northern's Zephyr route to California back in the '60s. That was the source of the bulk of his retirement income, but Kanter found it hard to believe that the railroad would have hired a blind bartender. All the while, Anderson seemed happy to be Terence's "seeing-eye person," and the old black man was just fine with the arrangement. He didn't relinquish his hold on Anderson's arm until he was climbing onto the MedBed.

"Here you go, brother," Hoop said, easing Terence's head into the nest of targeting arms.

"What part of Georgia are you from?" Terence asked.

Hoop, his eyes wide, glanced at Anderson and Kanter. "Macon," he answered. "How did you know I was from Georgia? I haven't lived there in years."

Terence put a bony finger to his ear. "It's still in your inflection, at the *back* of your words."

Kanter explained how the procedure worked and waited for the bed to read the contour of Terence's head.

"Why are we at a farm?" Terence asked just as the last arm pricked him between the eyes.

Kanter looked at Anderson and mouthed, "*What do I say?*"

"It's where Dr. Kanter set up his lab for the summer," Anderson said. "The owners are friends of his."

"Well, we're west of town, so who's he friends with? The Krupens or the Nelsons?"

This time, it was Anderson's eyes that went big. "Nelsons," she said.

"Good," Terence said. "Jake Krupen is a horse's ass."

The scanning took about 20 minutes, and Terence hummed through all of it. When the bed released him, Hoop caught him as he slid off.

"I'll tell you what," Terence said. "That table of yours, Dr. Kanter, has a mind of its own."

"So I've been told," Kanter replied.

Hoop passed Terence his hat. The old man adjusted it onto his head and ran his fingers along the brim before he pulled it down across his brow.

Anderson took Terence's arm and began walking him towards the front door, but he stopped her and turned to the room.

"So, what are you really doing up here?" he asked.

It felt to Kanter as if all the air in the lab had suddenly escaped. He looked from Anderson to Hoop but didn't find any help.

"What do you mean, Terence?" he asked.

Terence smiled a large, toothless grin. "I remember you, Dr. Kanter. You invented some medical thing a few years ago. It was all over the television. I got a head for names, you know. And you don't need guards to see what's inside an old blind man's brain." He rocked his head from side to side as he spoke. "Scott Nelson was a war hero, so I figure the government is probably involved. Plus, you didn't have me sign any papers.... I've done this kind of thing before, and I always signed a bunch of forms."

The last of the air left the lab. Kanter felt his stomach tighten. He leaned against the workstation.

"You're up from Chi Town, in the middle of nowhere, so I'll bet someone's after you ..." Terence tilted his head, as if some imaginary friend was talking into his ear, "... and your fancy machine. You must be working on something important, Dr. Kanter. If you can't tell me, I understand."

"I wish I could tell you, Terrance, but–"

"We've discovered a way to image memories," Anderson interjected. "We were just curious to see what yours might look like. I apologize for not being honest with you." She glanced at Kanter and mouthed, "*I'm sorry*."

What the hell, Kanter thought. The old man had most of it figured. He deserved to know the truth.

Terence, his fingers bent from arthritis, waved off her apology. "No worries, there. I've been lied to all my life. You see, people think since I'm blind, they can get away with anything. Truth is, I can see plenty, just not with my eyes." He let go of Anderson's arm and tapped the side of his head. "I got memories, Dr. Kanter. Lots of them, you'll see. But I feel there's more to your tests than memories, right?"

Kanter was floored. "Terence, are you sure you're not psychic?"

The old man let out a raucous laugh. "I *have* been accused of that a time or two."

"We believe we can also view the memories of a person's past lives," Kanter added.

The smile faded from Terence's face, and he nodded like he didn't have a retort for this revelation. He took Anderson's arm and shuffled with her a few steps toward the door before he stopped again.

"William?" he called out.

"Yes, Terence?"

"You be careful, you hear me? All of you!"

"We hear you," Kanter said. "No worries there."

Terence laughed. "I *know* that's right."

32. Notebook.

July 23

7:34 p.m.

I pray that God will give me His blessed guidance.

> Days warm. A lot like Rome this time of year, but with more bugs!

> Wisconsin people are nice but talk like they have a sinus infection.

> Kanter went to Wal-Mart. Protection went with him. Plain clothes, 2 of them: man, woman. Very capable. From prior observations, their PDWs are Uzi Micros – 9mm, 32. The man carried a sidearm in. No ID, but it didn't set off the door scanners.

> Bald man was also there, as before. Part of a bigger group? He used

his cell phone twice and left before Kanter. Still can't trace calls. Must be filtered. American government? NSA? CIA?

> Dr. Anderson accompanied Kanter. They appear closer than 1 month ago. They picked up A.A. male, mid-80s, blind, store employee. Probably to test.

> Kanter spent long time in W.C. Black guard followed. Bald man, too. Maybe they met?

> Have to change my plans. There might be something happening. Connection between bald man and Kanter? Presently unknown.

In Christ, I seek all strength and forgiveness.

Forgive me, dear Lord, for I do not know what my actions will be in the next days. Grant me thy Holy blessings and mercy, for I will have to sin.

In Jesus' name, amen.

<End log>

33. We have a situation.

It was almost six o'clock when Anderson and Gibson dropped off Terence at Wal-Mart. Terence had maintained a death grip on Anderson the entire trip, and his chattiness had abated. Anderson wondered if learning the truth had unnerved him.

Terrance slightly reminded Anderson of a waiter she had known in her undergrad days who had worked at a bar she frequented with friends. His name was Kip, but she never learned if that was short for anything. He had been close to Terence's age and had taken a liking to her during her junior year. He would give her advice about boyfriends and life, and although she suspected he was gay, she had never asked.

"Here we are," she said to Terence as the Wal-Mart's sliding doors opened.

A woman pushing a shopping cart piled with a year's worth of Budweiser almost rammed them. Anderson had to guide Terence in a little dance trying to figure out which way the woman was going to push her cart.

"This damn place gets busier everyday," Terence said. "People are in just too big a hurry."

After they navigated the entrance, Anderson flagged down Betty. She was standing near a life-size cardboard cutout of a guy who renovated homes on one of those reality home makeover shows. The position of the display made it appear he had his hand on Betty's butt.

"There's my Toothie," she called and waved.

Terence frowned. "I hate that name," he whispered.

Betty gave Terence a faux hug. "How did he do?" she asked.

"He was the perfect gentleman," Anderson said.

"They're going to find out what kind of a genius I am." Terence laughed while Betty took his arm.

"I hope we didn't keep him too long," Anderson said.

Betty rolled her eyes. "The place almost shut down, but we made do."

Anderson leaned in and kissed Terence on the cheek. "It was an honor to meet you," she said.

Terence bowed slightly. "The honor was all mine." He motioned her close. "You like that boy, don't you?"

The question caught Anderson off guard. "If you're referring to Bill, he's a very nice man, but–"

"No, no. You *like* him, right?"

Anderson leaned down to his ear. "I think so," she whispered.

Terence smiled and wagged a bent finger. "I know a thing or two about love, Dr. Anderson. I can hear it all up insidc your voice. Now you keep an eye on that boy, you hear? He might be brilliant, but I'll bet you he could screw up his own funeral."

* * *

On the ride back, Gibson didn't say a word. That was fine with Anderson. She stared out the Suburban's window as the neighborhoods around Wal-Mart gave way to cornfields. Kimberly had mentioned that River Point was surrounded on three sides by farmland, but a gigantic national forest hugged the west. The Nelson land was nestled against the forest, and Anderson was utterly content watching the corn morph into beech, ash, and box elder.

Gibson dropped her off at the lab, and the guard, the one Kanter dubbed "Mantis," opened the door for her.

"How's the old black man doing?" she asked.

"Terence is fine," Anderson said. "He's back at Wal-Mart, safe and sound."

"Good thing he can't see. Makes our job a lot easier."

Anderson didn't understand exactly what she meant by that and didn't want to know, either. She opened the inner screen door and entered the lab.

"Get over here, doctor," Kanter called from the main workstation. "Maybe you can explain some of this."

"Did Terence's scan have anything on it?" Anderson was curious to see what Kanter's machine might reveal about how congenitally blind people perceive the world.

"I thought *Eric's* scan was weird," Hoop said. "But this is just downright crazy."

"Really?" Anderson asked. "What does it show?"

Kanter stood and offered his chair. "We were hoping you might be able to tell us."

Anderson eagerly sat and scooted close to the workstation. On the screen was a paused image that looked like a child's attempt at a modern painting. It contained almost no detail, however, and the shapes of the objects were skewed as if there were multiple perspectives within the frame of vision. It was hard to tell what the scene was, but Anderson hazarded a guess that it was a one-bedroom apartment with a couch, a coffee table, and a galley kitchen at the back of the room.

"Why is it so dark and monochromatic?" she asked.

"Don't know," Kanter said. "The whole scan is basically like this."

"There's no sighted past lives?"

Kanter shook his head.

"You're kidding? Let it run."

Kanter reached over and clicked the scan into motion. As it sequenced, the imagery reminded Anderson of when she learned to scuba. It had been in a man-made lake, and the water had been so murky that when she had swum up to something – a rock or a piece of junk – she wasn't able to make out much detail until she was right on top of it. Even then, its form was distorted by all the silt in the water.

"What do you think?" Kanter asked after a couple of minutes passed. He was leaning over her and looking at the monitor.

"It's always been thought," Anderson mused, "that people who were blind from birth wouldn't be able to form any imagery in their minds."

"Then how do they dream?" Hoop asked.

"Their dreams have all the other senses, except sight."

"I read about this study done in Israel," Kanter said, "where they discovered that people who were blind from birth developed different memories than sighted people."

Anderson nodded. "The part of the brain that normally develops to process vision rewires to process the other senses, so a blind person's sensory skills become hyper-developed. Without vision, blind people experience the world as a sequence of events through smell, touch and hearing. One man who had been born without eyes could actually paint in perspective. I saw his work. It was incredible."

"That makes sense," Kanter said. "They must perceive their world in a linear order, from one thing to the next."

"But that doesn't explain what we're seeing here," Anderson said. "Plenty of studies prove blind people don't have a visual memory unless they were blinded after the age of six or seven."

"It's weird," Kanter said. "All these forms are dimensional. Look at this." He paused the sequence. "This looks like a residential street. Aren't those trees?"

"And that's a car, with a person standing next to it. How could he perceive this kind of detail?"

"Third-eye chakra," Hoop said to himself.

"Third *what*?" Kanter asked.

"The third-eye chakra."

"I've heard of this," Anderson said.

"You have?" Hoop asked.

"I had a boyfriend who was into all that New Age stuff. He did yoga and Transcendental Meditation. He was always aligning his chakras. I never thought much of it. He was very passionate about opening his ... what's it called ... Ajna?"

"That's the third eye," Hoop said.

"Are you talking about that symbol on the dollar bill?" Kanter asked.

"No," Anderson said, "I think that has do with Freemasonry."

"I've taken a lot of yoga," Hoop said, "and one of the ideas is to open your third eye. It's a way to achieve a higher consciousness, or something like that. I did these exercises once where I crossed my eyes and tried to concentrate on my third eye."

"Did you open it?" Kanter asked.

Hoop shook his head. "No. All it did was give me a bitching headache. I stopped taking yoga after that."

"None of this explains what we're seeing here." Anderson looked at Kanter. "There's nothing else on the scan except for this kind of imaging?"

"Nothing," he said, still staring at the monitor. "Seems Terence has been blind throughout all his lives. Your guess is as good as mine as to how many he's had."

"Didn't the program determine how many?"

"It works on digital pattern recognition. There wasn't enough change in the data for it to recognize any start or end points. His scan is about as long as mine, so we know he's had several past lives. I just can't tell you exactly how many."

Were blind people destined never to experience life visually? Anderson wondered. *Or was Terence an exception?* She hoped for the latter.

"You know, I met this blind dude once," Hoop said. "He could play trumpet like nobody's business. He told me that he could see the audience and play to them when he opened his third eye."

"What are you saying?" Kanter asked.

"Maybe that's what we're seeing here. Maybe Terence has learned how to do that."

"No offense," Anderson said to Hoop, "but it's taken a lot for me to buy into the fact that past lives exist. The evidence is too compelling. But I think this musician's ability has to do more with talent than with some Hindu mysticism."

"I agree," Kanter said, stretching. "The blind don't *see* the world in three dimensions, but they certainly experience it in three dimensions. They have an awareness of the position of their bodies in space; they can feel relative sizes and shapes of objects; and they can judge distance by sound. Add it all up, and it's not hard to understand how they could have a rough, though skewed, *visual* image of the world in their mind's eye." He motioned at the monitor. "Besides, I can't make heads or tails out of most of this stuff."

"He's pretty perceptive," Hoop offered. "He picked up on me being from Macon after just a few words and figured out our little scam on him. He even knew about the Primus guards, back at Wal-Mart."

"That doesn't surprise me," Anderson said. "That's his hyper-developed senses at work."

"Jesus," Kanter said under his breath.

"What's the matter?" Anderson asked.

"The more we test this machine, the deeper we get. I have a feeling we're just touching the tip of the iceberg."

"First things first," Anderson said. "We need to establish that the machine is accurately scanning current and past memories. There'll be plenty of time to study every other known disorder out there." She felt Kanter's hands at her shoulders.

"I knew there was a reason I brought you along, doctor," he said, rubbing. "To keep us focused on–"

"Excuse me," a voice behind them interrupted.

It belonged to the redheaded guard from the front door, the one Kanter called Mantis. She stood about five feet away; her pistol drawn and ready at her side. The weapon didn't register immediately, but as soon as she noticed it, Anderson couldn't take her eyes off it.

"Hey, Mantis," Kanter said with his back to her, still studying the scan. "What's up?"

"Claymore needs to see you."

"Okay, but we're a little busy here."

"Now."

Kanter turned. His eyes locked onto the gun. "Mantis, what's going on?"

"We have a ... situation."

"What do you mean?"

Mantis opened her stance as if what she was about to say would require fortitude. "Somebody tripped one of the screamers out by the road. A red truck came up the drive. It, ah, didn't stop."

"And?"

"One of our guys got suspicious."

"What kind of red truck?" Anderson asked.

"I don't know," Mantis said. "New. Chevy. A One-Fifty, I think."

"Bill," Anderson said, "could that be Gerald Park's truck?"

"What's happened?" Kanter asked Mantis.

"One of our guys ..." The guard straightened even more. "... shot the driver."

34. We'll get physical.

"When will Kanter's tests be finished?"

"A week? A month? He's run into some issues. Says they're working on it."

"Mr. Smith, you and your team are being paid to deliver this technology, not observe it."

The old wound on his forehead tingled. When Smith rubbed it, his fingers slid through the indentation. It had been a one-in-a-million shot. The bullet had deflected at the precise angle: one degree lower would have blown his frontal lobe out the back of his skull. *Israeli bastards*. His client's image quivered as static cut the computer screen into an oscillating triptych. The motel's desk was cramped, which caused Smith to twist awkwardly to see his tech manager. "A little help?" he asked.

The manager, leaning against the twin bed's headboard, looked up from his laptop. "Man, we're piggybacking here. Give me a second." He tapped in some commands. "There."

The static cleared. Smith crushed out another cigarette and almost tipped the ashtray. He caught it, and some ash spilled across his knuckles. His father had owned one just like it in their family's basement in Moscow, except his had the Ministry of Defense seal embossed in its tray. It always remained filled with ash and bent Troikas. As a child, Smith would sometimes steal one of the larger butts and smoke it down till it almost burnt his lips. His father had caught him once and made him eat the ash from the tray.

"Are you sure we're secure?" his client asked.

"For Christ's sake," Smith said, wiping his hand with a used KFC napkin, "we're tighter than your ass. And don't worry, you'll get the technology."

"What if Kanter refuses?"

"He won't. He's a pussy."

"Don't underestimate him."

Smith glanced at his watch. "We have to disconnect."

"You didn't answer my question." There was a trace of inflection, a slight lift on the word "didn't," that lent a moderate strain to the man's usual baritone. Smith had pushed too far.

"We'll get physical," Smith said, keeping his voice matter-of-fact.

"But isn't he being guarded?"

"Rent-a-cops. Not a problem."

His client rubbed pensively at his tightly cropped beard. The computer screen jumped with static, then cleared. "That would not be wise," he said. "Too much risk."

Smith scooted his chair nearer and leaned on the desk. "They're in the middle of fucking nowhere. We can scrub it in less than two hours."

"What about the family?"

"The typical murder-suicide. With Nelson's record, it'll stick. Look, I'm going to have to break off."

"Do I need to remind you what will happen if you–?"

"No, you don't." The old wound was tingling. Smith fought the urge to scratch it.

His client smiled and lifted his hands. "Then there's nothing to worry about. Praise Allah."

35. Clarity.

"God, I hope they didn't kill him," Kanter said to Anderson as they ran down the driveway. Several "what if" scenarios ricocheted through his mind.

"Amen to that," Hoop said.

Mantis was running in front of them. "Negative," she said over her shoulder. "He's alive."

A pick-up truck was halfway up the long drive. It looked like it had veered off and wedged into the wooden slat fence that ran alongside.

As Kanter ran up, he saw the bullet-hole fracture in the middle of the windshield. *Jesus.*

Gibson and another Primus guard had the driver propped up against the front driver's side wheel. Claymore and Nelson stood together like they were supervising a road gang.

The driver turned his head, and Kanter recognized Park. He seemed remarkably calm considering a bullet had torn through his shoulder. He forced a grin. "Hey there, Dr. Anderson, Dr. Kanter, Hoop." He didn't seem in much pain. "Was it something I said?"

Kanter and Anderson knelt. Park's shirt had been pulled off his shoulder, and the area above his collarbone was awash in blood. Gibson was working from a small duffle bag and working the wound with a wad of cotton balls.

"How bad does it hurt?" Kanter asked.

"Like a sonofabitch." Park grimaced as Gibson poured some iodine over the wound. The blood kept trickling. "Did it break the collar bone?"

"I don't think so," Gibson replied. "But it's hard to tell."

"I was fishing in the area, and I thought I'd stop by and say hello," Park said. "I would have packed my gun if I had known *this* was waiting for me." He gave a nod to his wound.

"I'm sorry, Gerald." Kanter angrily took Claymore's arm and lead him away from the truck. Anderson followed.

Claymore jerked out of Kanter's grip. "Get your god*damn* hand off–"

"Shut up." Kanter got in Claymore's face. "What in the hell happened?"

Claymore didn't waver. "Your friend should've stopped."

"Do you know what kind of exposure you've created? I thought you guys were professionals."

"This man needs to get to a hospital," Anderson said, stepping up. "If we don't treat that wound, he could bleed out."

Claymore pressed within an inch of Kanter's nose. "I'm well aware of the exposure, Dr. Kanter." His eyes shifted to Anderson. "And he's not going to any *damn* hospital."

Anderson, appearing like she was about to slug Claymore, leaned in. "The *hell* he isn't!"

"He's right," Park called out.

Kanter, Anderson, and Claymore turned in unison.

"Gerald, that wound needs immediate attention," Anderson said.

A slight smile formed at the corners of Park's mouth. "With all due respect, Dr. Anderson, I nearly lost my face in Iraq. I think I can handle a flesh wound. Besides, this guy, here, is right. If this machine of yours, Dr. Kanter, is what you say it is, you can't risk taking me to a hospital. That would mean paperwork, and questions, and police."

Claymore, clearly frustrated, glanced at Kanter then Anderson. He began to say something, but hesitated. "He should be sedated," he said finally.

"*Sedated?*" Anderson was pissed. "For how long? A week? A month?"

"It's my fault," Gibson said, winding a large gauze wrap under Park's armpit and over his shoulder.

"That'll be enough," Claymore ordered.

Gibson shot a vicious look at him. "This isn't the Corps, Sam. I jumped, and now we got a situation." The gauze reddened as he wrapped Park's shoulder.

"I don't care *what* the exposure might be," Anderson said. "He needs a doctor."

Claymore peeled off his sunglasses and raised his hands in a gesture of civility. “Mr. Park is right. We can’t involve the police. He’ll have to mend here. The real question is who can sew this wound up.”

“Aren’t you guys trained in this sort of stuff?” Kanter asked.

“Usually there’s a med person assigned to each team. But …” Gibson’s eyes went to Claymore.

“What?” Kanter asked.

“Strachan wanted a minimal profile,” Claymore said. “I didn’t think we would need one of our med people.”

Nelson squatted and inspected Gibson’s dressing. “I’ll bet the muscle’s been cut.” He glanced at Gibson. “Do you have an antibiotic drip and more sterile gauze?”

Gibson nodded. “We could almost set up a damn operating room if we had too.”

Nelson spat. “I can do it, but I’ll need some help.”

“I’ve assisted before.” Anderson was the only one who answered.

Kimberly walked up, but kept her distance. Her arms were folded against her chest like the whole scene was painful. Eric stood on the porch, craning around one of the columns.

Nelson looked at her. “Start boiling some water and get my kit from upstairs.”

Kimberly nodded and ran toward the house.

“Do you know what you’re doing?” Park asked.

“Believe me,” Kanter said. “He does.”

Nelson flashed Kanter a knowing a smile.

Kanter’s cell phone vibrated in his pocket. He pulled it out and read the ID: *Blocked*. He flipped it open.

“This is Bill Kanter.”

"How do you like your protection *now*?" It was the agent.

Kanter strolled away from the group as casually as possible. He looked to the tree line around the property and wondered. "What do you want?"

"Just checking in. Your new friend's wound is going to hurt like hell in the morning. Do you think Nelson's got any morphine? I know he doesn't have any booze."

"Get to the point."

"How are those problems coming along? Got them fixed yet?"

"We're working on them, but it's taking longer than we expected."

"We have people who could assist you, Bill."

"I can handle it, thanks."

"So independent. You and I are a lot alike."

"I doubt that." Kanter caught Anderson staring. He turned away. "Are you going to be up my ass the whole time?"

There was a pause. "It's not just me, Bill. The whole national security complex is up your ass. And yes, we will be."

"Are we done?"

Another pause. "For the moment."

*   *   *

Kanter hadn't hit the weights in weeks, and it was good to release some endorphins. He rarely felt the burn, so had never understood why the term was so popular. "*Feel the pain a dozen Advils might cure*" was a better catch-line, he mused.

"Bill?"

"Over here, Tren."

Anderson's figure emerged from the lab's darkness. "How can you work out this late?" She wore a pair of cargo shorts, flip-flops, and a black T-shirt.

Kanter did two more sitting militarys and let the weights down as quietly as he could. He grabbed a towel and wiped under his arms. "I don't know. I just felt like doing some reps. I haven't worked out much over the last couple of weeks."

Anderson rolled a chair over and sat. She propped her feet on the edge of the weight board. "You were awfully quiet at dinner tonight."

"It's been a crappy day, you know?"

Anderson nodded.

"Do you think Scott did a good job with Park?"

"Sewed him up like a pro. That kit of his has everything, and Primus has enough stuff to set up a battlefield triage."

"I guess if I were around as much machinery as Scott, I'd have a kit like that, too. How's Park doing?"

"I just came from his room. Hoop gave up his bed. Primus had some Demerol, so he'll be asleep for a while. It's going to take some time for the wound to heal, but he was in good spirits. He's such a nice guy. He kept going on about what a burden he was. Thank God Primus didn't kill him."

"Don't say that. I can't imagine where we'd be right now if it had happened."

"In deep shit," Anderson said.

"I've heard that before."

"What's that?"

"Nothing." Kanter took a swig from his bottled water. "Something on your mind?"

"Who called you this afternoon ... when we were all with Park by his truck?"

"Why do you ask?"

"After it, you didn't seem yourself."

"How'd I seem?"

"Anxious."

Kanter's pulse jumped. "It was just a friend."

"Bill?"

"Yeah?"

"What are you hiding?"

Damn psychologist. "Look, it's nothing to be–"

Anderson straddled the bench and sat across from Kanter, their knees pressed together. "Bill," she said, talking out the side of her mouth again, "you can't lie to me. I'm a professional, remember?"

"I thought you just worked with kids."

She grinned. "Why do you think I can read you so well?"

Kanter would have laughed if it weren't for the huge knot in his stomach. He thought he felt the back of his head throb where he had hit the rock. "Remember when I mentioned that the Department of Defense had funded much of the MedBed?"

"Yes."

"Well ... I've been approached again."

"When did this happen?"

"When I was kidnapped."

Anderson's face went momentarily blank. "Bill?" She blinked. "What's going on?"

"I wasn't kidnapped by radical fundamentalists. It was the CIA. They staged the whole thing and told me that if I didn't give them usage of the machine for the first two years, they'd..." It suddenly occurred to Kanter that the agent had never threatened anything specific.

"Bill?"

"They'd kill me, or that's what they intimated. They said that they had killed Phillip and Kelly, and they'd do the same to me. Then they beat the shit out of me to make it all look real. They told me to use a fake story about Muslim radicals to make Scott get on board and protect us, except we brought in the calvary, and now the CIA boss is pissed. I'm trying to stall him until I can think of some way to get us all out of this fucked up mess–"

"*Bill!*"

Kanter realized he had bunched the towel into a tight ball.

Anderson scowled. "Why didn't you tell me?"

"I thought it'd be safer if you didn't know."

"My God, Bill, what about Hoop and the Nelsons? What about *Eric*?"

"I know, I know. Stupid, right? But your life wasn't threatened, mine was. I'm not built for all this spy shit!" Something was working its way up from a new and untapped area inside Kanter. He jumped to his feet and hurled the water bottle into the darkness. It clattered to the ground somewhere by the trashcan. He tried to throw the towel, but it opened and landed softly just outside the light around the workout machine. "*Dammit!*" he yelled. He felt Anderson's hand at his shoulder. Her face was drawn tight with worry.

"Bill, calm down."

"Easy for you to say."

"It's doubtful that whoever ... what's his name?"

Kanter thought for a second. "You know, I don't even know

that."

"Are they really CIA?"

Kanter realized that the agent had never said exactly whom he worked for. "I-I don't know."

"God, Bill, what *do* you know?"

"*Listen*." Kanter stepped close. "My life has been threatened, and whoever these people are, they mean business." He pointed at his still-discolored cheek. "I didn't ask for all this. I just wanted to find a better way to image the brain, make some cash, and maybe land a teaching position somewhere warm." Frustrated, he kicked one of the leg curl pads. "Fuck, I hate Chicago." He leaned against the machine's armature.

"I doubt whoever this group is will kill you," Anderson said. "You're too valuable to them."

"I don't know, Tren." Kanter stared at a long tear in the bench's black vinyl and thought about the agent's words. "They know a lot about us and our current situation with Park. They seem pretty determined."

"Anyone with good electronics and a staff of researchers can dig up *anything* on *any*body. You don't even know if they *are* CIA. Say they were. Would it really be that bad if the machine was used to protect our country? Even if you do publish, they'll eventually get the technology, right? At least this way you're involved and possibly have a say in how it's used."

Kanter sat again on the bench and leaned back against the cold metal of the weight bar. "It's not like that, Tren. When I created the MedBed, it was used to save lives, so I could justify letting the DoD have it for a year. But this is different. This machine can be used to extract information. I don't want to be associated with black prisons and torture. There's no way I'll have any say in how they use it. My only chance is to publish before I have to turn it over. I know it will be only a matter of time before the CIA or the DoD or whoever gets their hands on this technology. I just want to delay that as much as possible. Or at least try, you know?"

Anderson sat next to Kanter. She brushed the hair off his forehead. "Is there anyone at the university who can help you publish?"

The knot in Kanter's stomach tightened. "Not really. Even if there were, I wouldn't bring them into this mess. I've already screwed up with you, Hoop, and the Nelsons."

"Not if Cole Strachan has anything to say about it."

No shit. Strachan wouldn't let anything happen to his prize investment.

Anderson moved her hand down to Kanter's. He watched her fingers massage his knuckles and wondered how such a simple gesture could prove so comforting. The clarity was liberating.

"What are you thinking?" she asked.

"That it's about time I started acting like a guy who's going to change the world."

36. Shit happens.

Kanter's revelations had Anderson worried. She thought she had a pretty good understanding of his quirkiness, but now, after tossing and turning through much of the night, she wasn't so sure. Why hadn't he felt comfortable enough to confide in her? It was one thing not to talk about something. But to conceal it, especially when it could have drastic consequences, was, well ... fucked up.

Depending where Anderson stood on the driveway, getting a strong cell signal was a crapshoot. The call failed again, and she thumbed the redial.

"*Tom?*"

"Hi, Trenna. How's it going? I haven't heard from you in ages."

"Oh, okay. We're in sort of a lock-down mode up here." Anderson glanced down and noticed the tip of her flop-flop in a patch of something dark. She realized she was standing where Park had been shot and quickly backed away.

"That doesn't sound too good. I can hear it in your voice. What's up?"

"I can't really get into it all right now. Let's just say that I think I've misjudged Bill."

"How *much* have you misjudged him?"

"Hmm. Maybe a lot."

"Is it bad?"

"It might be."

"What can you tell me?"

Anderson hesitated, then explained the kidnapping, Primus, and the CIA agent – if that's what he was. She tried not to make it sound too bad, but it didn't come out that way. And she definitely didn't go into what happened to Park. Tom was the kind of guy who would have driven to the farm and confronted all of them, especially his sister, and she couldn't deal with that right now. She was more concerned about Kanter and what he might do. If he *was* going to start taking charge, she wanted to make sure he didn't get them all killed in the process.

"Gosh, Tren," Prost said. "This is some serious business. Did Bill elaborate at all on what he planned to do?"

"No."

"Maybe that's a good thing."

"I don't know, Tom." Anderson turned away from the morning sun. "Some people have tried to change the world and gotten themselves, and others, killed."

"Do you think my sister's family is in any danger?"

"I don't think so. These Primus folks have their act really together."

"You said this CIA guy beat up Bill?"

"Kind of. Something about making Scott more protective."

"I don't know, Tren. I don't like the sound of this."

"If it get's too weird, I'll leave with Kim and Eric."

"They can stay with me. I'll call Kim later."

"I'd hold off on mentioning anything just yet. We don't want her freaking out over nothing."

"All right. I'll wait, but keep me abreast of anything that happens. So what do you think Bill is going to do? Maybe you should just have a heart-to-heart with him."

"I was going to this morning."

"Listen, Tren, no invention's worth putting your life on the line for, right?"

Tom's words caused a shift inside Anderson. She had never considered herself a gung-ho type, but Kanter's invention *was* important. Anderson was proud of her service in the military, and even though Iraq had been brutal, she took pride in the fact that she had done something noble. In her civilian practice, she often had found it hard to empathize with people whose problems seemed insignificant compared to what the soldiers in her care had faced. The truth was, though she hated to admit it, that's why she had moved into pediatric care. Looking back, she now felt her only real work of consequence had been with the Chicago Inner City Youth Program. That had been years ago. What had she done with her life since? What happened to the person who wanted to contribute to the world?

"Tren? You there?"

"Yes."

Static crackled. "So what *are* you going to do?"

"Get busy."

*   *   *

The edginess Kanter displayed yesterday had dissipated, as far as Anderson could tell. Given the state of the situation and how he reacted last night, however, it was hard to judge what he might be thinking.

Hoop and one of the Primus guards had ventured to Milwaukee for supplies, so she and Kanter were alone in the lab. He was at the main workstation while Anderson was checking the backups of the Cores.

"Bill?" she asked to his back.

"Yeah?"

"How's it going?"

"It's going."

"I've been doing some thinking."

Kanter swiveled around and leaned back. "And?"

Anderson shoved her hands into the pockets of her jeans. A rivet in the stitching dug at a cuticle. "One of the main reasons I took you up on your offer to come up here was the fact that I wanted to make a difference."

"Tren–"

"Please, let me finish. When I first saw what the machine could do, I knew it was important. But now that we've confirmed so much more, I agree with you … we *do* have an obligation." Her thoughts raced ahead of her words.

"To help the world?" Kanter offered.

"Exactly."

"Tren, I don't know what's going to happen when this all comes to a head. If I had known how screwed up this was going to become, I would have never asked you to join me."

"Too late."

Kanter grinned. "Something to tell the grandkids, eh?"

Anderson saw in his face that he instantly regretted the remark.

Kanter stood and approached her. "I'm really sorry I just said that. I-I wasn't thinking."

"It's okay," she said. "Who knows? Maybe I'll adopt."

"So, what were you going to say?"

"Just that if you need any help with deciding how to proceed, I'm here for you."

"Thanks, Tren. That means a lot."

The email chimed at the main workstation.

Kanter leaned on the counter and read it. "Oh, shit," he said, more to himself.

"What's the matter?" Anderson asked.

"How's your poker face?"

"Why?"

"Strachan is landing in fifteen minutes."

* * *

Strachan's helicopter circled the farm once before it settled on the far side of the main barn. It was a sleek, corporate number that exuded power. There wasn't a single marking on its black fuselage except for a small, bright blue Strachan Media logo on the pilot's door. When Strachan finally emerged, it was as if the President had stepped out; the Primus folks practically peed themselves getting the staging area ready.

"Sorry to drop in like this, Sam," Strachan shouted over the backwash of the rotors. "I have a meeting in Milwaukee, and I thought I'd see how things were going."

Claymore did a little anxiety dance and rose on the balls of his black work boots. "Not a problem, sir. Except the bird," he gave a nod to the helicopter, "is a little conspicuous."

"I know. I have a packed day and this was the easiest. You'll think of something to tell the police." He turned to Kanter and stuck out his hand. "Bill, how are you?"

"Great, Cole," Kanter said, taking it. "I want you to meet Dr. Trenna Anderson."

Strachan's gaze went to Anderson's chest, then to her face. *Pig.*

"I liked your work with inner city kids," Strachan said. "Not many people wanted to touch that one." He thrust out his hand.

Anderson shook it half-heartedly. "Thank you. I'm surprised you know anything about my work."

"I make it my business to know all about the people who work for me."

"I'd like to show you what we're doing up here," Claymore said.

"Actually, Sam, I'd like to talk with Dr. Kanter first." He faced Kanter. "Lets go for a walk, shall we?"

Kanter didn't seem fazed and motioned for Anderson to join.

"Good idea," Strachan said. "You'll want to hear this too, Dr. Anderson."

Strachan had arrived with two bodyguards dressed in the obligatory dark suits. They fell in line behind Anderson and Kanter. The morning sun was higher now, and Anderson was beginning to regret wearing the warm-up top.

"So how's it going, Bill?" Strachan asked. "Having any problems?" They were walking beside the fence that enclosed the perimeter of the main farm. Strachan let his fingers glide along the top rail.

"Okay for the most part," Kanter replied. "But we have run into some snags."

"Really?"

"I don't think it's anything we can't figure out. It's just going to take some time, that's all."

"How much time?" Strachan swished through the tall grass with his low vamp Italian shoes.

"At least another month. Maybe two."

Anderson could tell Strachan was deliberating. His fingers were now tapping a rhythm only he could hear.

"I usually don't like to meddle in my R&D ventures," he said finally. "I believe you research types do better when you're left alone."

"I appreciate that," Kanter said.

"So tell me, what have you discovered so far?"

"It's pretty amazing, Cole. We've confirmed that we can image current and past memories."

"Splendid," Strachan said. Anderson thought she caught a little skip in his stride.

"Wait till you see the scans."

"I can't stay long, so I'll take your word on it."

Usually, Kanter would've worn his disappointment, but his expression remained neutral.

"Tell me more about these problems," Strachan said.

"We keep overloading the system. I think it has to do with the lab's electrical situation. When we scanned Dr. Anderson, she got caught in the machine after a system overload. It took us almost an hour to disconnect her."

"I'm sorry to hear that." Strachan stopped and produced a small leather case from the inside pocket of his suit coat. He removed a cigar and gestured it toward Kanter, but Kanter politely declined.

Anderson was beginning to suspect something was up with Strachan. For a guy who had invested close to five million in an untested theory, he didn't seem too interested in its successes. His attention kept shifting from the landscape to the ritual of clipping the cigar's end. She'd read a theory once that suggested many CEOs had attention deficit disorder. It proposed that ADD allowed them to manage the multitude of problems faced by owners of large corporations. Maybe, in Strachan's case, he just had too much money and regarded Kanter's project as a hobby.

"Nasty habit, these things," Strachan said. "My wife calls me 'ashtray breath.'" He took out a high-tech pocket blowtorch and began scorching the end of the cigar. After a few puffs, the smoke wafted between them. "Bill, let me ask you something. You too, Dr. Anderson."

"Sure," Kanter said, "what do you want to know?"

Strachan took a long drag and let the smoke float off his lips. He looked into the noon sun. Anderson noticed for the first time the thin scar that ran the length of his right eye just above his cheek. "You wouldn't be lying to me, would you?" he asked.

"Of course not," Kanter said calmly. "Why would I need to lie?"

One of the bodyguards sneezed, and Anderson didn't remember them having their coats open.

Strachan stepped closer to Kanter. "Don't *fuck* with me, Bill." He blew a sideways puff of smoke. It drifted across Anderson and irritated her eyes.

"Look, Cole. I don't know what you're thinking, but I can assure you–"

Strachan angrily flicked some ash over the fence. "I know all about your plan to publish your findings. I don't like it when my employees get too independent. It doesn't serve the company's needs."

Kanter's casual act disappeared. "I haven't signed your contract yet," he said. "So I'm not technically *your* employee."

Strachan laughed. "Bill, come on. You've blown through three-quarters of the funding. I'd say that's as good as a signature. Besides, there's a lot more at stake now."

"What do you mean?" Anderson asked.

Strachan glanced at her, eyebrows raised as if to say, "*You talking to me?*" "Strachan Media has been awarded a contract from the Department of Defense. They're very interested in the technology your discovery might spin off."

Kanter appeared on the verge of going postal. "What the hell are you saying? I thought you were going to use this for gaming!"

"Bill, don't worry. I'm a reasonable man. I won't take advantage of you like Genonics did. We can all profit from this. Besides, you and the DoD are old running buddies. I thought you wouldn't mind having them back in the picture."

"What gives you the right to shop *my* invention?"

Strachan picked some tobacco from his teeth. "We've been trying to get a government contract for some time now. Your project was the perfect catalyst to make that happen. In fact, we're working with an old friend of yours, Colonel Marcus. He said to say hello."

"I won't finish," Kanter said. His fists, Anderson noticed, were so clenched his knuckles were white.

"I'd really like you on board, Bill," Strachan said. "It just wouldn't be right not to have you on the project. But if you want to leave, we'll be forced to finish without you."

"You can't," Kanter declared. "I've destroyed all of my notes. Only I know how the machine really works. I designed the main program, remember?"

Strachan drew a relaxed puff from his cigar. "You don't understand," he said. "We already have copies of your notes."

"How could you? They were kept in a safe deposit box."

"Come on, this is America. Everything's available for a price. It was just good business."

"But you don't have the new programming from my work here. I've destroyed that, too. It's all in my head now, and that's where it's going to stay!"

Anderson couldn't believe what she was hearing. "Bill, you *what*?"

Kanter faced her. "It was the only way to protect you and the others."

Strachan smiled through the cigar's haze. "That's not a problem. From what you've said, you haven't gotten very far. Anyway, it doesn't matter. I have people who can reverse-engineer what you've done. Did I mention I play golf with the CEO of the company with the rights to the MedBed? I don't really need you to continue, do I? Plus, I'm sure Hoop can be bought. He got his kid's education to think of."

"You son of a bitch!" Kanter yelled as he raised his fist.

The guard's feet shuffled in the gravel.

Anderson and Kanter turned at the noise, and it took Anderson a second to register the Uzis aimed at them. An icy feeling shot across the top of her head, just like it had back in the campus park.

"Beautiful country up here." Strachan was now leaning on the fence, his right foot on the lowest rail. He was taking in the view and puffing like he was contemplating what he might have for lunch.

Anderson thought about punching him herself. "You're not seriously considering killing us?" she asked. "Bill is a valuable asset to the University, with ties to your company. You wouldn't risk the PR nightmare. And what about Hoop and the Nelsons? Are you going to kill them, too?"

Strachan's shoulders pulled back, as if he needed to fortify the citadel of his corporate nature. He regarded her over the end of the cigar and gestured toward the main barn. "What do you think the Nelsons owe on their new milking equipment? Two hundred thousand? Three, maybe?"

"We can't be bought," Kanter said.

The wind kicked up and blew ash across Strachan's suit. "That's noble, Bill, but people die every day from all sorts of things." He brushed his lapel. "Overdoses ... *car* accidents." He looked at Anderson. "Shit *does* happen."

37. Everything is just fine.

Still dressed, Kanter leaned against the headboard and watched the curtain's pattern of bucking broncos dance in the gentle night breeze. As a boy at his grandfather's cottage, he used to lie awake at night and study the play of the wind on the drapes of his bedroom. He often wondered where the wind came from and what made it move. Tonight, though, his thoughts were far from science.

The door to his room opened a few inches, which caused the curtains to billow. A dark forelock and one of Anderson's hazel eyes appeared in the opening.

"Bill, are you awake?" she whispered and stepped in.

"Can't sleep?" Kanter sat up and patted the bed beside his thigh.

Anderson, still dressed in cargo shorts and a warm-up top, crept over and sat. She scooted close, and a finger of moonlight highlighted the side of her face. Kanter had never noticed the length of her eyelashes.

"No, I can't," she said.

"Me neither."

"What are–?"

Kanter put a finger to Anderson's lips, reached over, and clicked on the clock radio. An old Patsy Cline song, *Walkin' After Midnight*, blared from the speaker. He turned the volume down a little, then motioned her to the closet.

Anderson followed.

Kanter opened the door and shoved his clothes to one side of the rod. Anderson squeezed in and pulled the door shut.

"Sorry." Kanter reached up and clicked the light on. "I don't trust my room."

"Do you think it's been bugged?" Anderson asked.

"I think the whole damn farm is. How else did Strachan know about my plan to publish?"

"Bill, I'm scared."

"That makes two of us."

"What are we going to do?"

Damn good question. "You and Hoop should leave. Go back to Chicago first thing in the morning."

"Bill, no. I can't speak for Hoop, but I'm not leaving."

"Tren, this situation might get dangerous. There's no need for you and Hoop to get more involved than you are. If you can get out now–"

"What about the Nelsons?" Anderson asked. "Primus isn't going to let us leave, and I don't think this CIA guy is going to let word of your invention get out. They probably have our email and cell phones monitored." Anderson's brow creased with concern.

"Tren, what's the matter?"

"I made a call to Tom."

"So?"

She hesitated. "I told him about what was going on."

"Everything?"

"No. Some."

"Tren, my God. That means the CIA – and probably Primus – know that we know."

"I'm sorry, Bill. I wasn't thinking." Anderson rubbed her forehead. "So, what do you think our options are?"

Kanter had been mulling the exact question for much of the night. "I guess my only real choice now is to go with the CIA," he said, not really sure of his conviction. "If they did kill Kelly and Phillip, there's no telling what they'll do."

"Yes, but Strachan implied that *he* killed Kelly and Phillip."

"One of them is bluffing, and my guess is Strachan. The CIA is in the business of making people disappear. Strachan's not."

"I don't know, Bill. Strachan's guards looked like they meant business."

"He's just posturing. I can't believe a guy as high profile as Cole Strachan would cross that line. That's some major shit for a corporation to do, especially one that's not used to dealing in this kind of work. You made him think today with that comment about PR. Did you see the look on his face? His wheels were turning. You're right, if it ever got out that Strachan Media was involved in a muder plot, it would be a public relations nightmare, especially with our attachment to the University."

"Can you trust this *agent*?" Anderson asked.

Kanter had spent the better part of the last four hours trying to figure a way out of their mess. He shrugged. "I guess I'm going to have to. I don't see any real way out of this. I'm screwed any way you look at it. If they want it for the first two years, that's not really too bad, right? The DoD wanted the MedBed for the first year, and that flew by. I probably could find a little funding and kill the time by working on this new idea I've been thinking about ... maybe at some quiet, under-the-radar college. It has to do with monitoring the heart, but with–"

"Bill?"

"Yeah?"

Anderson cracked a tiny, if only slightly sympathetic, smile. "Will you *please* just shut up."

Kanter could only chuckle a little. "Is it me, or is this situation completely fucked up?"

"Oh *no*," Anderson said, sarcastically. "Everything is *just* fine." Her attention moved to the screwdrivers knotted at the ends of the drawstrings on Kanter's U of C sweatshirt. She began playing with the one that hung the lowest. "What are you going to tell the agent?"

"Nothing. He probably knows everything already." Kanter watched her wind the drawstring around her forefinger. She reversed her action and wound again. "I'm really sorry I got you into all this," he said.

Anderson's eyebrows arched, her finger unwinding.

"What?" Kanter asked.

"I was just thinking," she said, feigning fascination with her fingers.

Kanter moved closer. "About?" He could smell the heat from the day on her. It made him want to wrap his hands around her waist and pull all of her against him.

"When I first met you, you were wearing this, and I thought it was the weirdest thing."

"And?" Kanter took her hand into his. God, he wanted to kiss her.

"I've gotten to know you," she said, looking up, "and I think I understand, now, what these mean."

"Really?" He guided a stand of hair off her eyebrow and tucked it gently behind her ear. "Tell me."

Anderson stepped into his embrace. "That you're basically pretty screwed up. But that's what I love about–"

"Hey, Doc? Where are you?"

Both closet doors swung open. "Well." Hoop passed his gaze over them. "It's about time you two quit dancing and got down to it."

"We're not getting down to anything," Anderson said, walking out.

"Hoop, what do you need?" Kanter, feeling like a kid caught in his girlfriend's closet, could barely mask his frustration.

Park was standing in the bedroom doorway.

"Gerald, are you okay?" Anderson started inspecting the dressing on his shoulder. "Oh my God, you're bleeding again."

Kanter could see Park was struggling with the pain.

"I'm fine," he said, although he clearly favored his shoulder.

"Yeah, he's okay," Hoop said, "but the Primus folks are running all over the damn place. Something's up!"

"They look like they're at high-alert," Park said.

Kanter heard footsteps and went to one of the open windows. Anderson came up beside him. Hoop and Park went to the other window.

The moon was almost full, which lit the farm in a patchwork of soft light. Mantis, in full battle gear, was standing in one of the patches about 20 feet from their window. She had a hand cupped to her ear and was scanning the area like she had lost something. Her machine gun hung from her shoulder.

"What's she doing?" Hoop asked.

"She's on a throat mike and ear bud," Park said.

"Like the Secret Service?"

"Yes."

"What's going on?" Fear edged Anderson's voice.

"I don't know," Kanter said, "but it can't be good."

Gibson, also in full battle gear, ran up to Mantis and pointed to Kanter's windows. Kanter couldn't hear the exchange, but it seemed they were arguing. Mantis stepped away and listened intently to her ear bud. They exchanged words again before Gibson sprinted in the direction of the main barn with his machine gun drawn. Mantis swung her weapon off her shoulder and started to approach the house.

"That's the guard for the lab," Hoop said.

Who's guarding the computers? "Hey Mantis," Kanter called out.

She looked up and made a cutting motion across her throat.

Kanter leaned out more. "What's going on?"

Manits started to say something, but the collar of her body armor silently exploded in a crimson spray of pulverized flesh and she crumpled to the ground.

38. They mean business.

Anderson had seen death before, but something about the way the Primus guard was laying made her want to cry. She recognized her as Mantis. After the bullet had torn through the woman's neck, she had collapsed to the ground and crawled into the fetal position. She hadn't screamed or called for help, just balled up and stopped moving. A small puddle of blood gathered near her head.

"Jesus fucking Christ!" Hoop yelled behind Anderson.

Kanter looked in shock and had a death grip on the windowsill. Anderson thought he had said "*Oh my God*," but the words had come out as one.

"I did *not* sign on for this *shit*!" Hoop started pacing the room.

"It's them," Kanter said, still staring down at Mantis.

Hoop stopped and angrily folded his arms. "*Them?*"

Kanter raked both hands through his hair. "Man, there's something I need to tell you."

Hoop marched over, hefted Kanter by the sweatshirt and slammed him against the armoire. The miniature stagecoach on top fell to the pine floor and splintered into pieces.

"What the *hell* is going on?" Hoop growled.

"Let him go!" Anderson said. "He hasn't done anything!"

Kanter was gripping Hoop's wrists and kicking the armoire with his heels. "Damn it," he said, struggling. "Let me explain!"

Hoop let Kanter drop and backed away.

Kanter doubled over and coughed. "When I was kidnapped," he managed, "I was really taken by the CIA." He straightened and rubbed his throat. "They know all about the machine. They said if I didn't give them the technology, they'd make my life hell."

"What about those A-rabs?" Hoop asked.

"They're a CIA cover. They were used to influence Scott. You got to understand. These people know everything about us. Everything!"

"They threatened his *life*," Anderson said. "Bill, tell him about Strachan."

"What about Strachan?" Hoop's nostrils flared.

"He's tight with the Defense Department, and he's threatening to kill me if I don't cooperate. The whole gaming angle was just a bunch of bullshit."

"That's it," Hoop said, "I'm out of here!"

"Just how do you plan to leave?" Park asked.

Hoop glared. “Who the hell *are* you?”

“If you leave now, you’ll be killed.” Park was leaning against the window frame and clutching his arm. The blood spot on the gauze had grown. “Whoever is attacking, their bullets went through that guard’s collar armor.”

“Listen to me,” Kanter said. “These CIA people will kill just because it’s the easiest option.”

“I don’t get it,” Hoop said. “Why are they attacking?”

“I’ve been stalling.”

“*What?*”

“I thought if I could stall them, I could publish my findings before I had to hand over the technology. The farm is probably bugged, and they found out.”

“Preemptive strike,” Park said.

“Do you even know if it *is* the CIA?” Hoop asked.

Kanter hesitated. “No.”

“Then I say we just let whoever it is fight it out with Primus, and we’ll deal with the winner.”

“Deal with who?” Nelson asked from the doorway. The Mossberg was propped against his thigh and pointed up.

Claymore appeared at his side, night-vision goggles perched atop his head. “We’re under attack!” Claymore said. “I’ve already lost one of my people, but we killed at least one of theirs.”

A tensioned silence permeated the room. Claymore and Nelson seemed to have picked up on it.

“What’s going on?” Claymore asked.

“There’s something I need to tell you,” Kanter said. He explained the situation again.

Nelson and Claymore took it in like they were receiving special mission orders. Anderson had worked with soldiers like this, and she was always amazed at how they could remain perfectly calm, even in the face of something like an elite CIA black ops squad.

"Why didn't you tell me this before?" Claymore demanded.

Kanter hesitated. "I didn't think I should."

"Hell with it. It doesn't matter now." Claymore turned to Nelson. "This is going to get ugly. It'll be Special Forces against Special Forces."

Nelson shook his head. "Son of a bitch," he muttered, "I knew this was going to be a bad deal." He pointed angrily at Kanter. "When this is over, I want you gone."

"Where's your family, Scott?" Claymore asked, eyeing the Mossberg.

"In the basement. The old coal room. They should be safe there."

Claymore pulled the collar of his body armor aside and touched his throat mike. "Turner, these aren't the rag heads we thought. Probably ex-special-op types. Mercenaries, most likely. Maybe even Agency types. Pass the word and arm up. I need you at the main house to secure the Nelson family. They're in the basement." He turned to the room. "These people are using some goddamn impressive tech. The one we tagged got through our outer perimeter like it didn't exist. We think they're on foot about a click from here in the outer fields, so we're going to have to act fast." He looked at Anderson. "You're former Navy, right?"

"Yes," Anderson said.

Claymore pulled a gun from under his body armor and handed it to her. "You're going to need this."

Anderson recognized it as a Heckler and Koch .45. It was standard issue; a Marine friend of hers said he never slept without his. It had a compact laser sight and a silencer screwed into its barrel. Claymore reached over and clicked the laser to emit a red beam.

"I had it set for night-vision," he said. "You're ready to go."

Anderson checked the safety, then tucked it into the back of her shorts. She caught Kanter staring.

"You four come with me," Claymore said. "Mr. Nelson, you need to be with your family. Turner should be here soon. He'll meet you downstairs."

"Where are we going?" Kanter asked.

"To secure the lab. It's thick-walled with high windows and will offer some protection."

All the lights were off in the house, which made descending the stairs a little tricky. Anderson followed directly behind Claymore and could hear the faint chatter from his ear bud. As they rounded the landing, someone screamed a string of expletives into Claymore's ear.

"Come on, people," he said. "We've got to hustle it up!"

"Has something happened?" Anderson asked.

Claymore's only reply was to start taking the stairs two at a time.

Anderson stepped off the last stair, and Hoop's fingers dug into her shoulder. She could feel his breath on the back of her neck.

"We're in a fucking nightmare," he whispered.

As they approached the front door, Claymore hand-signaled for them to crouch. Nelson left their line and low-trotted back toward the kitchen.

"On my mark," Claymore said. "I'll open the front door, and we move onto the porch as low as we can without crawling. Got it?"

Anderson gave a thumbs-up, and everyone followed suit.

"Anderson, you move with me to the left. Kanter, Hoop, Park, to the right." Claymore reached for the doorknob, held his hand there, then yanked it open.

Anderson scurried onto the porch in such a low squat she almost hit her chin with her knees. She had instinctively drawn the HK and clicked off its safety.

Kanter and Park shuffled behind an old rattan couch, but Hoop stumbled and ended up crawling to it.

Claymore signaled for them to hold their positions. He edged his way to the long planter box that ran along the porch's front railing. It, along with the tall hedge, made for some cover, but no real protection. He peered over the top of the planter and motioned for Anderson to join him.

Anderson came up to Claymore's side on hands and knees.

"The best route to the lab is this way," Claymore whispered, motioning to the right with a crisp jab of his hand. "We're going to have to run like hell, but it's our only option. You think those three can do it without tripping all over themselves?"

"Bill's in great shape," she said. "Park was a Marine in Iraq, but he's hurting pretty badly."

"What about Mr. Dreadlocks?"

Anderson knew Hoop could run the distance. It was his mental state that worried her. He had flipped out upstairs and didn't look much better cowering behind the Nelson's cheap outdoor furniture. But given the situation, there wasn't a choice.

"He'll be fine," she lied.

"When's the last time you fired a weapon?" Claymore asked.

Iraq. "It's been awhile."

"Don't worry," he said, "it'll come back. It always does." Claymore glanced at the others. "On my mark, we'll line up and low-run toward the lab, but *follow* me. I'm going to go around that shed over there." He pointed again.

"Cover?" Anderson asked.

Claymore nodded and began to stand, but a figure about 10 yards from the front porch caught his attention. Claymore dropped to his hands and knees. He motioned for them to scrunch down as low as they could. Hoop went to his stomach and looked ready to dig through the wooden porch to get even lower.

Anderson pointed to the man, then to Claymore.

Claymore shook his head and mouthed, *"Not mine."*

Anderson lay flat and peered through a small gap in the hedge. The man was dressed in black and hooded like some kind of ninja warrior. High-tech equipment encircled his waist, and he didn't appear to be wearing body armor. His night-vision goggles were half the size of Primus's and hugged his face like an insect.

Claymore also had gone flat and was lining up his gun through the hedge.

Anderson watched a red dot traverse the front of the ninja's stomach. The man must have sensed something. He raised his machine gun and aimed right at their position.

Claymore squeezed, and his gun made a muffled crack.

The chest of the ninja puffed out about the size of a baseball, and he was lifted off his feet and thrown backwards.

"Shit!" Hoop said.

Anderson angrily gestured for silence.

The ninja was flat on his back and not moving. Claymore, his gun still trained, peered over the planter.

The ninja struggled to a sitting position and aimed a handgun.

Anderson raised her HK and sighted him through the hedge when a loud gunshot lacerated the air behind her.

The ninja's stomach tore open. Bits of flesh and blood burst from his side. He screamed and slumped over.

Anderson, her ears ringing, opened her eyes. She was spread-eagled on the porch, her chin resting on shards of glass.

"What in the goddamn *hell*?" Claymore whisper-yelled.

Both he and Anderson turned and saw Nelson standing behind what was left of the living room picture window.

"Get back with your family, soldier!" Claymore said.

Nelson lowered the Mossberg as smoke curled from its barrel. "You're welcome," he said before he retreated into the darkness of the house.

"Fucking boy scout." Claymore stood. "We're trying this again, people. On my mark, file up and follow me."

Anderson and the others fell in. They ran down the porch stairs and past the dead ninja. Hoop almost tripped sidestepping the blood spray from the guy's stomach. When they rounded the shed, Claymore made them hold their position.

"Everyone okay?" he asked, breathless.

Everyone gave a thumbs-up, except Hoop. He seemed to be at the brink of panic; his forehead was slick with sweat.

"Are you all right?" Anderson asked.

Hoop glowered. "Do I *look* all right?"

“Listen up,” Claymore said. “The lab is about fifty yards from this position. We’re going to run in a kind of zigzag pattern. It’s a bit of a distance, but I know we can make it.” A gunshot echoed through the farm, and Claymore’s expression went grave.

“What was that?” Kanter asked.

“I don’t know,” Claymore said. “We’re all using silencers. It better not be Nelson.”

Another gunshot rang out.

“Get in line,” Claymore barked. “Ready? Go!”

The zigzagging made it seem to take forever to reach the lab. Anderson was still behind Claymore, and the guy could run pretty well, considering he was probably in his 60s. About halfway, Anderson caught a figure out of the corner of her eye. He was hauling ass across the open area between the main barn and the house. In the moonlight, it appeared to be one of the ninjas, but it turned out to be Gibson. He came up next to Hoop and matched their pace.

“Whoever these people are,” he said between gasps, “there’re coming in heavy!”

“How many?” Claymore asked over his shoulder.

“Hard to tell, maybe–” But the next sound he made was a tortured, guttural cry.

Anderson turned to see what was left of Gibson’s right shoulder splattered across the front of Hoop. There hadn’t been any sound, except for Hoop shrieking like a teenage girl. Gibson fell into Hoop, but amazingly was still running. Maybe it was the moonlight, but Hoop’s eyes looked positively backlit. He shouldered Gibson away and took off around Anderson.

“Stay in line!” Claymore yelled.

The whole scene slowly unfolded like a video on frame advance. Gibson went down screaming and did a forward roll. Claymore tried to catch Hoop as he ran past, but missed and nearly tripped. Anderson clipped the back of Claymore's leg and stumbled, but she grabbed his body armor and righted herself.

When she looked up, she saw Hoop's form running full out toward the lab. Before she could yell for him to stop, a faint crack about 100 yards to her right cut her off.

Hoop's upper body jerked, and he began stumbling forward, his arms flailing.

"No!" Anderson screamed.

Another crack. Hoop recoiled and twisted sideways. He landed hard on his upper back, rolled several times, and came to rest in a bright patch of moonlight.

39. Wrong answer.

Anderson stopped, and Kanter slammed into the back of her, almost knocking them both to the ground. He had heard muffled gunfire but didn't know if Hoop had been hit. The dumb ass had taken off like a running back, and Kanter feared the worst. He looked over Anderson's shoulder and saw Hoop's body sprawled in the dirt as if carelessly tossed there by a giant.

Claymore screamed directions, but Kanter had disconnected into a vacuum of fear. It never occurred to him that the CIA might storm the farm when its patience ran out. He'd thought that destroying all of the data would make him the sole target. But after seeing Hoop's body, Kanter realized that he had actually placed everyone else in the

CIA's crosshairs. They were now, as the agent had predicted, in some serious and deep shit.

Claymore angrily pointed to the lab. "Keep *running*!"

Kanter took hold of Anderson's waist. He tried to push her forward, but she broke from his grip.

"No!" She cupped her weapon with both hands and took aim in the direction of the gunfire.

"Trenna, stop!"

Anderson squeezed off three rounds before Kanter tackled her. A fourth went into the dirt in front of them.

"Those assholes shot Hoop!" she said, struggling.

Kanter spun her around by the shoulders. Her face was etched with hate.

Park ran up, clutching his arm. "We have to keep moving," he said and winced.

Even in the dim light, Kanter could tell Park was in bad shape. He was hunched over, clutching his shoulder. Blood seeped between his fingers.

Anderson shrugged free of Kanter's grip and sprinted toward Hoop.

"Get in the lab *now*!" Claymore already was kneeling next to Hoop's body and waving Anderson away.

"What about Hoop?" she asked.

"I'll take care of him. Go!"

As Kanter passed, he could see blood sprayed across Hoop's chest. *Oh, God, please don't let him be dead*. Kanter glanced back and saw Park staggering. "Come on, man. You can make it." He slowed to let Park catch up.

A burst of muffled gunfire kicked up gouts of dirt in front of Hoop's body. Claymore crouched and started firing.

"Go! Go!" he screamed at them while he fired.

Kanter took Park by his good arm and helped him run.

Anderson made it first and opened the outer door.

"Hurry!" she yelled and motioned them in.

Kanter practically shoved Park inside the hallway. Anderson followed.

"Help Park," he said to her. "He's really bleeding."

Anderson kicked open the screen door, and they disappeared into the lab's darkness.

Kanter turned to the open doorway. "Come on!" he yelled. Past Claymore, he could see Gibson who, remarkably, was sitting up and unloading his machine gun with one arm. The sporadic light from the rounds revealed the severity of his wound. Gibson let loose another burst, then motioned Claymore to the lab.

"Go Sam!" he yelled, and laid down another round of covering fire.

Claymore's head swiveled in indecision; he stood and sprinted for the lab.

"How's Hoop?" Kanter asked.

"Shut the door!" Claymore ordered as he ran past.

Kanter pulled the door and bolted it. He tried the lights, but there was no power.

Claymore twisted on a small flashlight and began interrogating the lab with its beam. "Do you have any flashlights?" The sound of Gibson crying out eclipsed the question. The firing stopped. "God-*damn* it," he said through clenched teeth.

The moonlight from the high bank of windows illuminated the

lab in narrow slivers. Kanter felt his way to the main workstation and found a flashlight in the bottom drawer. It was a big Maglite, and its long black casing felt good in Kanter's hands. He held it like a baseball bat and wondered how it might fare as a weapon. "We've got to go back for them," he said and clicked on the flashlight.

"Negative!" Claymore said. "My team knew the risks."

"But Hoop is out there!" Anderson said. "He could be bleeding to death. You checked him. How was he?"

"I don't know." Claymore shook his head. "I sprayed some gel, but I couldn't see an exit wound."

"Where was he shot?" Anderson asked.

"Right side, just above the hip bone." Claymore stepped away and started barking orders into his throat mike.

"God, no." Anderson, her hands to her mouth, glanced at Kanter, then toward the front door. "Bill, we have to do something. He could be dying out there." She walked past Kanter's light.

"Tren, stop." He took her arm and pulled her around. "You can't. It's too dangerous."

"We don't leave anyone behind."

"Tren, you can't go out there." He grasped her other shoulder. "Even if he is alive, getting yourself killed won't help him. We'll have to go back when it's safe."

Park coughed and spit. Kanter swung his flashlight around and found him slouched against one of the Cores. His shoulder and arm were streaked in blood.

"Can you look at Park's shoulder, please?" Kanter asked.

Anderson forced a nod, walked over, and examined Park's bandage. "It looks like some of his stitches have torn open." She pulled off several sheets from a roll of paper towel, soaked them with bottled water, and began wiping the blood away.

Kanter watched her and thought of the rage she had displayed outside. He knew she was a strong woman, but to stand up and shoot back at an elite CIA team was just plain ballsy. Kanter warily eyed the lab's front door and thought about Hoop lying in the dirt, dead or dying. The guilt was overwhelming.

Don't go there, he thought. *There's too much else at stake.* Hoop had broken from the line and gotten himself killed, and there just wasn't a fucking thing Kanter could have done to stop it.

Claymore was pacing, and panic tinged his voice. "Taylor, how many are there?... What's our status? Taylor, are you there? Simmons? *Mitchell*?!"

"What's wrong?" Kanter asked.

"Son of a bitch!" Claymore's beam swung around. "I've lost contact with my team."

"You mean what's left of your team," Park said.

Claymore's flashlight found Park. "We don't know that yet."

One of the high windows shattered. Something metal landed near the electrical box and rolled to a stop by the U of C trashcan.

"They're going to storm us!" Claymore yelled.

A hissing sound rose near the trashcan, followed by a faint smell of sulfur. Smoke began filling the room.

Claymore started shoving the workstations together. "Come on, we need to build a barrier!"

Kanter and Anderson pushed three of the computer stacks in front of the screen door. Park shoved a filing cabinet up against them with his hip.

The lab quickly filled with an eye-stinging haze. Kanter couldn't catch his breath; Anderson and Park were experiencing coughing fits.

"Get behind the desks!" Claymore said between hacks.

Kanter, Anderson, and Park waved their way through the smoke and crouched behind the old wooden desks they used for storage. They ripped off several sheets of paper towels, wet them with water, and held them to their mouths.

Claymore pulled out all the ammo he had. "Here," he said and handed Anderson a new clip for her gun. He pulled two small objects, each about the size of a bar of soap, out of his thigh pockets. He handed them to Kanter and Park. They were flat gray with a thin metal armature running from top to bottom.

"These are high-density frag grenades," Claymore said. "Pull this pin and toss it in an arc. Don't throw it hard, just an easy lob. And only after I tell you to."

It weighed heavily in Kanter's hand. "Okay," he said, although he wondered if it would make any difference.

Claymore jammed a new cartridge into his machine gun and looked at Park. "How bad are you, son? Can you throw that, if needed?"

"I'll throw it to Milwaukee if I have to," Park said through a cough.

"Good. Now listen up. This room is big. The smoke's already beginning to dissipate. They'll probably batter that door down and come in on each side. Anderson, I want you to focus on the right side of the door. I'll handle the left. It'll take them a bit to push all that out of the way. Kanter, Park – be set to throw, but only on my command. Everyone ready?"

Kanter, Anderson, and Park nodded.

"All right then." Claymore cocked his machine gun. "Let's do this."

Several minutes passed. Kanter optimistically began to think that Claymore's team might have defeated the CIA when the front door of the lab exploded. The blast pressed Kanter to the ground and showered him with what was left of the three computer stacks. It felt like a gigantic airbag had gone off in his face. His ears were ringing.

Claymore signaled to Anderson, and they both came up shooting. His machine gun hardly made a sound as he sprayed the opening that had been the front hall and screen door. Anderson ticked off shot after shot like she had never left Iraq.

Claymore signaled Anderson to stop. Kanter peered over the top of the desk and saw two red laser beams cross in the smoke and sweep the lab.

"Sam?" someone called out. It sounded like the agent.

Claymore looked at Kanter, his brow knitted. "Do you recognize the voice?" he whispered.

Kanter nodded. "It's the head guy from the group that took me."

Claymore slammed another cartridge into his machine gun. "Yeah?" he called out.

"What are they paying you at Primus?"

Claymore glanced back at Kanter, even more puzzled. "None of your business!"

"Come on, Sam. What are you making? Over two fifty? I doubt it."

"Who are you?"

"I'm curious. Is your life worth whatever they're paying you? I mean, think about it. We've tagged your assets, so it's just you and, well, hello Dr. Anderson. So how 'bout it, Sam? Do we have a deal? Let's make it an even three-hundred thousand and call it a night."

Claymore rose, sprayed the opening, and scrunched back down behind the desk. Shell casings littered the floor around Kanter.

"Sam?" the agent called out.

"Yeah?"

"Wrong answer."

There was a muffled bang, and something passed through the desk Claymore was behind. It obliterated one of the drawers, impacted the back wall, and exploded. It had grazed the top of Claymore's thigh, but his wail made Kanter think it must have done more damage. Kanter passed a wad of paper towels that Claymore pressed against the wound. The paper quickly reddened.

"You gotta love our R and D folks," the agent said. "That bullet is kind of like a mini cruise missile. It goes through old desks like *budder*."

Claymore, his eyes tight with pain, glanced to the grenade Kanter held.

"You want us to throw these?" Kanter asked.

Claymore frantically nodded. He pressed the whole roll to his thigh and groaned.

"On three," Kanter said to Park, "we pull and throw."

"Okay," Park said.

"One–"

"Gentlemen, I wouldn't arm those," the agent said.

Kanter and Park froze.

"Sam, you know better than to use those cheap French units. They're going to hurt you a lot more than us. What do you have left in the clip, Trenna? Four, maybe six rounds?"

"Okay!" Claymore said. "We're coming out."

He heaved his machine gun over the desk. Anderson followed suit. Kanter helped Claymore to his feet. Park struggled but managed it with his good arm. Anderson stood with her hands on top of her head.

Red laser beams jittered through the smoke, and two figures approached. Both were hooded and wore night-vision gear. The ninja uniform turned out to be a black mesh body suit of some type of armor. Parts of its surface were covered with tiny electronic elements. Their vests were multi-compartmented military jobs, which made the whole outfit seem like the Borg had met Prada. The man on the right aimed a weapon that appeared more video camera than gun.

The second figure had a similar weapon, though without the optical gear. When he peeled off his night-vision, it made a sucking sound as it released from his skin. It was the agent from the motel room and Wal-Mart.

"Damn, that thing is hot." The agent tossed his night-vision onto one of the red tool carts, where it curled into a ball. He pulled back his hood and eyed Anderson. "You can put your arms down, Trenna. You're not a prisoner."

Anderson lowered her arms and folded them across her chest.

"How are you holding up, Bill?" the agent asked.

"What do you think?"

The agent grinned. "Go get the Nelsons and bring them here," he said to his partner. "And restore the power so we can have some lights."

The guy, still aiming the video weapon, gave a crisp nod and slowly backed out through the large smoldering opening that just minutes prior had been the lab's foyer. Kanter could see out to the yard and watched him zigzag between Hoop and Gibson's bodies.

"Who the hell are you?" Claymore asked.

Ignoring the question, the agent sat on the edge of one of the tool carts, and positioned his weapon to raise and shoot with minimal effort. He unzipped a shoulder pocket, and dug a cigarette out from a pack and placed it in his mouth, then fished a chrome lighter from the shoulder pocket, flicked it open, lit up, and stuffed it back into the pocket. He did all this with his free hand, and the action looked almost choreographed.

"You have, well, *had* a good team, Sam." He gestured with the cigarette. "I haven't lost a person in years, let alone three. Do you think Strachan would spring for a collection crew?"

Claymore didn't answer.

The agent's eyes went to Claymore's wound. "Did that bullet cut any muscle?"

Claymore pressed the only clean area left on the roll against the wound and grimaced.

"Look, Sam, I know we can work something out so everyone goes home happy." He took a long drag.

"Fuck you," Claymore said.

This kind of tactic could get them all killed. Kanter grabbed Claymore's arm.

"*Listen*, man," he said. "You need to start cooperating. These people are–"

A muted crack interrupted. Something ripped Claymore out of Kanter's grip. He flew backwards, almost clipping the MedBed, and landed about five feet from the back wall. The bed bowed and scooted back.

Anderson screamed.

Kanter's face felt wet. He cautiously touched it, and came away with bits of flesh and blood.

"What were you about to say?" The agent bit down on his cigarette and bared his yellow teeth in a grotesque smile. Smoke rose from the barrel of his weapon.

The lights came on with a jarring brightness, and sparks popped from a destroyed computer.

Kanter couldn't process the question and glanced back at Claymore's body, now fully illuminated. There was a horrific wound in the center of his flak vest that exposed part of his ribcage. Blood and bright pink clumps of torn tissue were splattered across the vest. Kanter swallowed the urge to throw up and looked away.

"*Bill*?"

Kanter cautiously lifted his eyes.

"Finish your sentence." The agent flicked some ash. "These people *are*..."

"I-I don't remember."

"Bad mother*fuckers*."

"*What*?"

"That's what you wanted to *say*." The agent stubbed out the cigarette on top of the cart. "And do you know something? We are."

40. Blah, blah, blah.

A tear had already slid down Anderson's cheek before she realized she was crying. It had happened unconsciously, probably because she had reached her limit of seeing death. She tried not to look at Claymore, but his lifeless body was unavoidable, sprawled in an ever-growing pool of blood.

"*Okay*!" Kanter yelled. "You can have the damn machine. Just stop *killing* people." He yanked out his shirttail and frantically wiped his face.

Anderson fought for control of her emotions, but her mind returned to a severely wounded Marine who had been brought to her surgical company. The forward resuscitative unit had written his name in black marker across his bare chest. *Taylor*. After trying to save him, the docs had ordered Taylor moved to the triage area where casualties were sent to die. In this case, it had been a kitchen, and she always wondered if the soldiers ever knew their last moments were spent near where some chef had prepared Hussein's *yalanchi*.

She had held Taylor's hand all the way to the stainless-steel counter, whispering across his swollen eyes how proud she was of him, until a corpsman had put a stethoscope on the bloodied "Y" and shaken his head.

Now, Anderson couldn't stop looking at Claymore's body, wondering what his name would look like in black marker. She tore her eyes away and for a second was gripped in the sheer atrocity of it all. A hand grasped her shoulder.

"Tren, are you okay?" Kanter's face still had blood speckled across it.

"Yes," she said, toughening.

"It's going to work out," Kanter said, although not convincingly.

"It will, Dr. Anderson." The agent let his eyes drill into her. "Because Bill is going to cooperate fully. Aren't you, Bill?"

Kanter let go and lunged. "You *fucker*!"

The agent jerked his gun up. "Bill." He jabbed the barrel into Kanter's sternum. "Don't tempt me. Now get back there, before I go tactical on you."

Kanter held his ground, but another jab convinced him to return to Anderson's side.

"Jesus, Bill. Don't do that again." The agent wiped his brow with the back of his hand. "I'm under a lot of pressure here, and you might end up like Sam over there."

The Nelsons appeared out of what little smoke remained in the air. The agent's partner trailed behind them. He had taken off his headgear and held his weapon aimed at their backs. His baby face and spiky peroxided hair reminded Anderson of a young Johnny Rotten.

Oddly, Eric appeared more concerned than terrified as he clutched his mother's hand. Kimberly, though, looked on the verge of a psychotic break. Her husband coolly ushered in his family. Nelson, Anderson noticed, seemed to be assessing every detail of the situation. His eyes surveyed Claymore's body, and he steered his family away. Kimberly glanced at Claymore and gasped. Eric tried to look over one of the desks, but Kimberly pulled him back.

"Ah, the Cleavers." The agent lit another cigarette. "Throw something over that, will you?" He exhaled and gestured toward Claymore's body.

The agent's partner, still training his weapon on the Nelsons, took Kanter's U of C sweatshirt off the back of one of the chairs and draped it over Claymore's chest and face.

"Stand with him," the agent instructed the Nelsons and pointed with his weapon toward Park. "I'm sorry you had to get mixed up in all this, mister?..."

"Park."

"Well, Mr. Park, maybe I can make this worth your while."

The Nelsons shuffled over and huddled next to the Cores.

Kanter stepped forward. "Can't you just deal with me?" He looked at the Nelsons. "They don't need to be a part of this."

The agent raised his hand. "Bill, remember? The stress?" He made a shooing gesture before he sucked in a long drag and puffed out two tiny smoke rings. “First off,” he said after savoring a third, “I want to formally apologize to the Nelsons.”

“Who are you?” Anderson asked. If they might die tonight, she at least wanted to know who was responsible.

The agent scrutinized her through the third ring. “My name is Smith,” he said dryly.

Sure it is. “Okay, Mr. *Smith*. Who do you work for? The CIA?”

Smith half-grinned. “Rarely. They don’t pay well.” He shifted his attention back to the Nelsons. “On behalf of the American government, I want to apologize for any and all inconveniences, blah, blah, blah. The bottom line, Scott, is that we’d like to compensate you for any damages, as well as for your family’s silence in this matter. I know you’re strapped for cash, so take a moment and think of a number.” He crushed out the second cigarette on top of the cart. “As an added bonus, if you want to relocate, we might be able throw that in, too. Maybe Florida. You could grow oranges. I’m sure they’re easier than cows.” He smiled at Eric. “And a lot less messy, right kiddo?”

Park suddenly threw his arm around Kanter’s shoulder, grabbed his throat, and jammed a black pistol to his temple. “Put your weapons on the floor and kick them to me,” he ordered.

Park had moved so fast and with such precision that Anderson wondered if he’d somehow injected himself with epinephrine. She’d seen the docs use it in Iraq, but usually it made a soldier sit up, not move like this. And what was with Park’s voice? He’d said “*veapon*” with an accent that sounded ... *German*?

41. Mercy.

Smith and his companion trained their weapons onto Park in unison.

"Whoa there," Smith cautioned. "Take it easy."

Kanter hardly noticed Park talking like a Nazi; his entire focus was held by the thumb and forefinger that grasped his throat like a pair of pliers. When Kanter tried to resist, Park dug in even harder. The muzzle of the gun felt like a baseball bat against Kanter's temple.

Smith's eyes narrowed. "Look Park – whoever you are – don't be a hero."

"If you shoot me," Park said, "my reflexes will pull this trigger and kill the only man who knows everything about the invention. You won't have, what is the word, *squat*?"

Park's hold was so close Kanter could feel Park's breath on his cheek. The German accent finally registered on him, which made the whole situation even more terrifying.

Smith frowned. "How do you know that Bill destroyed all his notes?"

Park's grip tightened, and specks of white shot across Kanter's vision.

"*Sir*?" the other agent asked.

Smith, scrutinizing Park, placed a hand on the barrel of the video gun and pushed it down. "Hold on," he said.

The other agent relaxed. "Sir, we don't need Kanter. We can tap the CIA for all the data. Let them buy Strachan out."

Smith shook a finger at Park. "Wait a minute. Aren't you with DARPA's Frankfurt bureau? There was a guy there, Carl something–"

"Silence!" Park yelled. "Put down your weapons!"

The other agent raised the video gun.

Smith jumped off the cart. "*I* give the orders around here!"

Kanter thought, *I'm going to die right here-* A loud crack exploded next to his ear. He felt himself scream, but all he could hear was an excruciatingly high-pitched ringing. He reached for his temple, expecting to come away with bits of his own head, when he saw the other agent stumble backwards.

The dark hole in the middle of man's left eyebrow was hardly wide enough for one finger. The shock on his face as he groped at the wound was sickening. He backed into a desk, toppled over and landed behind it with one of his boots sticking up. "CAT" was embossed in thick yellow rubber on its black sole.

Above the ringing, Kanter heard something that reminded him of the time he ran over a dog. He turned and saw Kimberly screaming. She had Eric pressed against her leg; a hand barely covered his eyes.

Kanter felt himself jerked back into a standing position. The pliers reappeared at his throat. The muzzle of Park's gun was hot from the discharge and burned as it dug into the soft spot at Kanter's temple.

Smith wheeled around to see his partner, then Park. "God*damn* it!" he screamed, spittle flying.

Park shook Kanter and pressed the gun hard. "Do what I say," he said, the German accent even more pronounced, "or I *will* kill Dr. Kanter."

Smith, eyes wild, stood there seething.

"You want Kanter alive, yes?" Park asked.

Smith's expression relaxed, like he suddenly didn't give a shit. "Hell with it," he muttered. He raised his weapon.

Oh God! Kanter squeezed his eyes shut, anticipating the pain. Every muscle involuntarily flexed.

The shot echoed.

"Son of a *bitch*!" Smith yelled.

Kanter forced his eyes open. Smith had dropped to one knee and clutched his forearm. Blood oozed between his fingers. His weapon had landed at Park's feet. Something silvery edged into Kanter's periphery. He recognized the vintage Colt .45 he'd seen on the Nelson's dining room table. Its long barrel seemed out of place compared with the tech Smith had wielded.

"Pretty crappy for a Marine sharpshooter," Smith said sarcastically as he struggled to stand.

Nelson jammed the muzzle of the Colt against Smith's forehead and shoved him back against the desk the other agent had flipped over. Smith tried to hold firm, but he slumped to the floor.

Park kicked Smith's weapon behind them and pivoted Kanter to face Nelson, who was now in his sights. "Think of your family, Scott. You don't want them to see you kill anyone."

Nelson wore the creepy stare Anderson had once described to Kanter. She'd seen it in soldiers who had been pushed too far – a kind of predatory *what-the-hell* attitude, as if they could close a door on their rational selves and instantly become cold-blooded killers. Now, with the Colt leveled and cocked, Nelson looked like he had closed his door and thrown away the key.

"He's right, Scott. You're better than this."

It was Anderson. She slowly approached Nelson, her hand outstretched to take the Colt.

"You left this anger back in the Zone, right?" she asked.

Nelson gave her a steely sideways look.

"Scott." Anderson's hand was an arm's length from the Colt. "*Please*."

"Trust in the Lord, with all thine heart," someone said. "And lean not unto thine own understanding. In all thy ways acknowledge Him, and He shall direct thy paths."

The voice was full and oddly unfamiliar. It took a second for Kanter to realize it was Eric. He stepped from behind Kimberly and casually walked in front of the Colt. The end of its barrel was barely an inch from his nose. His eyes fluttered and then calmed.

Kimberly reached for him. "Eric, stop–"

Nelson, staring at his son, gestured for Kimberly to hold her ground.

Eric raised his eyes to his father. "You have many days ahead of you." His voice was deeper somehow. "Don't give in to temptation."

Kimberly gasped and covered her mouth. Park looked on in amazement. Smith, cradling his wrist, stared as well. Anderson looked on with a strange mix of reverence and awe.

Nelson slowly lowered the Colt.

Eric smiled and walked over to Smith. He put a hand to his shoulder. "Andrei, do you remember what your father told you, in your basement in Moscow?"

Smith's face filled with disbelief. "How do you know *that*?"

Eric leaned near and whispered something into Smith's ear. "Mercy," Eric said, pulling back, "triumphs over judgment."

Smith started to respond, but reconsidered and looked away.

Eric took Smith's head with both hands and held it with reverence. "In *Him* we have redemption through His blood, the forgiveness of our trespasses, according to the riches of *His* grace. You must learn to forgive." He stared at Smith for a second, then kissed him just above the dent in his forehead.

Kanter was utterly gripped by the spectacle. He couldn't quite process what he was witnessing. Was it a miracle? God incarnate? Just another one of Eric's personalities?

Kimberly was crying quietly; Nelson moved to comfort her.

Eric turned and regarded Park, who had retrained his aim on Smith. He considered Park with what seemed benevolent curiosity and motioned him closer. Park shuffled forward, bent to one knee and bowed his head. Eric took his head with both hands and whispered what sounded like Latin into his ear.

Smith, still sitting on the floor, shifted his weight. Nelson swiftly drew the Colt, but Smith waved it off.

Eric stepped back and motioned for Park to raise his head. "You've done well, my son. But there is much more to do. Are you able to serve the father?"

"*Ja ihre anmut.*" Park stood, but it was obvious that his newfound strength was waning. He raised a shaky aim onto Smith.

Eric passed a knowing gaze across each of them, then shuffled over to Kimberly and took her hand. When he smiled up at her, innocence had returned to his eyes.

42. I wouldn't want to be in your shoes.

A silence settled that felt like what Anderson's C.O. had called "the infinite moment" – the few seconds after a doc called the time of death for a soldier. It was an unspoken time when everyone in the OR could reflect or say a silent prayer. And now Anderson was thinking about her own faith, and why it wasn't a larger part of her life.

"Get up," Park said.

Smith gathered himself and stood. He was still holding his forearm, but the bleeding appeared to have slowed.

"Your mission has failed."

"Monumentally," Smith said.

"You're in the business of making people disappear, yes?" Park asked.

"Sometimes."

"I think that is what *you* should do."

Anderson could see Smith working out the alternatives in his head. As he surveyed the lab, he rubbed some of the torn fabric from the shirt under his body suit against the wound. The fabric dissolved into a foam that spread across the gash. Anderson had read that the military had developed smart fabric that could clot a wound in seconds, but she'd never seen it up close.

Smith announced to no one in particular: "I'm not being paid enough for this bullshit." He reached for one of the pouches on his vest.

"Don't!" Park ordered.

"Relax. It just some tape." Smith removed a small roll of clear medical tape. Claymore's body drew his attention. "It's a good thing your farm is isolated, Scott," he said, wrapping his forearm. "You'll find three Primus men drugged and zip-tied behind the main barn. They'll be awake by sunrise, and they'll know what to do. Primus will have an extraction and bag crew that can tie all this off. You better get these bodies into something cold, in the meantime. I'm sure you'll get a call from one of Primus's lawyers, too." Smith tore the tape with his teeth and patted it tight against his forearm. The foam had changed color to match his pasty skin. "Don't let them bully you." He zipped shut the pouch that held the tape. "Stand firm and ask for the moon. You'll get it." Smith removed a business card from one of his thigh pockets and placed it on the red cart. "I've lost four good people. Give this to the lead tech of the bag crew. Tell him the truth about what happened. My team deserves to be properly handled."

Nelson took the card. As he examined it, Anderson saw that all it contained was an international telephone number.

"I'm sure Mr. Nelson will be able to handle the arrangements." Park gestured with the pistol to the large gap where the front door had been.

Smith looked hard at everyone, then edged between two of the desks. He knelt next to his dead partner and removed something from one of the pouches on the guy's vest. "He was a good kid." Smith stood and stepped through the destroyed opening. He stopped a few feet outside the lab. "Bill?" Smith's form was silhouetted by moonlight.

"Yeah?" Kanter replied.

"You know there'll be others."

Kanter glanced at Anderson, then back to Smith. "I'll take my chances."

Smith turned and ran toward the tree line on the west side of the farm.

Park's arm was streaked with blood. He lowered the pistol and looked wearily at Kanter. "I'm very sorry," he said. "I didn't mean to hurt you."

Nelson grabbed Park from behind, took the pistol, and twisted him into some Special Forces neck lock. "Who the hell are you?" Nelson demanded as he tightened his hold.

"Let him go!" Kanter said.

"We don't know who he is."

"He just saved us our lives! Let him speak."

Nelson relinquished his hold and shoved Park against one of the Cores.

"My name is Ulrich Boxler," Park said, clutching his arm. "I'm a

Vatican Special Guard. I was sent here to protect you. To make sure you finished your project."

Anderson glanced at Kanter and Nelson. She saw her own shock mirrored in their faces.

"You're *who*?" Kanter asked.

"Ulrich Boxler. And I bring blessings from his Holiness, the Pope."

Anderson still couldn't believe what Boxler had said, and neither, it appeared, did anyone else.

Kanter shook his head. "You have *got* to be kidding me." He grabbed a half-empty bottled water off the main workstation counter and rubbed his throat.

"It *is* the truth," Boxler pleaded.

"Man, you've got a mean grip," Kanter muttered, rubbing.

"I'm terribly sorry."

"So you're a Swiss guard, sent to protect me and my invention, by the *Pope*?"

Boxler nodded. "Correct."

Kanter opened the bottle and washed the last of the blood from his face.

"Remember when you were shot at, back at the University?" Boxler asked.

"How did you know about that?" Kanter leaned against the workstation and wiped his face with his sleeves.

"The other shots," Anderson mused, "from across the park." Now it made sense. "That was *you*?"

"What I don't understand is how the Vatican learned of my discovery," Kanter said.

Anderson walked up to Kanter and wiped a spot of blood off his cheek with her finger.

"I can't tell you that," Boxler said. "I can only say that the Church has conduits for information throughout the world."

"Scott," Kimberly interrupted, "is it safe to go back to the house?" She had a death grip on Eric's hand, and Eric looked like he could fall asleep standing right there. "He's back to normal, and I want to get him away from all this." Her eyes moved from the dead agent to Claymore's body.

"It should be safe," Nelson said. "But be careful."

Kimberly hiked Eric onto her hip and hurried out of the lab, all the while shielding his eyes from the carnage.

Kanter watched Kimberly leave. "What the hell did we just experience?" he asked.

"It's simple," Boxler said. "The boy was filled with the Holy Spirit."

"Like an angel?"

"No. The Holy Spirit is God himself."

Kanter looked at Anderson. "What do you think?"

In all her clinical work and studies, Anderson had never witnessed a child do anything near what Eric did. She had seen her share of disorders and children acting out deep-seated traumas, but Eric had displayed a much greater presence. How did he know Smith's first name, and how could he reference one of Smith's past experiences? And what did he say to Boxler? Had God truly been present in an 8 year old? Anderson was at a loss. There was nothing in her professional background that could even come close to offering an explanation. She hesitated.

"Tren?" Kanter prompted.

"I'm not really sure."

"You're the expert," Nelson said.

"I've never seen anything like this," Anderson said. "I guess it could be another personality coming forward...."

"What does your gut say?" Kanter asked.

"That Mr. Boxler might be right."

Kanter stared for a second, as if such profundity had locked him up. He shuddered off the realization, righted one of the workstation chairs, and rolled it up to Boxler. "I'm not buying this whole Vatican thing," he said, sitting. "You could be another Smith, from another black agency."

Anderson agreed. "Why would the Pope be so interested in Bill's discovery?"

Boxler eyebrows arched. "Is it so hard to believe?"

"Frankly, yes," Kanter said. "I was raised a Catholic, and to my recollection the church is pretty conservative. I would think they would want to stop technology like this from happen–" Kanter's expression grew serious while he slowly rose from the chair.

"Bill?" Anderson asked.

"Scott, get your gun out," Kanter said.

Nelson removed the Colt from the front of his jeans, but didn't aim.

"I'm not here to bury your discovery!" Boxler exclaimed.

"Then why *are* you?" Kanter asked.

Boxler leaned forward. "His Holiness is very progressive. When he learned of your invention, he felt it was in the best interest of the church to embrace the technology. We've been losing the faithful for many years now."

"I don't buy it."

"You must! The Pope wants to reform the Church. Your discovery will have a profound effect on humanity. His Holiness wants to make sure that the church is *in front* of this discovery."

Kanter folded his arms. "Why?"

"Because," Boxler said weakly, "it may prove the resurrection." He slumped against the Core and slid down its side. A streak of blood trailed him.

Anderson rushed over and felt his forehead. "Bill, he's burning up."

"The wound's become infected," Nelson said as he pocketed the Colt.

"I'll be all right," Boxler said.

Anderson examined his bandage. "We need to clean this out and fix these stitches."

"It can wait." Boxler looked at Kanter. "Didn't you tell me once that you wanted to help mankind?"

Kanter nodded. "I did."

"Then what better way to achieve that than by using one of the world's largest and most powerful institutions? Think of it. When His Holiness speaks, over a *billion* people listen. If you truly want to serve mankind, let us help you trumpet your message. We have the infrastructure, the distribution network, and the worldwide reach. This is too important, William, not to consider!"

"You forgot I'm tied to another organization."

"Don't worry about Cole Strachan or the American government. The church will deal with them." Boxler pulled a small parchment envelope from his shirt pocket. Its blood-red wax seal was embossed with a simple cross. "This is for you." Boxler's hand wavered as he held it out. “It is from his Holiness.”

Kanter took the envelope and sunk into the chair. He turned the envelope over in his hands, broke its seal, and began to read. After a minute, he slowly folded it and stared blankly at the bank of high windows. There was a faint yellow glow at the edges of the panes.

Anderson glanced at her watch. *4:39 a.m.* “Bill, what does it say?”

Kanter leaned forward and regarded Boxler. “Will the Vatican take care of all *our* needs?” His eyes went to Anderson.

Boxler relaxed against the Core. “Yes,” he said, clearly relieved.

What is he doing? Anderson thought. “Bill, wait. You need to think this through.”

Kanter flashed a confident smile and raised a hand to her. “Will I own the complete rights and patents?”

“Of course,” Boxler said.

Kanter stood. “Well then,” he said, stuffing the note into the front pocket of his jeans, “who am *I* to argue with God’s emissary?”

Epilogue. What's in the past.

It had been almost two months since Kanter had left the Nelson farm, and the *Hotel Vitelleschi Vaticano* had served as his home for most of it. He thought he would tire of its five-star elegance, but in fact he had come to love many of its details, such as the shower the size of his first apartment. He had been only mildly curious about his room's bidet, a feeling affirmed when he made an off-hand comment to the concierge, who assured him that women appreciated it much more than men.

The room's doorbell rang, and Kanter barely heard it over *Passioni Infinite*. He clicked off the bathroom TV and spit out the last of the toothpaste. Boxler had suggested that he learn Italian by watching their daily soap operas, but Kanter was terrible with languages and once ordered a filet of plaster at an expensive restaurant, much to the disdain of the waiter.

Kanter peered through the peephole at the distorted face of a plain-clothes Vatican security man. He thought his name was Antonio, although that might have been the night man.

"Welcome to Rome, Dr. Anderson," Kanter said, opening the door.

The security man stepped aside and allowed Anderson to strut in, her brow knitted.

"Have you seen the business section of the *Times* today?" She tossed the paper onto the foyer's bureau. Her purse followed.

"Good to see you, too," Kanter said as the security man rolled her suitcase against the wall.

Her expression relaxed. "Sorry." They hugged – a little longer than usual. The security man swept the room with his eyes and closed the door behind him.

"Which *Times*, London or New York?" Kanter picked up the paper and scanned the headlines. The lead article caught his attention. VATICAN TO ANNOUNCE PROOF OF AFTERLIFE.

Anderson's brow tightened again. "New York, why?"

Kanter gestured to the newspaper on top of the ornately carved antique coffee table that dominated sitting area.

Anderson picked it up and read. As she stood in a shaft of soft afternoon light, Kanter noticed how her tailored suit clung to her body perfectly. Her two-inch pumps only exaggerated the elegance of the ensemble. He couldn't recall ever seeing a more beautiful sight.

"Shit!" she exclaimed, breaking Kanter's reverie.

"That's a word for it." He folded the *New York Times* business section and slid it under her purse. "That paper you're reading is a week old."

"This article even has excerpts from the speech you're going to give." Anderson turned. "How did they get that?"

Kanter shrugged. "Seems my secure T-line isn't so *secure*. Have you seen the markets?"

Anderson, her expression pained, shook her head.

"NASDAQ is holding steady, but the Bombay and Asian exchanges are tanking in high-tech. They're calling it 'The Samsara Effect'."

"What's that?"

"*Samsara* means reincarnation in Hindi, or something like that."

Anderson read further. "It says your discovery could spark regional wars within the Middle East and Asia."

"I know. And don't even read the op-eds. *L'Unità* says I'm the anti-Christ." Kanter made a monster gesture and growled.

"Bill, it's not funny."

"Oh, *please*. Once the independent testing confirms the discovery, things will settle. It's not like we've proved the existence of God, or something. Anyway, it's too late now. In a couple of hours, the genie's out of the bottle."

Anderson made a face.

"Come on, Tren. This is exciting. We're going to impact the world in a way few people ever do. Besides, you're going to be in front of millions of people with the *anti-Christ*!"

"So what do I call you?"

Kanter folded his arms gangsta style. "I'm down with the

Diabolical AC."

Anderson laughed. Her attention was drawn to Kanter's hair. "You've done something different."

"What? Oh, right." Kanter passed his fingers through it. "Boxler said I needed to embrace Italian fashion. This is as far as it went. So how was your flight over?"

"I could get used to First Class."

"I know. It's a whole different experience." Kanter noticed the delicate stitching that bordered the neckline of Anderson's suit. It met at a point between her breasts in an embroidered flourish. "Who's the designer?"

"Armani."

"Smart choice. We wouldn't want to piss off our new benefactors."

Anderson surveyed the room. "I see the Pope spares no expense when it comes to growing his church." She nodded toward the door. "How do you like being under guard?"

Kanter leaned against the top of one of the room's wingbacks. "I guess it's like having Secret Service. You get used to it after a while."

"Hey, before I forget, Hoop wanted me to give you this." Anderson dug out of her purse a bright yellow square envelope and handed it to Kanter.

The card inside had an illustration of a dog clapping enthusiastically and the words *Thank You* in a crazy jagged typeface. Inside was a loose photo of Hoop in his hospital bed, surrounded by his family. The handwritten inscription looked like it could have been penned by the little girl sitting at the foot of Hoop's bed. It said, *"Thank you, Dr. Kanter, for saving my daddy's life."* A large smiley face replaced the dot in the "i" in life. The woman on the other side of the bed looked like a lineman for the Bears.

"Is *this* his wife?" Kanter pointed to the woman as he handed Anderson the card.

"Yes." Anderson smiled as she read the inscription.

"Hoop said she was tough. No wonder Strachan agreed to pay for everything. I wouldn't want to tangle with her, either." Kanter took the card back and placed it on the coffee table. "How *is* Hoop doing?"

"The doctors think, with time and therapy, he might get some use of his legs. Right now, it's fifty-fifty."

An ache of remorse coursed through Kanter. "It's amazing he's alive."

Anderson sighed through a faint smile and approached the picture window that looked out onto St. Peter's Square. She parted the sheer curtains with the back of her hand. "I shouldn't have listened to Claymore," she said, her head shaking imperceptibly. "I should have gone back and helped Hoop."

"Don't beat yourself up," Kanter said. "We were thrown into an extraordinary situation. We did go back, and he *was* alive. Thank God Primus had that med kit."

"Well, I know Hoop's grateful for you pressuring Strachan."

"Speaking of, how did the Nelsons make out?"

"I spoke with Tom the other day," Anderson said, staring out the window. "Kim and Scott won't have to worry about retirement or Eric's college education. And you'll be pleased to know that Eric hasn't had any episodes since his..."

"Angelic performance?"

She released the curtains and turned. "You still think it was one of his personalities?"

Kanter shrugged. "Maybe. I'm more concerned about him seeing Smith's partner getting shot in the head. That's going to mess with him."

"Both Kim and I had long talks with Eric about the events of that evening. He doesn't seem to have any memory of the shooting, thank God."

"Why's that?"

"Professionally speaking, I think he was already into his, um ... incarnation. The real Eric wasn't present, so there was no memory implanted."

"But what if it did? Couldn't it manifest someday as repressed memories or something?"

"Only time will tell. Right now, he seems to be a normal 8-year-old boy, which is all his parents want. If he does have any more episodes, I'll let you know." Anderson's attention traversed the room again, as if she was searching for a new subject to talk about. "So how *did* it finally go down with Strachan? Your last email said he was meeting with the Pope this week?"

"The Vatican flew him over on Monday." Kanter joined her at the window. "I wasn't asked to attend, but Boxler assured me that an agreement was reached that met all of Strachan's requirements. It must have been a huge payoff. I doubt Strachan would let go of his investment without a fight. I guess it pays to have friends in high places."

Anderson stepped closer and began adjusting Kanter's tie. "Well, aren't we the new papal treasure."

"I wouldn't go that far. The Vatican has more money than God."

She pushed the knot tight.

"Easy, doctor." Kanter pulled at his collar. "I have to make a speech to the world media, remember?"

"By the way, I wanted to thank you for inviting me to the press conference."

"Are you *kidding*? Without you, I wouldn't be here. I'm just sorry Hoop couldn't make it. He deserves it, you know?"

"The satellite link should make him happy." Anderson smoothed out his tie.

"So how's it going – getting ready for your fall semester, I mean?"

"Oh, you know the drill. Boring paperwork. Endless department meetings."

"Tren?" Kanter put a hand to her shoulder.

"Yes?"

"Join me. Here in Rome. The lab is state of the art, and they have *six* Cores."

"Bill, we've talked about this. I have obligations to my students *and* patients. I can't just abandon them."

"I know." Kanter bit off his frustration and removed his hand. Maybe at dinner he would try again.

"Bill?" Anderson tucked his collar under the lapel of his coat. "There's something I've been putting off asking."

"What's that?"

"Why did you accept Boxler's offer so quickly, back at the farm?"

"Once a Catholic boy, always a Catholic boy?"

Anderson raised an eyebrow.

"Okay, the truth is, I just wanted all of us to be safe. And the church offered that."

"Are you sure all this safety," she gestured to the room, "isn't just a pair of velvet handcuffs? The church doesn't exactly have the best track record when it comes to keeping their word."

Kanter thought back to the night at the farm where he had been introduced to the overwhelming clarity of death. "Look, Tren, I'm not wired to be a hero. I've never been in combat like you and Scott. When all that came down at the farm, I guess it ..." Kanter flashed back. He and one of the Primus men, the morning after the attack, were struggling to hoist Claymore's body into one of the large black industrial trash bags Nelson used for cleaning out the milking stalls. Claymore's arm fell out when they had pushed his body bag against Gibson's. The hand had fallen palm up, one finger pointing at Kanter like Claymore was blaming him. The Primus man, without any hesitation, just kicked it back into the bag with the tip of his boot.

"Bill?"

Kanter pointed to the windows that looked out onto St. Peter's. "No one's going to get at me behind *those* walls," he said, feeling his throat tighten. "No one."

Anderson started to say something, but hesitated.

"What, Tren?"

"I just don't want to see you get used again, like with the MedBed."

"I'll be okay," Kanter assured her. "The university has a team of lawyers watching my legal back. I own all the rights and patents. Besides, we're about to announce to the world that there *is* an afterlife. I don't think the Church is going to suddenly lock us away."

"Still, be watchful." Anderson smiled and brushed off his lapels. "There, now you're perfect."

"I am?"

She searched his eyes, then leaned forward and brought her lips to his.

Kanter pulled her close and for a moment was lost in their kiss.

Anderson pulled back and scrutinized his face. She wiped his lips with her thumb. "My color isn't going to work with your new suit."

Kanter gently stopped her and took her hand into his. "Thank you," he said.

"For what?"

"Everything."

A coy smile spread across Anderson's face. "This is only the beginning, Dr. Kanter. I plan on coming to Rome on a regular basis." She made a final adjustment to his collar. "And the pontiff better spring for more first-class airfare."

Kanter took her by the waist. "I think I can arrange that."

A knock at the door interrupted, and Kanter went to open it.

The same security man was standing there. "The cars are here, *signore*."

"*Darci un minuto, per favore*," Kanter said and closed the door.

"Your Italian is getting better." Anderson glanced at her watch. "A little early, isn't it?"

"Rome traffic is a bitch. It'll take at least forty-five minutes to make the event hall. I still have to do a mic check and make sure the MedBed is set to perform." Kanter hefted his backpack off the coffee table. "On the way, you can catch me up on what's happening at our illustrious university." He caught Anderson's reflection in the foyer mirror as she reapplied her lipstick. Her eyes were drawn to his backpack.

"Bill, don't you think it's time you dropped the grunge look?"

She dabbed at her lips with a tissue and turned to face him. "You can afford a nice Italian briefcase."

"Some things, Doctor, will never change." Kanter zipped the top of the backpack closed.

She laughed. "Whatever."

"You know, you never answered my last email," Kanter said. "How did it go when you went home?"

Anderson's attention moved to the windows again and lingered. "I've decided never to bring anything up about my uncle or the events surrounding my birth parents." A faint edge of resignation colored her voice.

Kanter thought about saying something like, "You should at least ask them what they knew," but he figured it wasn't his place to question her decision.

She glanced back. "I lied to my folks about what was in my scan."

Kanter nodded. "It's probably just as well."

Anderson's face brightened. "The way I look at it, what's in the past should stay there." She gathered her purse from the bureau.

"You know, after today," Kanter said, hiking his backpack over his shoulder, "that might not be an option any more."

PAUL BLACK always wanted to make movies, but a career in advertising sidetracked him. Born and raised outside of Chicago, he is the national award-winning author of *The Tels*, *Soulware*, *Nexus Point*, *The Presence* and *The Samsara Effect*. Today he lives and works in Dallas, where he manages his graphic design firm, feeds his passion for tennis and dreams of six figure movie deals. He is currently working on a new book of fiction tentatively called *CoolBrain*.

ACKNOWLEDGEMENTS

I would like to thank the following for their assistance, inspiration and patience: Lisa Glasgow, Bridget Boland, Brian Moreland, Pat O'Connell, and Max Wright...you all were there for me when I needed you.

For future trends in technology: *www.socialtechnologies.com* and its wealth of future forecasts and models of global trends. And to NASA News and the Langley Research Center website for its white papers on the future of technology.

Special thanks to my editor and friend, Jay Johnson, for his faith in my talent.

And to Trish, as always, with love.

Dallas, 2011

WINNER of Writer's Digest's 2005 Book of the Year for Genre Fiction
FINALIST for Science Fiction Independent Publishers Book Awards.

"...this is definitely **ONE OF THE BEST SCIENCE FICTION NOVELS** I've ever read...the book is remarkable."

~ *Marilyn Meredith, Writer's Digest's 11th Annual Book Awards*

THE NEAR-FUTURE A new revolution has spread across the human landscape. The Biolution and its flood of technology have changed almost every aspect of life. Also changed, is the face of terrorism.

Throughout his life, Jonathan Kortel always sensed he was different, but never imagined how different, until two rival factions of a secret group called the Tels approach him out of the shadows of government. He has a gift that could change his life, and possibly the world, forever.

This is his story. A battle for the loyalty of a man who could change the course of human evolution. And the struggle inside this man as he comes to terms with his destiny. Deeply intriguing and powerfully suspenseful, Paul Black has created a future described as "mind-bending" by the *Dallas Morning News*. Part *X-Files,* part cyber-thriller, *The Tels* unveils a view of a world that could be just around the corner.

Available at all online retailers including **Amazon.com** and **BN.com**.

WINNER ForeWord Magazine's Book of the Year

"...**A RIVETING SCIENCE FICTION** novel bt a gifted author..."
~ *Midwest Book Review*

"...**HIGHLY ORIGINAL**...Mr. Black has quite an imagination and puts it to good use..." ~ *John Strange, The City Wide Web*

DESTINY AWAITS Jonathan Kortel is the most powerful telekinetic ever. There are others like him, and they're called the Tels. Able to manipulate gravity, they exist out at the edge of the next century, where the Biolution and its wave of new technology have changed life forever.

Blamed for the deaths of the Tel leadership, Jonathan escapes to a life of anonymity. But there's something strange happening in space that threatens all life on earth, and only Jonathan Kortel has the ability to stop it.

Here ends the Tels trilogy, author Paul Black's fascinating near-future series, introduced in his award-winning 2003 novel *The Tels*. Nexus Point continues where *The Tels* and *Soulware* (2005) left off, following the saga of Jonathan Kortel as he fulfills his prophetic destiny.

NOVEL INSTINCTS

www.paulblackbooks.com

Available at all online retailers including **Amazon.com** and **BN.com**.